Holiday Hearts

Dana Volney lets her imagination roam free in Wyoming, where she writes romances and helps local businesses succeed with her marketing consulting company. Splitting her time between telling sexy, fast-paced suspense stories and sweet holiday romances, she likes to try new adventures in real life whenever she can (which, let's face it, means tasting all sorts of delicious cuisines). Dana is bold, adventurous, and—by her own admission—good with plants, having kept a dwarf lemon tree alive for six months.

Also by Dana Volney

Kisses for Christmas
Holiday Hearts

DANA VOLNEY

Holiday Hearts

CANELO

First published in the United Kingdom in 2020 by Canelo

This edition published in the United States in 2025 by

Canelo, an imprint of
DK Publishing, a division of Penguin Random House LLC
1745 Broadway, 20th Floor, New York, NY 10019

The authorized representative in the EEA is Dorling Kindersley Verlag GmbH.
Arnulfstr. 124, 80636 Munich, Germany

Print ISBN 979 8 217 25308 1
Ebook ISBN 979 8 217 25348 7

The December Deal first published in the USA in 2015 by Crimson Romance, an imprint of Simon & Schuster. *A Heart for the Holidays* first published in the USA in 2016 by Crimson Romance, an imprint of Simon & Schuster. *December Deception* first published in the USA in 2017 by Crimson Romance, an imprint of Simon & Schuster.

Printed and bound in Great Britain by Clays Ltd, Elcograf S.p.A.

Look for more great books at
www.canelo.co | www.dk.com

1

The December Deal

To my family, for their unwavering support.

Chapter One

Lilia Carrigan set her cup down on the small table in the coffee shop and took her seat in the corner with a view of the mountains. There had to be something she could do to raise money quickly. She opened her laptop and slouched in the hard wooden chair. She and her siblings had set up a GoFundMe campaign to ask for donations and pooled what little extra money they each had, but it wasn't nearly enough. A fundraiser at the pub was a viable idea, but they needed hundreds of thousands of dollars, and their friends weren't that rich. Twelve thousand dollars was only five percent of what they actually needed.

Out of the corner of her eye, she noticed a tall man walking straight toward her. There was no mistaking his intention. She glanced up and took in his luscious brown hair, intense blue eyes and his business attire down to his shiny black dress shoes. The man was stunning – his cobalt eyes smiled at her, and his entire face radiated sexy with a self-assured smile. Great. She was going to have to be a jerk, tell this guy she wasn't into small talk and move him on his merry way.

He pulled out a chair at the table next to her, unbuttoned his black peacoat and sat with an ease that was a tad intimidating. An older, shorter man appeared behind him, plopped down across from him, and proceeded to continue a conversation about metal prices.

Good. Crisis averted. She focused on her computer screen, hoping she hadn't made a fool of herself by keeping eye contact with the could-be *GQ* model so long. Well, he'd looked like he was going to talk to her, so whatever. She'd probably made his day.

Snow flew by the window on the other side of her as the Casper, Wyoming, December wind started to pick up. The trees down by the river were still white from the snowfall a couple days ago.

She clicked on her travel and food blog, *Made to Wander*, to upload a post she'd written earlier that day on what it was like to return home after being gone so long – the city seemed bigger; she hadn't realized how much she'd missed being near her family and how good her old haunt restaurants tasted. Her emotions were all over the place these last couple weeks. Writing about stabilizing subjects had helped her feel normal again and not like her world was falling apart. She was personable in her writing but left family stuff out of it. If she didn't, there'd probably be tons of posts she could write to deal with the sadness tearing at her over her dad's recent diagnosis. But she wasn't ready to talk about that experience so far – putting it out there would make it too real.

"This isn't a surprise." The older gentleman had a stern voice. "You know the terms of the will."

Mr. *GQ* just got a lot more interesting – certainly more entertaining than trying to think of her next topic to write about.

"There's got to be a way to change it." Her chair neighbor, who had gently sun-kissed skin, kept a cool voice even though it sounded like things weren't going his way. "Or another clause."

"This is the same conversation we've been having for a year."

"And I've tried diligently for a year to make it go away." The cute one sat back in his chair and crossed one ankle over his other knee.

She'd normally put in earbuds and click on iTunes, but this was by far the most interesting thing to happen in the last two weeks. Interesting in a good way, not the bad reason she'd come home.

"Unless you're married, you cannot maintain control."

"But it'll just cost more money in the long run with a divorce. This entire situation is asinine. Tell me you didn't encourage his idea."

"Your father was of sound mind when he decided on this clause years ago. He didn't want you to live just for work. He wanted you to have a life, a family."

"My life is perfect the way it is." Mr. Suave was losing patience.

The hottie needed a wife. It was hard to believe that would be an issue for him. He wasn't her type, but surely with that smile he was someone's. She preferred her men a little more exotic, more like Zenzo, her Italian boyfriend – ex-boyfriend.

"Be that as it may, if you're not married by New Year's Eve, I'll be forced to start the paperwork to give the company to your uncle."

"I don't want to get married because I have to."

"No one said you had to."

"But then I lose everything." Resignation was loud and clear in his quieter words.

Sucks to be you, man. Her predicament wasn't great, but this guy's sounded like a rock and a hard place. Not that she'd ever admit this, but hearing someone else wrestle with bad luck was oddly comforting. Turned out not everyone else's life was all rosy.

The bearer of bad news checked his watch and stood. "I have a meeting on the East Side. Let me know what you decide."

Lilia clicked on her email, trying hard not to look at the stranger and give him a knowing frown to commiserate with his situation. He needed a wife, but she needed the impossible. She couldn't just pick up the next person she saw and make her troubles go away. She had to figure out how to make a miracle happen. But she would. There was a way to get her dad the treatment, and she was going to find it.

She opened a message from her contact at a travel magazine. The subject line was "READ ME NOW" so something was happening.

She scanned the email and her heart rate kicked up with each sentence. "Holy crap." She sat up straighter and tried to read slower from the beginning. "Holy crap."

"Everything okay?" Her eavesdropee swiveled in his chair toward her.

"Yeah. More than." Her smile could not be tamed. "My latest blog post was just picked up by a fantastic magazine, and they loved it so much, they are offering me a contract for the next year." All twelve issues, with online exposure for the full twelve months as well. They paid top dollar and were well respected in the industry. This was huge. And why she was rambling to this stranger, she did not know.

"Congratulations." He sipped from his white cup.

"Thank you." It was probably rude to crow about her triumph to a guy who had just been kicked in the nuts from the sound of it. "I couldn't help but overhear." She glanced at his friend's vacant seat. "Bum deal, man."

"Yeah. It is pretty much ruining my life." He reached behind him for the jacket he'd shed at some point when she wasn't prying and stood. "Your day is going much better. Congratulations again."

She nodded, her smile still intact. "You just need to bite the bullet and pay for a wifey to get what you want." She chuckled and pulled up the calculator on her computer as he reached for his to-go cup. Damn, this new contract was a sweet paycheck, but in her reality, it meant she could afford dinner at the pub a few nights a week rather than fixing Cup-a-Soup after visiting her father, who'd just been released from the hospital again. Not even good news solved her true problem. "Heck, I'd marry him for the right price."

"Excuse me?"

Her head shot up, and she looked right into his vibrant blue eyes, embarrassment sucking all of the moisture from her mouth. And here she'd been trying to avoid this type of moment again.

"I..." She shrugged, and her gaze darted around the little shop. Shoot. He wasn't supposed to hear her half-serious, half-joking words. When she was on her game, she might have had a clever comeback, but the truth was she was too tired. "I was talking to myself."

"About marrying me?"

"No." She pointed to her screen and shrugged. "Something else." Heat threatened her cheeks, but she absolutely refused to get embarrassed. It wasn't her fault he had great hearing. He was the one who should've felt awkward.

He peered over her shoulder at her calculator and email window, and then raised his eyebrows.

She crossed her arms over her black sweater. Was this fool really standing here judging her? "It was a joke." Men were so irritating sometimes.

"Are you married?"

"No."

"Dating anyone?"

"No." She'd asked Zenzo to come with her to Wyoming. Apparently he had no intention of living anywhere other than Italy.

"Jokes are funny because they are a version of the truth." He pulled out the chair across from her and sat.

"I'm not laughing." Did this guy really think she would marry for money? *It would solve all my problems. No, focus, you aren't a gold digger.* Well, so far she hadn't resorted to that.

"So then you are serious."

It wouldn't be the craziest thing she'd ever done – running off to Europe on a whim and then staying for a year still topped that list. "Tell me how this is something you are actually asking about." She moved her palm up and down, showcasing his face. "You have a problem dating?" The problem wasn't his looks. Maybe it was his personality.

"I'm not looking to date. I need a wife."

"Yeah, well, we all need something."

"I'll help you if you help me."

"I think that deal would be a little one-sided." Her brow furrowed. This guy looked serious. Too serious. And he wasn't walking away. Had she accidentally proposed to a stranger?

"How much?" He unbuttoned his peacoat and revealed a baby-blue button-up.

She had his full attention. And, holy crap, was this something she could do? Could he afford her? Yeah, she definitely sounded like a prostitute now. "You can't be for real. Listen, I'm sorry I listened in on your conversation."

"Then you're well aware of what is going on."

"I got the gist. It's not my problem."

"So I'll ask you again, what's your price?"

She should shut the conversation down right there. Or try to again. They were talking about falsifying a marriage. The thought made her skin feel dirty. This wasn't right. But if this guy was for real and had enough money, all her dad's problems would be solved.

She sipped her coffee. The insurance company was refusing to cover an "experimental treatment," and the estimate was seared in her brain. "A lot."

"Okay, how much?" His nicely defined cheekbones made her a little angry – he probably could have anything he wanted and thought she was just another easy deal to be made. She was also steamed that she was entertaining his ridiculous offer.

"Two hundred and forty-two thousand." She rounded to the nearest thousand. Why the hell not? She was already on the train to Crazytown; she may as well get the highest figure her dad would need. That should cover the hospital stays past, present and future, and a nurse to give her mother a break, on top of the treatment itself. One of the first things Lilia had done after his diagnosis was figure out the full financial strain pancreatic cancer caused.

"Done." He extended his palm for a handshake. "I'm Vincent Morgenstern."

She stared at his hand and blinked. "Just like that, huh?"

"You seem like a decent person." He returned his hand to the table.

"What if I'm not?"

It was no longer a joke. He was completely serious. Marriage had always been a great idea but not really for her. Not at this point in her life.

"Then my intuition has failed me."

What the hell? I'm not going to raise that money any other way. This is Dad's only shot.

She needed a mute button for the little voice nagging at her sensible side.

"What *exactly* are we talking about here?" She uncrossed her legs and sat forward. Butterflies danced in her stomach, and adrenaline made her palms a little shaky.

Vincent was desperate, that much was clear from the fact he'd taken her up on a whisper. But before she got anywhere near a white dress and a priest, she wanted to know all of his expectations. And lay out hers.

Maybe this time she could make a commitment since she knew it wasn't real. Like training wheels for the future when she met the guy she really did want to marry – or traveled back to Italy with the courage to tell Zenzo yes.

–

"Can we start with your name?" Vincent should've ordered a larger coffee.

Marriage shouldn't be mocked – and that was exactly what his dad was making him do. His views on marriage had always been clear to his father – if he was ever going to get married it would be because he'd fallen so helplessly in love he couldn't live without her. He'd yet to come across that woman – Rachel, Kiera, Laney and certainly the blond across from him didn't fit the bill.

"Lilia. Lilia Carrigan." She made no advance to shake his hand so he kept his palms on the table.

"It's nice to meet you, Lilia. My dad died a year ago." The words were automatic, but the pain remained. "He was the sole owner of Morgenstern Fabrication. He willed the company to me, but only if I married within a year of his death."

He'd been trying to beat the clause since he'd first learned of it – he was officially out of any legal options. The clause was staying. The reality of what he had to do to keep a company he loved so much had ground down his teeth.

"Is this real? I mean, this is a thing you're serious about?" Her eyes were intense and discerning. "Because I need this money, and I don't want to get my hopes up if this is a line or sick joke."

Did she owe a bookie this money? Was she involved in some sort of backward pyramid scheme?

"I'm as serious as the heart attack that killed my father."

He couldn't go to lunch without wondering if he could bring himself to say "I do" to the girl behind the bar at Olive Garden. And the ironic twist was that he and his family were rich enough without the company, so he could drop this nonsense – if he wanted, he could wander around aimlessly from one cocktail party to the next for the rest of his boring life.

But Morgenstern Fabrication was his life – he'd grown up watching his grandpa and dad work in the office that overlooked the machine floor, he'd landed big contracts in the last two years that meant he continued to provide jobs to people who'd become his friends, and he couldn't stand the thought of the company going to his loser uncle. He wasn't going to start over. He was willing to pay the price to stop that from happening. All other avenues had failed.

It was marry or be proof that third-generation businesses were the most likely to fail.

"What are your expectations here?"

"Actually getting married, license and all. Preferably soon. Like tomorrow."

"And people believing we really met, fell in love and got married so quickly?"

"Yep." There were people close to him, his mom and sister, to start, who would guess he hadn't meet the perfect girl so close to the deadline, but the charade had to stay intact. "For a year."

"What else is required in this will? We're not sleeping together, and I'm not having your baby."

Yeah, that was just what he needed out of the deal – child support payments for the next eighteen years.

"Whoa." He put his palm out to slow her down. "We live together, you'll have your own space, we'll be seen at events throughout the year, you change your last name. Nothing else." Then she could stay on her side of his house and he'd stay on his, and the year would fly by.

"My name?" She slowly twirled the cup sitting on the table.

Her big, round, dark brown eyes were almost too much because her face was already like a porcelain doll. Long, blond hair fell down the back of her petite frame.

"Everything has to seem legit. And for that amount of money, it better." The words *gold digger* kept flashing in his mind. "I'll have Dean, my lawyer, draw up a prenup so the divorce in a year will be clean." And he'd keep his business and money, and she could keep whatever weird crap she probably had.

"I don't know. This might be a bad idea."

It was. She was right. He could feel the urge to run all the way down to the tips of his toes. But he couldn't. He had let time run out instead. This woman sitting in front of him was his chance to keep the life he'd built. "This is real."

"I need the money up front."

"Logically, you'd get half on our wedding day and half a year later when we divorce."

"Then I'm out. I'm more of the instant-gratification type."

Not shocking news – he didn't get an "I have my life together" vibe from her. From her innocent, lost look, he'd guess when she woke up in the morning she had no idea what she was going to need to do for the day.

"That was a specific amount ready on the tip of your tongue. What do you need it for?"

As long as the money wasn't for something totally in left field, he would stay in his seat. If she said something like buying studio time, distribution and advertising for a new band she shacked up with at Burning Man, then he was out. His life had no room for impracticality.

"It's personal. I'd rather not share." Her chin jutted out, and she gazed down at her keyboard.

The woman wanted almost a quarter of a million dollars. His bank account could take the hit, but it would still hurt. "Then I'm not going to pay."

She shut her laptop and reached down for her bag on the floor. *There'll be a contract, don't let her leave. Let her have the money now.* He couldn't let another woman get away – this time he had to follow through.

As it was, he was a little embarrassed at how his love life was turning out. He'd never imagined it would be hard to get married – not until he'd tried. What kind of person had to pay someone to marry him.? This was a low point.

If he'd done this right after his dad died, he'd be almost divorced now and on his way to putting his life back together the way it was before.

"Hold on. Are you from here?"

"Yep. Born and raised. I actually just came back from Europe. I've been there for the past year."

"What were you doing over there?"

"Living life while I can." She held her coffee cup now with two hands and sipped. "I always wanted to pick up and travel, no plans necessary. Along the way, I had to teach English as a second language to fund my extended trip."

"You speak other languages?"

"Enough to get by, and then I learned as I taught. They were basic classes."

"Very cool."

"I write for my blog too. I've been blessed with a lot of popularity this year. Hence the magazine interest."

"My frat buddies and I had a bit too much fun racing cars in London once and nearly landed in jail."

"I didn't make it there. I meandered around the southern countries, trying to hit each one. My magnet collection about covers an entire fridge. Italy was my favorite." She stared behind him for a second before gazing back at him with guarded eyes.

"Magnets?"

"I collect them when I travel and write the dates on the back."

"How long were you over there?"

"About twelve months."

"Why didn't you stay longer?"

"Wanted to come back to see my family. I missed them."

Family values. Good. There was a chance she was going to get along with his family.

"Are you from Casper?"

He nodded. "Same as you. I love Wyoming as my home base, but traveling is always high on my priority list."

"Good. Glad that's settled." She chuckled, and he could hear her nerves.

This was foreign for him too. It was nice to know she wasn't completely comfortable with this wild plan.

He checked his watch – he had a meeting with a general contractor in fifteen minutes. "So… what do you think?" A proposal had never been finer.

"I still need the payment first." She sat forward, set down her cup, and clasped his folded hands in hers on the table. "We are basically strangers—" her brown eyes intensified "—but I promise you, I will stick to the deal and fulfill my end. No matter what. I can't do that, though, without the payment, in full, up front. That's the whole reason I'd do this."

Her eyes bore into him, and he sensed her seriousness and desperation. Her soft hands continued to try to cover his on the table, and he glanced down.

"Fine." Normally he played business close to the vest, but there was no other way to close this deal.

He was going to have to give her his mother's ring to sell the union. But first he had to make sure to get her down the aisle and past the hurdle of asking but not actually following through with the *I do's*. His gaze met hers again, but not before they rested on her lips for a moment – so pink and shiny and kissable.

This was fake. All fake.

Yep, he was out of his damn mind. And then there were her eyes. Beautiful brown eyes that stirred a sense of adventure he'd lost lately.

"Thank you."

"We'll live in my house," he blurted out. "I don't know what you have, and we'll take care of the payments, but my house is big and I like it."

She nodded, and her fingers slid away from his as she sat up. Her warmth was gone. It figured that he'd felt nothing for the slew of women who would have made great wives, but now that he was paying a gypsy-type woman for a fake marriage, his body was primed and ready to go.

"Will your family know this isn't real?" she asked.

"They'll probably guess – I'm really close to the deadline. How about yours?"

Her eyes darted around the room again, and four of her fingers ran back and forth over her thumb. "It would be best if they thought it was real. I don't want them to know about the money."

"Okay, then we tell no one. To everyone else, this is totally real."

She reached out her hand and they shook.

–

The little voice in the back of Lilia's head wasn't so little anymore. Or quiet. The name change had really set her off. Marrying a stranger wasn't a good idea – buying in so far as to change her name made her skin damp, her hands a little shaky and her mouth dry. *This is the right thing to do. This is the only way to give Dad a fighting chance.* A chance she'd never regret giving him and one she wouldn't tell anyone what she had to do to make happen. Unless her current last-ditch effort paid off, literally, and she could still call herself a moral person in the mirror.

She walked through the open door to Zack King's office and sat down in a semi-comfortable, standard-issue, North Platte River Bank chair.

"I didn't know you were back." Zack wrinkled his forehead to look over his thin-rimmed glasses without turning from his screen.

"Couple of weeks ago. How've you been?" She clutched her bag on her lap, trying to get rid of her nervous energy. She wasn't one for begging. But desperate times and all.

"Darla and I broke up. But other than that, all right."

"Oh, I'm sorry to hear that."

She'd known Zack from high school, and he was probably the unluckiest person in love she'd ever met.

"What brings you in?"

"Well," she said and cleared her throat, "I need a loan."

"Great. For how much?"

"One hundred and twenty-five thousand dollars." She'd take far less money, an amount that would still get her dad the treatment he needed, if it meant the next year of her own life wouldn't get highjacked.

"Are you buying a house?"

"No. I need the money for something else."

"A business?"

"Not exactly."

"What kind of collateral do you have?"

She'd always known that one day her drifter lifestyle would bite her in the butt. It's why she hadn't turned to Zack first. But miracles could happen at Christmas. *Couldn't they?* "Hmm. Clothes?"

"Lilia, you know I'd love to help you out. But I can't just hand out loans. I have to go through a process – one that involves collateral."

She took a deep breath and slumped into her chair. "I knew it was a long shot."

Perfect, she was so totally screwed. There was only one other thing to do. "What do you know about Morgenstern Fabrication?" The least she could do was ask one person in town about her future husband before she said her *I dos*.

"Oh, I know Vinny."

"Vinny?" She scrunched her face, and her nose wrinkled. No. Absolutely not. She'd be calling him Vincent.

"Ya, he owns the place. Good guy. We golf together in the summer."

Okay, that wasn't bad news. Zack was a good judge of character – male character, that is. He still sucked when it came to the women he chose to date.

She let Zack get back to his numbers and tried not to cry as she walked out of the bank. She was really going to have to make this commitment – something she'd never wanted to do even with Zenzo. And she'd loved him. *Still did* love him? She felt a lot of emotions for him, but more of the live-together kind than the forever type.

She angled into her car and couldn't breathe. She liked her last name, it was nice and strong and held her family ties. Lilia Morgenstern? That sounded like she should be a character in an Addams Family episode. Starting her car to turn on the heat, she reached for her cell phone. The seven-hour time difference made it evening in Italy.

She dialed, and with each ring, her heart beat louder in her ears. Why was she even calling him? They'd agreed breaking up was the best. Or rather, he'd suggested so. She hadn't said much.

"Lilia?" His familiar Italian accent caused the ends of her lips to curve.

"Hey there."

Music played in the background, and she could picture the little restaurant he was probably at with a gaggle of friends, wine and a live band. Life seemed simpler over there.

"It's nice to hear from you." The music softly disappeared from his end.

"How are you?" She really didn't know what else to say. She'd never told him why she'd had to leave in such a hurry.

"Doing well. Is it nice to be back home?"

"Yeah, it's been a busy couple of weeks." She picked at her steering wheel with her finger. "How's business?" His custom sandal business was how they'd met four months ago.

"Baby, come back inside." A woman's voice that she didn't recognize was clear on the other end of the line. There was a sensual laugh and what sounded like kissing.

Lilia froze, and chills zoomed down her spine. *Baby? What the hell?* Did their time together mean so little he'd moved on after only two weeks? Men. Pigs, the lot of them.

"I see you're busy," Lilia managed between gritted teeth. "I was just calling to tell you I'm getting married." Whoa. Yep, she'd said it.

"You're what?"

Oh, now she had his attention.

"Yep. So…" This could possibly be the only satisfying thing about her upcoming nuptials.

"To *who*? Is this why you didn't say yes to me?"

"No one you know." Or she knew. Zenzo didn't need the details. She hadn't said yes to him because committing the rest of her life to a person was terrifying – what if their love didn't last and she was stuck with someone she hated? Divorce meant absolute failure, and she hated failing. "Anyway. Take care."

She hung up and threw her phone on the passenger seat as if it were diseased. Before she could control her emotions, tears trailed down her cheeks. She'd left a wonderful life to come home because her dad was sick, Zenzo had moved on, and now she was going to get married and change her last name to make sure her dad got treatment. A treatment none of them knew would even work on his horrible cancer with a less-than-stellar survival rate. Was this really what she wanted to do? She stared at the bleak afternoon – the sun was gone and the sky threatened more snow.

No. But it was exactly what she had to do.

Chapter Two

The sun was bright in a blue sky, and he was going to start sweating soon, even though the air was crisp. He was getting married in a matter of minutes. Dean had drawn up the prenup with the money requirements, secrecy clause and the fact that this sham had to last for at least a year, along with the other standard you-can't-have-any-more-of-my-money clauses. Dean had also pushed the marriage license and all the details through the proper channels.

Vincent held an envelope in his hands and paced in front of the courthouse doors. A clicking noise intensified, and he glanced over to see Lilia striding toward him. She had gained at least four inches from the hot-pink heels she'd donned. He stopped breathing as he took in the full picture walking toward him – she wore an open pink coat that fell mid-thigh with a shiny white 1950s-style top that accentuated her collarbone. The mid-calf-length dress that cinched at her waist and flowed down to her legs swished in the light breeze. Her hair was pinned back, and a little bit of netting was secured in her hair, covering part of her forehead and part of her gaze.

Her half grin looked forced, ruining the fantasy that she was a true bride.

He took a deep breath. *At least she's not in jeans.*

"Hi." She stopped in front of him, leaving more than an arm's length between them.

"You look beautiful." For a fake wedding, she sure looked like a real bride. He wore a black suit, white button-up, and black shoes, plus a boutonnière. Which he'd probably have worn to his real wedding anyway.

"Thank you. You look good yourself." He got more of a smile now from her as she ground one heel into the cement.

"Shall we?" He opened the big courthouse door, and as she walked past, a whiff of pomegranate filled his nose. He took a deep breath as he fell in step beside her. "I also have the paperwork." He produced the envelope he'd toyed with earlier as they reached the elevator.

Somehow he felt odd giving her a contract before they promised to love each other forever.

She took the envelope from his hand and opened it, looking over the pages as they rode three floors up in silence. "Do you have a pen?"

"Yes." He retrieved a pen from his inside breast pocket and watched her closely as she found the signature page again. "Do you have any questions?" He'd gone to his uncle that morning as a last option and tried to strike up a deal to buy back the company if they just let the will take effect. But Barry had made it clear he'd never sell – more like he'd squeeze every cent out of it and run it into the ground and *then* sell.

"I sign it, we stay married for a year and here's my check." She waved the rectangle paper worth thousands.

He nodded as she shoved a chunk of his savings into her hot-pink clutch – money he'd worked late for, skipped family events for, and lost sleep over.

"Then I'm good." She scribbled on the paper and handed them both back to him. He folded the papers, returned them to the envelope and put all of it back in his inside pocket.

"You didn't have to go all out." He glanced at the length of her dress.

"What?" She followed his gaze down. "Oh, well, it's supposed to be real, right? No one would believe I didn't wear a dress. The rest of this story is going to be hard enough for my family and friends to believe. We'll need to take some pictures. In fact—" she opened her clutch and produced an iPhone in a bright pink case that had little gold hearts all over it just as the elevator door opened "—we should start now. Smile."

Her back and butt brushed up against him as she leaned in and held her phone up in front of them. Annoyingly, his body responded positively to her touch.

He wrapped his palm around her waist, and she tensed under his grip.

"For the photo," he felt obligated to explain. This was her idea. They weren't going to do anything half-assed.

She snapped some pictures of their smiling faces. The thumbnail haunted him—what would he think of the picture tomorrow or in a year? Today was surreal.

"Are you going to post them on Facebook?" he asked, anxious to get this marriage out there so it could disappear and he could go about his normal life.

"I'll think about it. I mean—" she stared up into his eyes and shrugged "—we're in it now, right? This is what people do when they get married."

"I guess."

He could see her chest rise and fall with the deep breath she took. "Okay. Then we're all in. Together." She laced her fingers in his as they continued to the office.

His chest tightened at her touch. No matter where they were in a year, and even though he'd paid her, he'd be forever in her debt for helping him keep his dad's company. He nervously smiled and held the office door open for her, making sure to keep her hand as they approached the reception desk.

"We have an appointment with Judge Hardwick," he said.

The young receptionist clicked her mouse a couple times and then smiled. "Fill out this sheet." She handed it to Lilia, which forced her to take her hand back. "When you're done, the judge is ready."

They moved back from the desk, and she started filling in the questions.

"How do you spell your last name?" she asked.

What if the receptionist overheard? He snuck a glance at the woman, who was, thankfully, interested in her screen. How reckless was Lilia to just blurt that out? "I'll do my parts, and you do yours. Quietly."

They should've just eloped to Vegas. People didn't think twice about couples getting married on a whim there. Still, they managed to fill out the sheets and only got one semi-suspicious look from the brunette behind the desk.

"Judge." Vincent shook the longtime family friend's hand.

"How the hell are you?" The white-haired man in a black robe stood to the side of his desk.

"Can't complain."

The judge, a name he'd called him his entire life, moved his attention to Lilia and shook her hand. "No kidding. I've known Vincent since he was yay high—" his hand moved level with his knee "—so be good to him."

"I promise." She crossed her index finger over her heart. When the judge turned to his desk, Vincent caught Lilia rolling her eyes and shaking her head, clearly uncomfortable.

"I'm surprised your mother didn't want to be here." The judge picked up a laminated paper on his desk. "And that you aren't having a grander affair."

"We wanted this to be our day," Vincent said, straight-up lying to his old friend. It was something he would have to get used to.

Lilia opened her clutch, and he clasped his hands in front of him. He'd figured she wouldn't open that sucker up until she was at the bank. Then, all of a sudden, she held a bouquet of little white flowers with hot-pink pearls speckled throughout the arrangement.

"What else do you have in there?" He smirked.

"Tic Tacs." She winked at him.

The judge laughed so hard, it was a wonder he could stand up. As it was, he bent over and wheezed for a few seconds.

As they stood there and listened to the canned speech, Vincent watched her out of the side of his eye. He was about to agree to marry someone who hadn't even known how to spell his last name. He took the vow of marriage seriously; it shouldn't be just another business transaction in his life. His heart beat a little faster. He hadn't slept much last night, worrying about anything and everything that could go wrong. The thought that he had to marry someone just to keep a company made anger boil just below the surface, and if he could punch his dad right now, he would.

Lilia pressed her light pink lips together, and he watched them plump back into place. There were worse things in life than marrying a nice, stunning woman – like paying to do it.

"Do you have the rings?" The judge raised his white eyebrows.

Vincent took the red velvet box out of his pants pocket, opened it, and picked out his mother's diamond engagement ring that went back two more generations, the wedding band he'd purchased to match it, and a gold band for him that matched as well. He should've been thinking ahead and given her the diamond ring to put on before this point – hopefully the judge wouldn't notice the flub.

He repeated the right words as he held Lilia's surprisingly cold hand. This was it. He was officially a fraud.

The rings, by the best luck of his life, fit her finger perfectly. He couldn't take his eyes off of the main marquise diamond set in a gold ring and the diamond-studded band below – it looked like it was always meant to be there. Then he gazed into her eyes, and the room stood still. For a moment this was really his life – marrying Lilia, pledging his love and meaning it.

The judge asked her for a ring, and Vincent had to reach back into his pocket, releasing her hand in the process.

The spell was broken. Neither of them meant these vows.

As soon as they said their *I do*s and signed a little piece of paper, his troubles would be gone. Marriage, in all its glory, boiled down to a contract – and contracts, he knew how to manage. This was another deal in a long list of deals he'd made for his company over the years. Nothing more.

–

Vincent held out a gold band similar to the one on her finger, only thicker. Her ring finger now bore a fat, sparkling diamond.

She hadn't told her parents what she was going to do, let alone asked them to the wedding. If she showed up married, they couldn't talk her out of it. She'd always taken her own path anyway.

She steadied her hand and pinched his ring between her thumb and index finger to stop her urge to puke.

"Repeat after me." The judge read off the standard wedding speech, and she barely recognized her own voice as she repeated it. She wasn't going to remember this moment tomorrow; it was a blur now. She might, however, remember the look on Vincent's face when he'd promised to love her forever. There'd been a hint of sincerity in his voice – more than just going through the motions. It was probably all in her head, though – no woman wanted to admit, even to herself, that she was standing before a magistrate and playacting her wedding vows.

Vincent's hand was hot as she steadied it to put the band on his fourth finger. She watched him as she said the words out loud. It was hard not to get caught up in the moment, to want him to really love her and to want to love him in return. But that wasn't her lot in life. Not today. After she slipped the ring on his finger, she held on a little longer.

She focused on the judge's forehead, trying not to cry or laugh or walk out as he listed all the good things about love. Who knew that a civil service got so touchy-feely? They should've just signed the license and been done.

A year. I can do this for a year – for Dad. One year of her life was nothing if it gave him even a minute more on this earth. She had the check, signed, and for the exact amount she needed. She would be able to help her dad receive a new drug treatment that aggressively treated pancreatic cancer over several months.

"I now pronounce you husband and wife. You may kiss the bride."

In all her crazy, up-and-down thoughts about what she'd agreed to do, never once had she ever imagined kissing him. Which was weird, because he was such a hottie.

Vincent stepped closer, and her arms fell to her sides. His warm hand cupped her cheek, and his lips grazed hers. She felt the tingles deep in her toes. Her lips parted, and the kiss deepened, their tongues touching. It was like strokes of fire, melting her common sense until she was on the beach at Waikiki, snuggling close to a wide, masculine chest that smelled of spice and bonfire and was all male. Then the moment was over as quickly as it started – he moved back but remained close as he searched her eyes.

Kiss me again.

His hand slid from her jaw, and she worked to reset her bearings on life. Her body buzzed with a mix of excitement and bewilderment. She wasn't going to date her husband. No. She'd decided to take this year and expand her blog and writing commitments. Plus, she'd sworn off men – they were all a let-down in the end.

"Sign here." The paperwork sat on the corner of the judge's cherry desk.

Vincent signed first and handed her the pen.

She signed her full name: Lilia Lucile Carrigan.

It was official.

"Would you like me to take a picture?" the judge asked after he scribbled his portion to send in for the official marriage license.

"Yes." Vincent put his arm around her again. He sure was quick to get handsy.

"Say 'marriage is forever.'"

They repeated the phrase that made her want to puke through her smile. She'd look at the pictures later. Right now she needed some air.

The judge was the only one smiling as they left the room.

"Congratulations, Mr. and Mrs. Morgenstern." The brunette receptionist waved to them as they left.

Vincent clutched her hand a little tighter.

"We're married. Holy crap." At least she waited until she was in the elevator to scrunch her face.

There were so many things about this she hadn't thought through. So many little details she didn't know the answer to – or even what the questions were. She rubbed the band of her new ring with her thumb.

You only live once. Make the most out of it. Her mantra while she'd traveled in Europe pacified her frayed nerves now. *This is worth it.*

His thumb rubbed over her palm. His touch was the opposite of comforting when it started to register. *Feelings are not part of this deal.* There was one reason she'd agreed to get married. Nothing more.

"Let's celebrate." He opened the front door to the courthouse for her. "Do you want go out to dinner?"

"Sure." That was a good, logical next step that would allow them to get to know each other. Possibly one they should've considered yesterday. She needed to start being rational.

"Where did you park?"

The sun was falling in the sky, and the chill to the air was brutal – more so than just the hour ago when they'd gone in.

"Down the block."

"Actually, why don't you come over to my house and I'll make dinner? We can talk about the movers, too."

"I packed up everything when I decided to travel last year. I only have suitcases right now. The rest is in storage."

"We can get it out of there if you'd like."

We. That was going to take some getting used to.

"I haven't even seen your home yet. So, I don't know." How much space would she have? Was he clean or was there underwear and socks scattered about? He better be tidy – she hated piles of crap everywhere.

Just another in a long list of bizarre conversations she'd be having with her new husband.

"Let's get your stuff before dinner then."

"My suitcases are actually in my car because I didn't know exactly how this was going down." Hopefully the level of practicality downplayed how pathetic that sentence was.

"Perfect. Give me your cell number in case we get separated, but you should follow me over now."

"Give me your phone." She added her contact information and then, just for fun, took a selfie and set it as her profile picture while Vincent laughed. She texted, "We just got married!" to herself from his phone to save his number.

"Hey, Vince." A voice from behind her caused her to whirl around.

"Jonathan." The men shook hands. "Nice to see you again, man. How's business?"

"Good. We need to have lunch and talk about a new project I just won the bid on." A confused silence fell as the shorter blond man looked between them.

"Lilia, this is Jonathan. He owns a construction company I do business with. Jonathan this is Lilia… my wife."

The word "wife" rang in her ears.

Jonathan extended his hand, and they shook. "Congratulations. I had no idea."

"We had a private ceremony." Vincent put his hands in his pockets and rocked back on his heels.

She didn't want to raise red flags for him and ruin their deal, or be a laughing stock over the sham. Even though this marriage was not for love, she didn't want other people to second-guess them – she couldn't take the sideways looks, humiliation and disgrace if people knew she'd sold out. They'd agreed this was their secret, and she intended to make sure it was kept.

"We eloped." She smiled warmly at Vincent and then directed her attention to the shorter man. "But when we throw the reception party, you'll be on the list."

They parted ways, and she said a quick prayer that they didn't run into anyone else he knew. Or that she knew. She needed to soak all this in and get comfortable without being bombarded with questions.

"Reception party?" Vincent faced her, amusement dancing in his eyes.

"Apparently you're quite the social butterfly."

He waited for her to continue, clearly not satisfied with her answer.

"I don't want anyone to get suspicious. So, yes, add reception to whatever list you're keeping. Oh!" She clapped. "We should have it on New Year's Eve. That's a fun theme."

"Have at it. Let's take this public."

Public indeed. She had a sinking feeling that people would be asking a lot of questions long before the party.

Chapter Three

Vincent set plates of shrimp linguine on the reclaimed tabletop in his dining room. *Their* dining room. He should probably change his terminology during the next year to avoid drawing attention.

"Smells delicious." Lilia crossed her bare legs. She'd opted not to change after he'd helped her pick out a room upstairs and unload her suitcases. She'd chosen the room farthest from his: a second master with a full bathroom en suite that was across and at the other end of the hall from his.

Having her way down the hall would be good. They'd both maintain their own spaces.

"Do you cook a lot?"

He poured a glass of Chablis for each of them. "When I'm home. It's the timing that's hard because I work late." He should treat her like his college roommate – that's all they were. Roommates.

"We'll probably miss each other a lot because I work from home during the day, so usually I try to get out at night."

Perfect. He breathed a little easier; she was clearly approaching this the same way he was.

"Do you not like to decorate for Christmas?" She sipped wine and gazed at the half of the living room visible from their seats. "It's like two weeks away."

"I've never really had a need for it. I spend holidays at my mom's, so decorating around here is usually a waste of time." He took a bite of food and watched her face fall a bit. She was beautiful, with her small nose and big brown eyes, no matter her mood. "I have a company Christmas party this weekend."

"This weekend?"

"Saturday." Two days from now.

She nodded. A lot.

"You don't have to come." He picked up the wine bottle, topped off her glass and added more to his own.

She was the one who was so gung-ho to fit in as a couple. It didn't matter to him. The night would actually go more smoothly if she didn't come. Although, then he'd have to answer questions by himself, because he couldn't very well take his wedding ring off – not when he'd gotten married for the company.

"I'd love to." She sat back in her chair and put her hands in her lap. "How formal is it?"

"Not very. It's a fabrication business, so we're pretty low-key." He rubbed his new ring with his thumb – the band seemed tight all of a sudden.

"Every time I've seen you, you were dressed up."

"I'm the owner. And today I got married." Because they'd only seen each other twice.

She laughed. "That you did." She lifted her glass toward him. "To impulsive decisions. May they always work out."

The ends of his lips turned up. He and Lilia were going to get along just fine. "Cheers."

His side of the deal had already worked out. But her toast implied that whatever reason she had for saying "I do" was still in the works.

"Are you going to tell me why you needed the money?" Sooner or later he'd find out – Dean could run a background check on her. Something he should've had done before he signed his name, binding himself to her. Vincent had never been so impulsive in his life or acted so recklessly without doing his homework.

"It's not important now, is it? I'm here. We're legal." She gathered her dishes and loaded them into the dishwasher.

It was important, for some reason, but he'd once again let it go.

He brought his dishes into the kitchen. When she whirled around, he tried to move out of her way but wasn't fast enough. She knocked into his plate and sent it flying to the linoleum.

"Whoops." She covered her mouth, and her big eyes widened. "I'm sorry."

He grabbed a towel and knelt to pick up the plate and wipe up a couple drips of sauce. "Don't worry about it. I have a ton of plates that I don't need."

"What's this?" She pointed to large pieces of rolled up paper on the dark granite countertop.

"Plans for a meeting tomorrow." He unrolled them to reveal custom blueprints for a new restaurant. "I'm proud of this one in particular. It's got a lot of moving parts and timelines."

"And this is what you do at your company. Make stuff like this?" She opened the freezer.

"Yep. We do projects locally, statewide, and once in a while we bid on some bigger projects around the region."

She produced a carton of ice cream.

He had rocky road, mint chocolate chip, strawberry and phish food flavors stocked in his freezer – she'd gone for the phish food by Ben and Jerry's.

"Bowls are on the right of the stove."

She put two black bowls on the counter. "How do you find out about projects to bid on?" She glanced over her shoulder and raised her eyebrows.

He nodded. "We've been around for decades. I have a lot of contractor contacts and am on industry lists when people are looking for fabrication. I've started going after more nationwide contracts. Which will mean more travel." He welcomed the new challenge and change of pace. After years of helping to build the company, and after the year of stress he'd endured, getting out of the office to court new business was long overdue.

She walked past him silently, bowls in hand, to the living room. *When did she slip off her shoes?* She was still in her fancy dress, and the intimacy of her bare feet made him smile on the inside. He was still in his suit, too, just without the jacket and a couple of his buttons undone.

Lilia sat on the leather couch and handed over his favorite flavor as he took his seat on the opposite side. He'd always thought the vaulted ceiling was what made his cabin feel as cozy as the mountain range that paralleled it. Maybe the answer wasn't the architecture.

"Is this the first time you've been married?" She dug into her bowl and right into the meaty questions.

"Yes. You?"

He darn near held his breath waiting for her answer.

"Yep. Ever come close before?"

"No." He crossed his ankle over his knee and settled back into the plush cushion. He should light a fire or do something that would give him something to focus on other than Lilia in her white wedding dress with her legs curled under her slender frame, eating his favorite ice cream in his favorite room of the house. He might start to feel at ease, and where would that lead him? Neglecting his company like any other suckered newlywed, perhaps. No, thank you.

"But you tried, right?" Her spoon pointed far right. "Sounded like you had when we spoke at the coffee shop."

"No. Dated a couple wonderful women." And there he was, not being totally honest with his wife. He'd asked three women before Lilia to marry him, but each time he was the one who couldn't bring himself to say "I do." With Laney, he'd backed out as late as a couple hours before – and each time he had no idea why he couldn't just bite the bullet. Marrying Lilia hadn't been nearly as painful as he'd thought the commitment would be.

"And none of them fit your image of a perfect wife?" Her gaze narrowed.

"Something like that." He got the impression her assumptions put her off. Whatever. She could adopt a narrow viewpoint of his situation if she wanted. Her opinion on the subject didn't much matter.

"You're lucky you met me. You don't have to worry about this being anything but professional. You can treat this arrangement as work all you want."

The fact that they were on the same page now was a good thing. Although the notion she had no intention of looking at their relationship any other way was a little harsh. She was good-looking and he was good-looking – to say it wasn't possible was a little ridiculous. Not that he was hoping for anything different than their original agreement. Because he wasn't. They were roommates with built-in responsibilities.

"What about you? Was there ever a fiancé in the mix?"

He wasn't sure he actually wanted to know the answer to the question he was asking. Or the ones that would inevitably come up. Knowing someone's past made the situation serious. Real. And all of this was not real. It was purchased.

–

Lilia purposefully took small bites. Her wild decisions were well documented – partying in college, job-hopping, picking up and moving to Europe on a whim. Heck, she'd blogged about most of it since starting her *Made to Wander* blog years ago. But she didn't want to share her story now – she wanted Vincent Morgenstern's.

"Nope. Never even close to a fiancé." Unless she counted Zenzo – who was perfect right up until she left and he immediately started seeing someone else. Commitment made her itchy – the real kind, anyway. "I'm not the type who likes to be tied down."

"You sure proposed to me quickly."

Her laugh sounded happy even to her own ears, a welcome relief after being down in the dumps about her dad the last couple of weeks. "That's how you remember it happening, huh?"

"Yep, that's what I'm going to tell people, that you couldn't live without me."

His blue eyes sparkled in the dim light. She wanted to run her hand through his thick brown hair. If she were interested in dating him, she'd be sitting much closer and batting her eyelashes. Vincent was a catch; she'd have to be an idiot not to know or see that.

"Did I get down on one knee?" She sat forward. "I recited a poem, didn't I? Classic romantic." She intended to playfully slap his knee, but her fingers lingered. She sat back quickly and cleared her throat before shoving more ice cream in her mouth.

"Okay, okay. I'm rethinking this story."

"I thought so." She swirled her melted marshmallow, caramel and chocolate, not looking up.

It was getting late. There were tons of details she should still learn, like his mom's name, for one, but her brain was starting to slow from the lack of sleep she'd been experiencing.

"It's getting late." She stood. "I'm going to call it a night." Not exactly the romantic talk she'd pictured for a wedding night, but it was what it was. Her life wasn't exactly a romance at the moment – from any angle.

Chapter Four

Lilia woke up to new surroundings, taking a while to remember where she was and why. *Oh, right, I'm married.* The thrill of her big decision and the sheer stupidity of it mixed into one ball rolling around in her stomach. She tried not to focus on the consequences of her actions and more on the positive as she went about her morning. She threw on skinny jeans, her gray snow boots that went to her knee but looked like moccasins, and a heather-gray t-shirt scattered with small flamingos and curled her long, blond hair.

There had to be a good way to tell her family about marrying Vincent; she just hadn't come up with the right angle yet. They would be totally skeptical if she said she'd gotten married and then handed her parents a check for the treatment. The information had to be doled out correctly. Intentionally.

His house, her new residence, was beautiful. The garage entrance opened to a dining room on one side that led to the spacious kitchen, and on the other side was a loft-ceiling living room with a grand fireplace and stairs leading to the second floor that housed three rooms – hers being the one on the far right. There was also an office on the first floor and a big deck that had the most breathtaking view of Casper Mountain. Next time it snowed, she was going to sit out there under the canopy, drink peppermint hot chocolate and read or write, or just soak it all in.

She grabbed a banana for breakfast in the ridiculously nice kitchen, which went along with the rest of the expensive-looking house, and turned around to see all of Vincent's plans lying on the counter from last night.

I thought he needed those. He was long gone, but she could swing by his office on her way to have lunch with her siblings to spread the joy of her news. This would let her put it off longer.

She put all of his stuff in her bag and went out through the garage, using an opener he'd given her the night before.

She actually felt good about her decision this morning. Vincent was a nice guy. She had a rent-free place to live for the next year, and her dad was going to be okay – he had to be. The deal could've been much worse.

Zenzo had tried to Skype her last night, but she hadn't answered. She'd been foolish with her heart, and that wouldn't happen again. As a bonus, her marriage would force her to take a break from dating.

Vincent's office was close to downtown, so she'd pop in there and then go meet her family at Carrigan's Pub for lunch. And step one of her plan: tell them about Vincent Morgenstern.

When she reached his office, a plump woman below a big metal sign that read Morgenstern Fabrication smiled at her politely. "Can I help you, dear?"

"Yes. I have these for Vincent." She laid the rolls and folder on the counter.

"And your name is?"

"Lilia," a man's voice said, surprised.

She whirled around to see Vincent a couple doors down the hall, heading right for her. He wore dark jeans, square-toed shoes, and a white button-up under a dark blue argyle sweater. The man looked good in everything. She stopped from rolling her eyes at herself – of course he would still look good, just like he had the day before and the day before that. But her stance on men hadn't changed, so it really didn't matter how good he looked in his jeans. There'd be no dating, no blurring the line of their relationship. Her heart couldn't take another letdown if she ventured down the road with Vincent, and she couldn't risk losing the money – if she didn't complete the year, she owed him every dollar.

He looked happy to see her. And wasn't that nice.

"Hey. Did you forget something?" She jabbed her finger a couple of times in the direction of the counter.

"Thank you." His palms touched in the prayer position. "You're a lifesaver. I just noticed I was missing them and was on my way back to the house."

"No problem. You're on my way to the pub."

"Who's your friend, Mr. Morgenstern?" the receptionist asked with eyes that expected a juicy answer. And, boy, was she not going to be disappointed.

Vincent studied the receptionist's knowing eyes, finding amusement in their situation. "Jan, Lilia. Lilia, Jan. Lilia is my wife."

"Wife?" Her drawn-on eyebrows rose high on her forehead, way over her glasses.

"It's new," Lilia said. "Not many people know." She laced her arm through his, leaned toward Jan, and lowered her voice a bit, like she was telling an important secret with her lie. She'd have to come to peace with this subterfuge at some point, so why not have fun with it? "But we're planning a party to celebrate on New Year's Eve. You'll be invited."

Delight crossed the woman's face. "I'll tell Frank we have plans for a party."

"I better get back." Vincent gathered the paperwork.

She untangled her arm from his. Out of the corner of her eye, she could see the expectation in Jan's wrinkles.

"I'll see you at home later, hon." Lilia stood on her tiptoes to reach his lips on his six-foot frame. She closed her eyes and pressed her lips against his, letting her entire body relax into him. *I won't say no to more kisses, that's for sure.* She stepped back from him – those were thoughts she shouldn't be having.

She started to smile but didn't meet his gaze as she waved goodbye to Jan and then twirled toward the front door, not looking back once.

In the car, she closed her eyes and reminded herself, *Eyes on the prize.* On the way downtown, she practiced the sincerity she'd need to sell the story that she'd fallen in love, got married the next day – and all because she wanted to. And also the inevitable shock of her siblings' non-approval – mostly Luke's. "We fell in love," she said out loud as she stopped at a light. "I just knew." She took a deep breath and smiled. "I just knew." Then she practiced smiling. Yes, smiling.

By the time she opened the giant wood door to the pub, she was ready to sell the lie and had her story straight. *Bring it on.*

"Hey." She hugged her identical twin sister, Lena, tightly. "I haven't seen you all week."

"School has another week, then I'll be free as a bird." Lena pulled up a seat at the long bar top and shed her jacket, and Lilia did the same. "Thankfully, my free period is right before lunch hour."

There was probably a point in time that she should tell Vincent about the whole twin thing. The only difference between her and Lena was their personalities. Everything else was the same – down to their hairstyle, voice, and colors of nail polish they preferred.

"Yo, bro," Lilia called down to Luke, who was handing beers to a couple of guys eating lunch at the far end of the bar.

"There they are, my sisters squared." Luke, their Irish-twin older brother, owned the pub that had been in the family for three generations.

"I see your rush hasn't started yet. We should eat now." Lena, ever the practical one, nearly lay down on the bar to grab the menus sitting on the shelf that ran just underneath. "I'm starving."

"You can look at the menu all you want, but David is already making you guys burgers," Luke said.

Lena snapped the menu shut, and Lilia laughed. They never strayed from their burger order.

"The place looks nice." Lilia took note of all the white roses and poinsettias that now peppered the tables, bar and entryway. A lot had changed while she'd been gone, but this place and the town still felt like home. "I see Candace has been doing some decorating."

"Trying to make it festive in here." Luke cleaned a tall glass and set it under the bar.

"Looks great, really."

She'd planned to wait until they were all eating, but adrenaline had started seeping into her bloodstream already, and if she didn't say something soon, she was going to have to go on a run to burn off all the energy stockpiling itself. And she hadn't run since high school.

Without drawing attention, she reached into her jeans pocket and put on her diamond ring and band. She'd taken it off and examined it last night. It wasn't new, although definitely taken care of with love. The thin, polished, yellow-gold ring had filigree on both sides and held a marquise diamond set up high so the diamond-crusted band could fit nicely underneath. If these were really her wedding rings, she'd have the two fused together. But they weren't. Vincent was going to want these gems back for sure.

"I have something to tell you." She glanced between her siblings as she ran her four fingers across her thumb in her lap. "I got married." She flashed them the hand sporting the ice.

"What?" and "You've got to be kidding me!" came at her all at once.

"I met Vincent, and we decided to go to the courthouse and get married."

"Who is Vincent?" Lena's dark brows knitted all the way together. "And *when*?"

"Yesterday. He owns Morgenstern Fabrication, was born and raised here, and is one of the nicest men I've ever met." All solid facts, and basically the only ones she had about him. She crossed the fingers on her other hand, hoping they didn't ask any more specifics about him.

The men at the other end of the bar hailed Luke for a refill. He glared at her before obliging their request.

"Why didn't you tell us?" Lena asked.

Lilia controlled her breathing as she forced herself to keep eye contact with her sister. Sometimes, in moments like these, it was like she was trying to convince herself, not another person. It was either a twin thing or a sister one, but either way it was painful. "It was just a spur-of-the-moment idea. I got caught up in it." She pulled her phone from her jacket and showed Lena the couple of pictures she'd taken yesterday.

"Is this the Italian guy?"

"No." She grimaced a little at the ambush. She'd forgotten she'd told Lena about Zenzo – and, looking back, how stupid she'd sounded gushing about him. "I met him here in a coffee shop."

"How long have you known him? Have you dated him before?" Lena glanced at the picture on Lilia's phone again. "He doesn't look familiar."

"I met him three days ago." Finally, the part where she could tell the truth. The only way her family's feelings wouldn't be collectively hurt was if this was seen as another crazy Lilia move – marrying a man she'd just met. That way, she hadn't purposefully excluded the people she loved from sharing in her happiness.

"You're certifiable. You know that? I can't believe this."

David set down three juicy burgers in front of them, and Lilia gave him a hug before he returned to the kitchen to deal with the orders from the quickly filling tables.

"You love him?" Lena asked.

"Yes." She nodded and shoved a French fry in her mouth. "When I met him, there were… just, these sparks. When you know, you know."

Lena bit into her burger, and they chewed in silence. Lilia glanced sideways to see if Lena was buying her story, and all seemed to be going smoothly.

Say something normal for cripes' sake. "We should go get our nails done when you're out on break."

"Your dress looked beautiful. Do you have a better picture?" Lena studied her with knowing eyes.

Things weren't so smooth after all.

"No, this is it. I told you, it was quick. But we are going to throw a big reception party on New Year's Eve, and you're invited of course." If pretty much everyone in Vincent's life was invited, then the most important people in her life were welcome, too. It wouldn't really be a reception if the bride's side was absent. *Also, I should probably start planning that.* Her job left her more hours in the day than Vincent's, and it had been her idea.

"Did you tell Mom and Dad yet?" Luke finally joined the conversation again.

"Nope. You two are the first people I've told." She wasn't exactly eager to change her Facebook status. This year would be a good year to dive into her work, really market it and stay away from things that wasted time – or caused people asked you questions about your life choices.

"Obviously we need to meet him. Like, now." Luke sounded like their father when she and Lena used to switch places for events, classes and anything else they felt like. Luke was going to make a great parent one day.

"We've an office party tomorrow, how about Sunday?"

Since news of their father's illness, the Carrigans had decided that Sunday dinner should be set aside for the entire family to gather, if only for a couple hours, at their parents' to catch up from the week.

"I look forward to it." Luke ate his burger, staying on the working side of the bar. He still refused to hire another person, even though business had picked up over the last year.

Lilia stayed on guard as questions about her news peppered the entire lunch.

After her belly was full, she bundled up for the cold and stepped into the daylight with Lena. Their cars were next to each other, and she gave her twin a hug.

Lena stepped back but kept her hands on Lilia's arms. "What's going on?"

"I fell in love."

"No, you didn't." Lena shook her head and pursed her lips. "You can tell me now or later, but you won't be able to hide it for long."

Lena had a point. They didn't have secrets from each other – from everyone else, yes. But not between them. *Don't do it. Don't say the words out loud.*

"I married him for money."

"You what?" Lena's eyes were five times as big as normal. "Where is this coming from?"

"I didn't marry him because he's rich. Well, sort of. I mean, at its basic level I did."

"Stop rambling."

"We made a deal." She lowered her voice. "He has his own reasons for needing a wife, and I said I'd do it if he gave me money. Dad's treatment isn't cheap, and we don't have enough, even when we pool everything."

Lena nodded, and her eyes filled with tears.

"Don't cry. Then I'll cry."

"There must be another way."

"There isn't. Not one that I've come up with. This just fell into my lap, and—" she pulled out the check Vincent had given her yesterday "—now Dad and Mom can start making the arrangements." Her next stop today was the bank.

"Holy crap, that's a lot."

"I know. You and Luke can take back your life savings, and we can use this for everything Dad should need."

"This Vincent just gave you this money for marrying him?"

"Trust me, he has it to spare."

"I can't even process this right now." Lena's hands dropped to her sides, and now it was Lilia's turn to rest her hands in the same spots on Lena's arms.

"You have to promise me this stays between us. You can't tell anyone, Lena. Not a soul." Small alarm bells started to ring in her ears. She should've said that sentence before the whole "I married for money" bit. "Look at me. Promise me. I've signed a contract and cashed the check. I'm not backing out now, and this whole thing needs to appear real to everyone."

"Or he'll take back the money?"

"Yeah, and I'd like to save face. If people think our marriage is real, then that's the end of it." He'd take back the money only if she left before the year was out.

"Oh, Lilia."

Yeah. She understood. This is what had to be done, so it was over. End of story. Her parents were going to meet Vincent on Sunday, she'd give them the money later that week, and life would go on.

–

There were still emails to return and projects to lay out, but Vincent found himself pulling into his garage at a decent dinner hour. With takeout.

Dean had filed the paperwork. They were married in the eyes of the government, and full ownership of Morgenstern Fabrication would permanently pass to him by the end of next week. Everything was working out as planned – even Lilia was a nice surprise, considering all she cared about was money.

The freezer door was open, and Lilia's back was to him as he set the bag on the counter.

She shut the door and whirled around with a spoon in her mouth. "Eggnog ice cream. Just got it. 'Tis the season." The apples of her cheeks grew as she smiled behind her spoon, and it was the sexiest thing he'd seen all day, except for her standing in his office earlier with the plans she knew he needed.

"I brought dinner." He started to unload the cartons of Chinese. "I didn't know what you like, so I got a lot of variety."

"I thought you liked to cook." She stood close to him, probably the closest ever, willingly. As the scent of pomegranate washed over him, he watched her inspect the food, her hair falling over the side of her cheek. He wanted to brush the strands away; the craving pulled at the tips of his fingers.

"Good. Sesame chicken."

His attention fell back to the spread. He was hungry for food and nothing else. Certainly not his wife.

"How was your day?" he asked as they made their way to the table.

"I saw my brother and sister." She poked at her chicken. "Are you free Sunday for dinner? We started a new family tradition."

"That depends. How'd they take the news?"

He braced himself for the good, bad and ugly.

If her family changed her mind before Dean used their marriage certificate to finalize the ownership transfer, he wouldn't be able to gain full control before it was taken away from him. There was a real sense of building a house in the sand – he could lose it all at any moment, and that was eating away at him. He hated uncertainty, and he'd been living it in now for far too long.

"It went as well as it could. They know we met and were married only a day later. Probably don't expect open arms and hugs on Sunday."

"I'm not much of a hugger anyway. Anything else?"

"I don't have a lot to share at this point." She searched his eyes.

It had been bugging him that he hadn't told Lilia about his multiple attempts to get married over the last year. He didn't owe her anything – hell, he'd paid her to marry him – yet he felt bad about the deception.

"How about your family?" she asked.

"They know."

The conversation with his mother had been simple and focused on the business side of what the marriage license meant. Of course, he'd stuck to the professional aspects on purpose. The fact that Lilia intrigued him he'd kept private. He was keeping a lot of things private lately.

"And what did they say about our quick vows?"

His chuckle was as humorless as they came. "I honestly think my mom wondered why it took me so long. And she thinks you're beautiful."

"How would she think that?"

"Remember your profile picture in my contacts?"

"Oh, yeah. Glad she approves."

There'd been a little smile his mom hadn't been able to hide when she saw Lilia's picture. She'd been pleased indeed. Probably because they made a handsome couple and the marriage looked real, but a tiny voice in the back of his mind nagged that his mom thought his marriage had a chance of succeeding. That voice was going to be very disappointed in a year.

Chapter Five

Vincent parked for the party the next evening and went around to the other side of the car to help Lilia through the snow – it hadn't stopped falling all day. Lilia had insisted they listen to Christmas music the whole drive because "it's only on once a year."

"Ready?" He held her gloved hand as they walked into the hotel where Jan and her party-planning committee had rented a conference room.

"How was your day?" She held on to his arm through the lobby.

"Good. My shot was crap at the indoor range though."

Lilia had crossed his mind more than once – did she like golf, what did she do to relax and when was the next time he was going to get to feel her lips on his? She kept things real and didn't make bones about what she was thinking. He'd originally thought they should have one meal together a week, to keep stories straight and stay in touch with each other's lives in case they encountered questions. But now, he almost missed her, which was crazy.

"There he is." Jan held a microphone in the middle of the floor.

"Are we late?" Lilia whispered through a grin.

"No. We're right on time." For what, besides a party, he wasn't sure.

Jan had specifically told him six o'clock. Many times throughout the day.

"Come here, you two lovebirds." Jan was all smiles as she beckoned them onto the wood square in the middle of the room. "This is Lilia, Vincent's wife."

Clapping followed her announcement. He clamped down his jaw as frustration started to mount, and the pleasant look froze on his face. He found Lilia's hand without looking and laced his fingers with hers. She grasped his palm tightly in return.

"While they did elope, they are having a reception New Year's Eve, and you're all invited," Jan told the crowd.

Hoots and hollers surrounded them. *Thanks, Jan.* He didn't remember asking her to blanket invite everyone.

"But tonight, along with our Christmas party, we wanted to celebrate," she went on, turning to Lilia and him, "so we got you a cake." Charlene, the head of his billing department, wheeled out a five-tiered cake. "And we know you'll do this at the reception, but we wanted you to have your first dance tonight." Mike, one of his main guys, brought out a stool and guitar, and his wife, Amber, took the microphone from Jan.

"Congratulations, Mr. and Mrs. Morgenstern." The couple, in their late thirties, performed around town at all types of events – he'd seen them a couple of times and they were impressive.

They started to sing "You and Me" by Lifehouse as Vincent raised Lilia's right hand still in his and brought it to his heart. He wrapped his palm around her waist as she settled her other hand on his shoulder, and they swayed to the music.

Her teeth seemed extra bright from the white, glittering sweater she wore with red skinny jeans and heels to match. In her four-inch heels, she was almost at eye level with him.

His throat tightened, and his chest squeezed a bit. He wished he was doing this with his real wife, someone who loved him. Not someone he'd paid to sign a piece of paper. He gazed at Lilia as she watched the crowd. He'd taken away that experience for her, too.

"Your people sure do love you," she spoke quietly into his ear.

"They're pretty great." He conceded to the affection of the people in the room. He wasn't hot on the personal surprises, but he wouldn't have it any other way either. He'd made the right decision to marry Lilia to keep ownership of the business. If he'd let the company fall to his uncle, all of these people would have been out of jobs within a couple years. "I know this is a little much."

"It's pretty cool." The sincerity in her eyes was warming. "You should feel good that you've fostered a fantastic environment."

Before he knew what he was doing, he hugged her tighter to his chest. Hopefully she'd chalk it up to their being in the spotlight and not his getting swept up in the moment.

"I've always wanted to learn how to play the guitar." He ripped his eyes from Lilia for a moment to watch Mike strum the melody.

"Why haven't you?"

"Never enough time. There's always something else that needs to be done."

"I'm a fan of living in the moment. If you want to do something, you'll find the time."

Lilia might be onto something. You could say his whole decision to marry her had been living in the moment, and so far it hadn't bit him in the ass.

He was thirty-three and never knew he'd enjoy a roommate so much. Her perfume had replaced the standard air freshener smells, home-cooked food had replaced takeout, and her voice had replaced television.

Glasses clinking cut through the song.

Here was another moment to live to the fullest. Without a second thought, as if his hands knew what they wanted before he did, they slid up to her jaw. He pressed his lips to hers, and chills danced down his body. The kiss deepened, and he felt her palms curl around his hip and side, pulling him closer. Their tongues intertwined, and he wanted more. He could feel her chest rise and fall, feel the heat of her skin. Or maybe it was his skin. They were too close to tell.

The clinking stopped, the music stopped, and all that was left was his blood pounding in his ears. He separated his lips from hers, placing a quick kiss on her cheek as millimeters turned into inches between them.

He couldn't get too comfortable – Lilia and all of this would be gone in a year. He'd have to remind himself of that every day.

–

Lilia plopped down on the king-sized bed in her new room. The holiday party had turned out to be more fun than any company get-together she'd ever attended. Vincent was clearly the hero of the company and greatly respected. Standing by his side was easy, and she'd even picked up a couple of stories about him that made her laugh.

Holding hands with Vincent was something she'd come to expect in public – Zenzo hadn't minded PDA, but it had never been tender and for solidarity. His affection had been to show off. Vincent and Zenzo were opposites on a lot of fronts – work ethic, responsibility, smiles. Vincent had the best smile.

She ran her hands down her face and rubbed her makeup-heavy eyes. They were frauds. Vincent had paid her so that he could keep his company, and he was lying to all those nice people he loved about his marriage. Staring into faces and straight-out lying was a lot more taxing than she'd expected.

Her phone vibrated, and she reached into her pocket. "Hey."

"Dad's in the hospital." Lena's tone was low and serious. "Mom just called."

Lilia sat straight up and grabbed her pink, rhinestone-studded bag. "I'm on my way. Text me the details."

She ran down the stairs and was halfway to the hospital before she started to process what this meant. She hadn't even had the opportunity to tell her parents about the money. That was going to happen tonight.

She picked up her phone and dialed. The smiling photo of Vincent she'd taken at the party when he wasn't looking popped up on her screen.

"Lilia?" Vincent answered on the first ring.

"My dad is in the hospital." Tears rolled down her cheeks. Saying the words out loud struck a fear she'd buried weeks ago when she'd found out the surgery hadn't removed his cancer completely – that's when her parents decided to tell Lena, Luke and her. Talk about receiving bad news.

There wasn't really a reason she'd called Vincent. It's not like she had to tell him where she was – he wasn't her real husband. But she'd wanted to call him. She wanted to talk to him about this upsetting news.

"What happened?" The urgency in his tone made her picture him sitting up and focused.

"I'm not sure. Lena just called."

"Where are you? In your room?" He sounded like he was on the move. "I'll drive."

More tears streamed down her face, and she closed her eyes at a red light. "I already left."

"Oh."

Was that disappointment? She could really use him holding her hand right about now.

"I don't know how long I'll be, so just a heads up." She'd missed the opportunity to have him with her, but it was still nice that he offered. Very nice.

"Okay. Let me know if you need anything."

She disconnected and wiped her eyes in the visor mirror. She'd worn a lot of makeup to the party – full eyeliner, many coats of mascara, and blue eye shadow – all of which was now running down her face.

It took another twenty minutes for her to arrive and find the room after one wrong elevator ride.

"How is he?" she asked Lena in the hall outside the room.

"Stabilized." Lilia hugged her twin just as Luke and his new wife, Candace, arrived.

"What'd they say?" Luke asked Mom as she opened the door. "Can we go in?"

"He's resting. It's been a long day." Her mom's kind eyes nearly made Lilia cry again.

"What happened?" Lena rubbed Mom's back.

"Side effects of the chemo." Her mom took a big breath and clapped her hands. "I need something to eat." She looked at Luke and Candace, and the three of them went to find the cafeteria.

"What do you think?" Lilia asked Lena once they were out of earshot.

"I think it's worse than they're telling us." Lena hadn't bothered to take off her jacket yet either. They should probably settle in, though. Lilia, for one, wasn't going anywhere until they saw him.

"Yeah. I do, too." Lilia crossed her arms.

"Have you told them yet? About the money?"

"No. Only about Vincent." Her parents had been so happy for her, she'd nearly cried. Their strong support never ceased to amaze her.

"How'd they take that?"

"Better than I ever expected."

They both chuckled, but it didn't contain much humor.

"Well, in a year it'll all be over, right?"

Lilia nodded and pursed her lips. In a year, Vincent would go his way and she could go hers. And her road still led out of the country, although she was thinking Australia now. Once she was traveling, life would be normal again. Only, she'd started to enjoy being back with her family. And maybe other people.

"Oh no." Lena shook her head as she scratched her forehead. "You didn't."

"What?"

"You're in like with him. You like your husband."

"As a friend. Sure." That was definitely true.

"I've seen that look before. Do you remember Luke last year? That man was head over heels for Candace and all her stubbornness."

"You're crazy." Lilia shrugged. Lena needed to stop making something out of nothing.

"Mmm-hmm. We'll see."

"I'm going to go find coffee. Want some?"

"Sure."

Lena was insane. Lilia wasn't in like with Vincent, she just plain liked him as a friend. She didn't have any feelings for him past friendship and being his fake wife. Her focus was her blog and her family.

Chapter Six

Vincent paced, tried to watch television, and checked his work email on his phone – four times. Nothing took his mind off of Lilia. He couldn't stand the thought of her at the hospital with her dad and not being by her side to help her.

That's it. A real husband would go. What kind of message would he be sending to her family if he didn't show up there to support her during a difficult time? It didn't matter that he hadn't met them yet. He would eventually; he planned to live in Casper many years, and he didn't want a reputation as a bad husband. There really was no other way to see it.

He found a nurses' station and, three floors later, found the Carrigan name on a board under room 219. He took a deep breath and rounded the corner. He could do this. She hadn't told her family much about them, so they could just make it up together.

Lilia stood in front of a door, pacing back and forth while looking at the ground. Her blond hair fell around her face, and her arms hugged her chest. *It's going to be okay.* His gut wrenched for her – he'd do anything to help her dad and get her back to smiles and sunshine.

A quick look down both hallways told him no one would see. They could have their moment.

"I'm so sorry." Shock filled her face as he gathered her in his arms, one around her back, the other cradling her head. "It's going to be okay." He closed his eyes and took a deep breath.

Something was different. She didn't smell sweet or like pomegranate. She smelled like flowers and energy.

"Vincent?"

His eyes shot open. Lilia's voice was not coming from the person he held.

"What are you doing?" Several feet away, Lilia cocked a hip and set her hand firmly on it, holding a hot cup in the other. Then she grinned.

"I thought..." He held the blond next to him at arm's length. She looked exactly like Lilia. "What the... ?"

Was he dreaming? Had he fallen asleep on the couch?

Lilia walked slowly toward him and her doppelganger, who now had her eyebrows fully raised, an expression of non-amusement in the eyes that looked exactly like Lilia's but felt different.

"Vincent," Lilia said, standing arm in arm with him, "meet Lena. My sister."

Lena took a step back. Then another before her gaze settled on Lilia. "You didn't tell him we're twins, did you?"

"Hadn't come up yet." Lilia shrugged and covered a smirk by sipping her drink.

"I guess that happens when you marry a stranger." Her sister's dark brown gaze squared with his. "Lena—" she extended a hand "—the younger sister by three minutes." Her gaze softened a touch but was still wary.

He got it. He'd be in disbelief, too, if he were in her shoes.

"Nice to meet you." He'd never known twins before, let alone dated one. But apparently he'd married one.

Good thing he hadn't picked that moment a minute ago to kiss her again.

The sisters were in a staring contest, presumably using twin telepathy. He focused on Lilia, her hair still pinned up from the party, with pink lips and bright eyes. There was a difference between the sisters, and he could see it now.

Lilia was hotter by a mile.

"What are you doing here?" Lilia turned to him as Lena pivoted and walked toward the elevators he'd just come from.

He opened his mouth, but the moment was gone. He couldn't be all heroic now, rushing to her side, after that mix-up. "I figured I shouldn't leave you hanging here."

Her brows furrowed.

"Being your husband and all."

Her head moved up and down cautiously. "Right. And the hug – for appearances, too?"

Busted.

"Yup."

"It didn't seem like it. Neither did what you said. I could keep going."

The hospital made her a wise-ass.

He was careful not to spill her cup as he put his arms around her for a hug, thankful for her scent once again. "Would it be so bad if I came up here because I care?" he whispered into her ear, but he was asking himself as much as her.

He needed to stop trying to flirt and go back to the spirit on which they'd both agreed: this was only a mutually beneficial contract.

"No, it wouldn't," she breathed into his chest, and his entire body woke.

Tomorrow. Tomorrow he'd remind himself of the terms of their agreement. Tonight he just wanted to be by her side.

"Lilia?" An older woman in scrubs opened the door they were standing in front of. "You can come in for a moment."

Lilia nodded to her and then turned back to Vincent. "Stay out here?" Lilia searched his gaze.

Yeah, he'd made the right call coming to the hospital.

"I'll be right over there." He pointed to a bank of chairs lined up on the other side of the hall then she went into the darkened room.

"Where'd she go?" Lena asked, sitting down next to him and crossing her legs.

"The nurse said she could go in."

Lena leaned closer to him. "I know why she married you."

"You do?"

"Yup. I also know why you married her."

"Oh." Disappointment stifled his word. He'd rather enjoyed that no one was aware of their deception. It was a secret only they knew. Now her twin sister was in on it.

"I think it's horrible."

Yeah, his night wasn't going so well.

"And why is that?" He'd play along. It was that or leave, and he wasn't leaving Lilia.

"Because you can't toy with your lives like this and not expect consequences." Lena rested her head on the light blue wall behind them, staring at the closed door to her father's hospital room.

"Like what?" Consequences like having full ownership of his business and Lilia cashing a fat check? Which she had. The next day.

"You'll find out. Sooner or later, you'll find out."

"Why did she marry me?" Maybe Lena would tell him what the money was for.

"Because that woman is crazy. That's why."

"She's not so bad." A smile tugged at the ends of his lips.

"I'm going to give you the PG version of what my brother will say when he gets back. Mind you, he doesn't know this is all a farce." She sat up straight and looked him dead in the eye. "You mess with her, you mess with me. And I have nothing to lose and all day to plan revenge."

"I appreciate that you care, but I have no intention of hurting Lilia. We have an agreement, and we're both adults honoring it." She should know that if Lilia had fully filled her in on the deal.

"You forget." The door to the room opened. "I'm the one you hugged."

Lilia appeared out of the darkness and nodded to Lena, who stood, then turned back to him. "Consequences."

A chill ran up the length of his arms as Lilia warmed the seat Lena had just vacated.

"What's that about?"

"Nothing." He sat forward and leaned his elbows on his knees. "What's wrong with your dad?"

"Pancreatic cancer." Her face flushed, and her cheeks sunk.

Not a good sign.

She looked like what he'd experienced a little over a year ago in the ER of this very hospital the night his dad died. He'd felt that same sadness down to his soul for four long hours. The beeping and voices surrounding his dad were a nightmare he could still recall in the blink of an eye. His dad hadn't made it up to a proper room before having another heart attack and dying. The hope in Lilia's eyes broke Vincent's heart.

"He's doing okay. They're going to go down to Denver and try a different type of treatment. It's experimental. Although I don't think the side effects are any easier with those drugs either."

"So close to Christmas?" At the very least, he hoped her dad made it long enough not to spoil the holiday season for her forever.

"Has to be."

"We can drive him."

She squeezed his knee, and he watched her hand. His knee warmed, and he didn't want her to move her palm.

"Arrangements have been made. I don't think we get to go. Just Mom. Hopefully he's back and better by Christmas."

"If not, we can bring Christmas to him."

Damn the "we—" he just couldn't stop saying it.

She smiled faintly and stood. "Let's go. I'll come back tomorrow."

He locked fingers with her and led her to his truck. It was late, and she'd had a long day; he could drop her off at the hospital to pick up her car on his way to work in the morning.

"Thanks for coming tonight." The darkness of the night prevented him from seeing her face clearly.

"No problem."

She reached over and set her palm on the top of his hand that rested on the center console.

"Have they tried surgery or chemo or whatever else they do these days?" There had to be more options than experimental drugs.

"He had surgery a couple weeks ago, but new tumors have already formed. Chemo is making him sick and weak. That's why I returned home."

"I'm sorry to hear that."

"What did your dad die from?"

"Heart attack."

She tightened her grip on his hand.

"It sucked. It still sucks."

His dad was probably laughing from his grave at the way his clause was actually turning out.

They rode in silence. Lilia had a lot to process from her night, and he wasn't in a chatty mood any longer. But their silence wasn't uncomfortable – nothing about Lilia was uneasy. And damned if that didn't scare the hell out of him.

-

Lilia tiptoed downstairs. She needed ice cream. She'd been tossing and turning in bed for hours – her lids hung low and sleep was appealing, but images of her dad in the hospital haunted her. The cool air from the freezer chilled her arms, but she just stood there. Vincent had a lot of ice cream and she'd bought more flavors to feed her habit, but now she didn't know what she wanted.

At all. In life.

She wanted her dad to be fine so everything could go back to normal with their family. But then where did that leave her? Away from those she loved? That was stupid. Her world was crumbling, and she couldn't breathe. She braced herself on the frame and hung her head. Her dad's condition was serious, she knew that. She knew the odds of him being alive in a year from now were in the teens.

But those were just numbers. Seeing him so sick – that was real.

Hopelessness bit at her cheeks, and she started to sob. She was helpless to fix this, to make her dad well again. The experimental treatment was all they had left, and even then, she didn't know the life expectancy rate. She wasn't strong enough to watch her dad die. What would she do without him?

"Lilia." Vincent's palm caressed her back.

Had she been crying that loudly? It didn't matter. She couldn't stop herself now.

She wanted to move, to shut the freezer and back away from him, but she didn't feel steady.

His palm moved to her side, and then she was in his arms, completely encased. She wrapped her arms around him and held on, catching her breath. His chest rose and fell in an even rhythm, and she could hear his heartbeat. She closed her eyes and listened.

He didn't say anything. He just held her.

Her tears, and probably a little snot, had soaked through his cotton shirt.

He slowly moved his hand back and forth on her lower back and gently moved her hair away from her face so it wasn't matted to her cheek any longer.

It would be so nice if this were real, if he were consoling her because he loved her. She took a deep breath, pulled back, and meant to look him in the eye and thank him. But she couldn't. She left his arms and turned away from him, unsure what to do next.

"Do you want ice cream?" His soft tone made her wish she was still in his comforting arms.

"Yeah."

"Which flavor?"

"Surprise me."

It didn't much matter, she liked them all, but eating this late hadn't been the point of coming down here. She'd felt she was going to crawl out of her skin if she had stayed in bed, picturing her dad sick, much longer.

She made her way to the couch, pulling a throw off the back and onto her lap. She curled her knees up to her chest and rested her head against her sweatpants. From her vantage point she could see Vincent move around the kitchen.

"I hope I didn't wake you." Her nose wrinkled, but she had to say it. She'd obviously woken him with her crying, which, dang it, was a little embarrassing. There were only a few people she'd ever comfortably cried in front of, and he wasn't on that list.

He is now.

"Here you go." He handed her a bowl heaped high with rocky road. She started to smile – this was the ultimate comfort ice cream. "It must have been years ago, I think I was still in college, and I came home early one weekend. I hadn't been back in a while." He balanced his not-as-full bowl in his lap as he put one ankle over a knee. "I was going to pop in to see Dad before dinner, and I heard him in a meeting so I stopped at the doorway."

He wasn't really looking at her, and his far-off memory made the apples of his cheeks rounder.

"He was in a meeting with a big client, and they were arguing. Something hadn't been done right according to the guy. That was the first time I'd ever seen my dad as… not perfect. Human. To me, he'd always been this larger-than-life business guy, family man." His gaze connected with hers, and she swallowed hard because the rest of her was paralyzed. "It's hard to see the ones you love go through something tough or to realize they aren't perfect and beyond life's perils."

"It's certainly not great." She knew people who had family problems or hated a parent or sibling, but that wasn't the case for her – her family had always been close and enjoyed each other. They weren't beyond their occasional fighting, but it never lasted long. She had no idea about, and couldn't even bring herself to picture, life without the patriarch.

"I can't even tell you it will get easier, but you'll make it through."

"How did you deal with your dad's death?" No one else she knew had lost a parent, and surely it was okay to talk about this with him, since he hadn't just left her down here to sulk. Her panic subsided. In this moment, she could talk to Vincent about anything. Once someone saw you sob your eyes out, it was all kind of out in the open.

"It was hard. Still is. Once in a while I forget and I still pick up the phone to tell him about a deal I made or something he'd like, and then I just sit there, stunned all over again."

"I'm so sorry." Tears welled in her eyes again. Life could be so sad, she could barely handle it. "I actually didn't think you guys were that close, with the clause and all."

"That was a shock and still makes me mad that I can't talk to him about it. I did ask Mom; she says it was because he didn't want me to miss out on having a family."

"Best of intentions, right?" He wasn't going to get a family with her, so his dad had failed, and she could see the pain across his face because he knew it, too.

"Apparently I'm a workaholic," he said.

"You don't seem that bad to me."

"That's because I've left the office before eight since our deal—" he nodded to her "—and I didn't go in today like I normally do."

Why hadn't he? Maybe orders at Morgenstern Fabrication were slower because of the holiday season.

"I'm sure you'll get back to the way it was soon."

Did he not date much? He said there were a couple other women this past year, so surely he had a social life.

The tip of her spoon sliced into the melting ice cream and clinked the bottom of the bowl. "I don't even know what my normal is any more." A month ago, she'd known exactly where her life was, and she'd liked it. Now, too much had changed, and she needed new bearings.

"Christmas is in a couple of days. Do you have any traditions? That could be a start."

"We have a party at the pub, and all of our family and friends are invited. That's been happening for as long as I can remember." And Christmas had come a little early this year – her mom's face had lit up when she'd slipped her the check at the hospital.

"Perfect. I look forward to the celebration. We should probably get our schedules straight. My mom wanted to have us over for Christmas Eve dinner. I'm not sure if Silver will be back in town by then, so you might have to meet her another time."

"Silver?" Did he have a daughter?

"My sister."

"Right. Looks like Christmas will work out." She glanced down at her empty bowl and then to the grandfather clock in the corner of the living room. It was beyond bedtime, and while Sunday had already arrived, she didn't want to sleep the day away. "We better get back to bed."

She stood and tried not to freak out that she'd said "we" like they were going to bed together.

"Any plans for tomorrow?" He let her go up the stairs first.

"Not really. I'll probably mess around with my blog and start drafting out some posts." About what, she wasn't exactly sure – she hadn't eaten anywhere amazing or traveled anywhere new to write about.

"Now who's the workaholic?"

She turned at the landing, at the spot where they'd go their opposite ways, in time to see him smile. "Guilty as charged."

He stepped up to the second floor and was closer to her than she thought he'd be. She should've taken a step back to give him more room. She glanced behind him – or he could've not stood so close. There was plenty of space for him.

Her gaze dropped to his perfect, not-too-thin, kissable lips, then slowly rose back up to meet his eyes. They were intense and hot and contained something she hadn't seen in them before. A lot of possibilities for their late night could play out. But only one of them ensured her keeping the money and her heart safe.

"Good night."

"Good night." He backed up and turned toward her room.

She crossed her arms in front of her and made her way to her bed. There were a ton of things she could think about now besides her dad – like what the heck had just happened between her and Vincent in the hall. His blue eyes stared back at her when her head hit the pillow and her eyes closed.

Light streamed in through the high windows that framed the snowy mountains. Vincent had gotten up early and decided it was time he bought a Christmas tree. A real one. He would've been lying if he claimed his newfound affinity for the holiday was purely without the intention of cheering up Lilia. Because it was.

After the tree was set up in the corner where the grandfather clock had been, he found a box in the back of his garage that contained Christmas decorations his mom had given him years ago – some bought, some from his childhood. He'd never looked in the box before.

It was nearly lunchtime when Lilia made her way down the stairs.

"Good morning." He looked up from the couch, where he'd started to take lights out of boxes.

"What's all this?" She'd belted her fitted jeans and had a red plaid button-up tucked into them.

"Christmas. Want to help decorate the tree?"

"Of course. I thought you didn't do decorations at home." Her familiar pomegranate scent filled his nose and made him more aware of how beautiful she looked with a lot less makeup and her hair straight.

"I thought it was time to buck up and embrace the holiday." *And your smile.*

"First, I need some coffee." She headed toward the kitchen. "It smells really good in here."

"I put a roast in for later." He'd definitely gone overboard. But the day was chilly, and a roast sounded good.

"There's no chance it's ready now, is there?" she called out from the kitchen.

"Nope."

"Want a sandwich for lunch?"

"Sure."

As soon as he had a string of lights ready for the tree, she appeared with two plates and ham sandwiches.

"Breakfast of champions." She chuckled as she set her coffee and plate on the long, rectangular table in front of the couch. "Are these your ornaments?" She slid the box on the floor closer to her. "You didn't say you actually had Christmas stuff to use."

"That's because I had no intention of using it."

"Well, let's dig in." She pulled out a circle of bubble wrap and gently pulled it apart. "Oh my goodness, did little Vincent color this?"

There was a self-portrait crudely drawn in the middle of what he vaguely remembered was combed-out green yarn made into a circle frame.

"Yes. And clearly I'm an artist who missed his calling."

She set it lovingly on the table and reached for the next handful of bubble wrap.

"Maybe this was a bad idea." There was no telling what else his mom had packed in that box. He should've checked it before leaving it out in the open.

"Nonsense." She pinched a golden thread and lifted another homemade gem. "You were crafty back in the day." She smiled and even the sides of her eyes crinkled. If he could take her mind off of the negative in her life for just a couple hours then he'd done good.

A family picture framed by Popsicle sticks colored red and green dangled from her fingers. "Wow, that was a long time ago." Definitely the eighties by the look of their patterned shirts and his mom's and sister's ratted hair.

She offered it to him, and he studied the picture, which was also framed in his mother's hallway. "This one will have to go right here." He hung it halfway up the tree so he could see it from his perch on the couch.

"We should put the lights on before we get to the rest of these fine ornaments."

He stood on the right of the tree, and she manned the other side. He started on the bottom, making sure the cord would reach the plug, and handed the strand off to her to wrap around her side. Their fingers didn't touch, but his heartbeat started to pick up in anticipation of the strand getting smaller.

One more round and nothing. Another round and nothing. Anticipation was growing as their eyes met. Was she thinking the same thing? Maybe. But should they be? She'd married him for money, and as far as he could tell, it was just because she wanted it. That wasn't exactly the type of person he wanted to be with. Or stay married to.

He watched the smaller ball of lights pass through her fingers and reached for it, his fingers grazing her wrist and palm. Prickles crawled up his arm, and he focused on the tree, no longer sure of what to do. He wanted to kiss her. He wanted to feel her lips on his and hold her close to him. There wasn't any good that would come of it, and they still had over eleven months to go on the deal. He didn't like messy. He didn't do messy. He kept things neat and clean and orderly. Starting a relationship with Lilia wouldn't be any of those.

"We're just going to make it." She stood on her tiptoes to reach a higher branch. "You'll have to do the rest."

He laced the lights all the way up, and she plugged in the strand. "Perfect." She stood behind but closer to him. "It's a good thing you have high ceilings since you went for what I imagine to be the biggest tree in the lot."

He took one step backward, and they were nearly arm in arm.

"We had a fake tree growing up." She chuckled as she reached for the green ornament she'd first uncovered. "It was kind of sad, but by the time we put all the decorations up, it shined like none other. I swear my mom had something for every inch."

They started unwrapping his childhood memories and placing them carefully on the tree. Lilia wasn't acting differently or awkward, so he needed to snap out of it – she didn't even know he'd thought about kissing her.

"What type of blog posts were you going to write today?"

"You know, I don't really know. I haven't done anything lately that I'd normally write about. No travel. No exotic food."

"Feel free to tell the tale of tree decorating."

"As riveting as that sounds, I probably won't." She winked, and he nearly forgot how to put a hook on a branch.

"Do you talk about your dad on there? What's it called again?" He should check it out and see what she did for a living.

"*Made to Wander*. And, no, I don't talk about it on there."

"Why not?"

"It's too personal." She sipped her coffee and looked at the tree, not him.

"Isn't that the point of a blog?"

"I don't want to share. Not yet anyway. It's all too real then."

His own life was becoming all too real. Had it been silly or just plain naïve of him to think he could make a serious commitment to someone and then not feel anything at all? Were whatever feelings he was having even real? His Christmas tree efforts had cheered her up, but now he was the one who wasn't sure where his life was headed.

Chapter Seven

"Merry Christmas." A short, brown-haired woman wearing a red sweater with a Christmas tree brooch answered the door.

Vincent went through the door first, giving his mother a big hug.

Lilia took a deep breath. Once all of the initial meetings were out of the way, then she wouldn't be so nervous. She had no reason to be anxious in the first place – she didn't actually need to impress Vincent's family or win over his mom. They were already married. There was no disapproval that could change that now. Besides, none of it was real. Everything he did was for show – like coming to the hospital to keep up the façade. And all of the things she'd done were for the exact same reason.

"Mom, this is Lilia. Lilia, Birdie." Vincent kept his hand on her lower back during the introductions.

Lilia extended her hand only to have it pushed to the side.

"Nonsense." Mrs. Morgenstern embraced her.

"I'll put this in the fridge." Vincent disappeared down the hallway with a jello salad she'd made and rolls they'd picked up at the store.

"It's nice to meet you." Lilia said as air left her lungs, and they weren't easy to refill with how tightly Birdie had her arms wrapped around her.

"I'm glad to finally meet the woman who wears the family ring."

"Family ring?" She held up her left hand. So her suspicions were accurate about the ring being old. She hadn't expected it to be a family heirloom though. She'd just thought he went to a pawn store and lucked out.

It sparkled in the recessed light of the living room, which could easily fit a twelve-foot tree with no problem.

"It's beautiful." She put her hand down, rubbing the smooth band with her thumb.

"And it's stunning on you. Come and sit. Dinner is ready." Mrs. Morgenstern sat on one side of a black, six-person table, and Vincent and Lilia secured the place settings across from her.

"I'm sorry to have missed the wedding." Birdie glowered at Vincent and then turned a pleasant smile to Lilia. "I'm pleased you will be hosting a party though. I've sent Jan the guest list for our side."

Lilia's stomach knotted, and suddenly the baked ham didn't smell so good. This reception deal was like the wedding all over again, except in front of people she knew and loved. What if they figured out they were faking it like Lena had? What then?

"No one was at the wedding, Mom." Vincent unfolded a napkin and placed it in his lap. "You weren't intentionally not invited."

"We moved pretty fast on the whole deal." Lilia sucked in a breath at her word choice and glanced at Vincent. "I mean, love. We just went with it." She picked up a dish filled with green beans cooked in bacon bits and spooned them onto her plate, not making eye contact with either of them.

When she passed the white dish, Vincent's sexy grin almost made her laugh. Yeah, she'd gotten tongue-tied. She certainly couldn't do that in a week around people who might not know why their marriage was suspect. She finished filling her plate and dug into the food – a full mouth couldn't make an idiot out of her.

"Do you want children, Lilia?"

The mashed potatoes she was swallowing almost went down the wrong pipe, and she started to cough.

"Mom."

"Well, I'm getting old, and I want grandkids. Silver is probably never going to settle down, so you're who I'm pinning those hopes and dreams on."

Talk about pressure. He said no kids. Lilia was starting to get the distinct vibe that Birdie did not know the marriage was merely to keep Vincent as the head of the company. And wasn't that interesting?

"Yes," Lilia said, "I do." She really did, just probably not with Vincent. Definitely with a real husband though.

Vincent slowly turned toward her, and a distinct look of panic flittered across his gaze.

"You do?" he asked.

"Wonderful. How soon?" Birdie smiled wide as she stabbed a piece of ham with her fork.

"Not yet," Lilia said. "Probably *years* from now." Her answer should satisfy both inquiring minds.

Now she was certain Vincent hadn't filled his mother in on what was going on. Lilia would be reading that contract tonight. If there was a provision about kids in there, she was gone. She'd specifically said that was not an option. She'd only thought about kissing him, and almost did when they were putting up the Christmas lights, but she was not going to bring a kid into a fake marriage.

It's not like she dreamed about him or thought about him when he was at work or ached to slip her hand in his.

She could play along. That's what she'd agreed to do. "We won't disappoint." She reached down and laid her hand on Vincent's thigh and squeezed. "Will we?" she said through clenched teeth as she locked eyes with him.

His blue eyes were apologetic, but hope also flitted across his face. Hope? Maybe, or she was just hallucinating.

Vincent gazed back at his mother. "Everything has been so fast that we'll probably wait a while to add more to our duo."

She smiled and removed her hand from his leg. She'd kept it there too long. And not long enough.

–

Vincent helped clear the table and do the dishes so that his mom and Lilia could talk. Leaving them alone wasn't ideal, especially after the questions his mom had pulled earlier in the evening.

His mom wandered into the kitchen to pour herself a cup of hot chocolate from the coffee pot, then leaned against the counter. He would have had a shot at his holiday not being completely ruined had she kept on walking.

"Lilia is lovely."

"She is." He wiped his hands on a dish towel and tossed it on the counter. "You seem to be forgetting what all of this is about."

"I'm not the only one."

"Please. I'm well aware of my situation." He glanced to the living room. Lilia's blond profile peeked over the couch as she sipped from her mug. What if they'd met under different circumstances? Would they have dated, or would he have found out that she wanted him for his money? He wished he could trust her, but he couldn't bring himself to do that. He liked her, wanted to kiss her, sure, but that didn't mean anything in the long term. They were destined to have a fake marriage and then go their separate ways.

"Sometimes it's best to embrace the path you've chosen."

"Now you sound like Dad."

"And you have the same look on your face that he gave me for forty years."

His mom was seeing what she wanted to.

"Good night, Mom." He kissed her on the cheek. "Merry Christmas."

He found their jackets and helped Lilia into hers, and they were in his truck heading home within ten minutes. He'd thought tonight would be no big deal. He'd been wrong. He hadn't brought a girlfriend home since high school, and having Lilia there was odd. It was odd that she fit right in, got along with his mom, and didn't seem uncomfortable at all. Which, in turn, pleased him. It made him downright happy, and that was the issue. Lilia was not supposed to make him happy. She was supposed to be the answer to a business problem.

"I thought you said your mom knew about our deal." Lilia did not sound happy. She adjusted her position in the passenger seat to face him on their way home.

"She would naturally suspect but I didn't say anything."

"So what exactly does she think the deal is?"

"Are you angry?" He wasn't going to sit here and try to guess her attitude.

"Yeah. Kind of." Her tone now wasn't as convincing. "I didn't expect those questions."

"I don't know what her deal is."

His mother was only making things worse – just like when she hadn't stopped Dad from putting in the damn clause. She could assume whatever she wanted, but in a year there would be a divorce.

Chapter Eight

Vincent set his keys on the hook by the garage door. The sooner Christmas Eve ended, the better for all of them. His mom was out of her mind. She knew the deal. This wasn't a real marriage; they weren't starry-eyed about their future and kids. He'd never admit that he'd held his breath, hoping to see longing in Lilia's eyes. But there hadn't been – she'd been stunned all right, but not happy at the prospect.

"Stay right there." Lilia ran up the stairs.

She'd handled his mom well tonight, and his wife's mood had vastly improved the closer they got to the front door of his house. *My wife. I haven't used that as much as I should.* The term was weird because in his reality that's not what they were – only on paper.

He sat down on the dark leather couch and marveled at the Christmas tree they'd decorated together. The white lights, gold ornaments mixed with ones from his past, and red accents made for a captivating view.

What was she up to? He glanced at the open staircase and second floor. His stomach grumbled at his influx of nerves. He was only one week in; there was no way he was going to survive fifty-one more weeks of knowing but not knowing what he wanted out of this arrangement. It was no longer about his company or her check. It was about more – he felt the pull toward her. He was ready to admit that now. Only he didn't know where she stood.

"I have a present for you." She sat near him on the couch and held out a very long, very large, red, neatly wrapped package.

"You shouldn't have." He took the weight of it in his hands and set it down in front of him. It was heavy, and he was baffled.

"I wanted to."

He tore into the wrapping, never having been so excited about a present before in his adult life. He couldn't wait to know what she'd thought he needed for a gift.

"A Fender?" He slid the guitar case out of the box and opened it to find an acoustic guitar he'd wanted since he was young.

How could she have possibly known? His throat tightened as he slid his hand over the body of the polished, light wood instrument.

He was such a jerk – he hadn't gotten her anything. He sucked as a husband.

"Thank you." He locked eyes with her and searched her face for some indication of why.

"You're welcome. Merry Christmas."

"Merry Christmas."

"Play something."

"I have no idea how."

"Well, I guess you're going to need this then." She produced a green envelope with her wide smile.

He raised his eyebrows. There was more – more to the already most perfect thing she ever could've given him. He was beyond words. Just when he thought he had her figured out, she went and did something like this.

He gazed at her wide eyes and perfect, silky skin and lips. He didn't care what was in that envelope, he wanted her kisses for Christmas.

He purposefully grazed his fingers over the side of her wrist. The soft touch hit him in all the right places. The delusion that he was going to keep his feelings for Lilia purely business was slipping away quicker and quicker with each day.

He flipped open the flap of the envelope and pulled out a thick card. "Lessons?"

"Yep. Now you have no excuse not to learn."

The Christmas party – that's when he'd told her he'd always wanted to learn. They'd only been married for three days at that point. And yet she'd been paying attention.

"You're amazing." His sincere, easy comment rolled off of his lips.

"I just wanted to let you know I appreciate you and our arrangement. You're the best fake husband I've ever had." Her eyes danced in the twinkle of the white lights.

Fake husband – the phrase he hated more and more with each day that passed.

Chapter Nine

On Christmas, Carrigan's Pub was filled with people, half of whom Vincent had been introduced to and all of whose names he wouldn't remember. He didn't feel like meeting any more people.

"How you doing?" Luke sidled up to him and slapped his back.

Luke had been frosty at first, but as the party had gone on they'd been able to talk more and Luke had settled down. Or maybe Luke thought Vincent was less of a scumbag now and just a guy in love.

"Faring nicely. There's no shortage of entertainment." There was poker happening in the loft area of the pub behind them, dancing, and tables filled with people chatting. Not to mention the food – he'd never seen that kind of spread before. This crowd could feast off the food in the room for a week.

"Nah, we do it up right." Candace caught his attention from across the room, and with a nod, he was gone.

Vincent spotted Lilia walking around the bar, and he headed straight for her. A Christmas song played in the background.

"Here ya go." She offered him a beer, but instead he took both of them out of her hand and set them on the bar.

"Dance with me?"

He held her palms, putting the right one on his heart and letting the other one go so he could slide his hand around her waist.

"Your family is big." He swayed them to the music, and his mind blanked for a second when she relaxed and leaned into him.

"Not everyone here is family. Most are just close friends."

"I'm glad your dad is back."

"Yeah." Her lazy smile touched his soul. "He'll have to go back down for another round of drugs and tests, but they are hopeful."

"He's out of the woods?"

"For now. Thanks for being a good sport about the party. I know this is a little overwhelming."

"It's easy as long as I'm with you."

"I'm glad we're friends."

He felt the pull toward her and couldn't resist – didn't want to resist. And it wasn't a friend type of attraction.

He kissed her. There was no expectation with the kiss; he needed to feel her lips on his, if only for a moment. Then she opened her mouth to him, and their tongues collided. His palm slid further across her back as he pulled her closer to him. There was no guarantee of a next kiss, and he wanted to soak this one in.

She pulled back, and the look in her eye was not anger but something else. He knew what he wanted it to be.

"I should get back—" her gaze fell to his lips "—to the juke box. I'm on quarter duty." She pulled away from him and picked up her beer from the bar.

He watched her walk away. She glanced behind her shoulder before taking a sip of beer and joining a group that included Lena.

Well, he couldn't stand in the corner all night, and he certainly couldn't up and leave. He took a deep breath to calm his buzzing body. He was falling in love with her. For real. His attraction to all things Lilia was undeniable and taking over his life.

He chugged his beer and helped himself to another before heading her way. He'd stand by her side all night, and maybe they'd never talk about the only kiss they'd ever had that wasn't prompted by an outside force.

Lena broke from the group and stopped him before he could reach Lilia. "What are you doing?"

"Pardon?" Drinking. Clearly. And not nearly enough.

"I may not agree with all of this, but you two have a good thing going on."

How many drinks had he had already? Lena wasn't making a lick of sense.

She leaned in closer to keep her voice low. "She needs to be able to keep that money."

"What are you talking about?" He'd never even thought about taking back the money, and their deal was still in full swing. Why did Lena think it wasn't?

"The reason she married you? The money? It was for Dad."

He furrowed his brows. There were too many questions to ask all at once.

"He needed that experimental treatment the insurance company won't pay for, and the hospital in Denver wouldn't do it without at least half the payment up front." Lena's gaze found her dad, and her eyes teared. "We tried to raise the money, but it wasn't happening quickly enough." She crossed her arms. "Because of your check, he was able to go down to Denver sooner to receive these new drugs, and now everything will be paid for so they don't have to worry."

He gazed at Lilia from across the bar – she was picking out songs with Candace.

From the outside, she looked so carefree, and she was full of spirit to boot. But on the inside, she was just as scared as he was. She hadn't wanted to lose something – someone – close to her either.

"I'm glad it all worked out." He took another pull from his beer. If he could've done something, anything to save his dad, he would've. He respected her choices.

And the fact that she'd needed the money for her dad changed his perception – she wasn't just all about the money for greed's sake.

Both of their stakes had been high. Talk about two people being at the right place at the right time – they had needed each other. They were each other's last resort. And possibly saving grace.

"Which brings me back to my original point," Lena said. "If you start bringing feelings into your perfect little setup, it's all going to fall apart."

What had Lilia told her twin sister? Was Lena here as a warning because Lilia wanted her to be?

"I don't know what you think is going on, but—"

"I can see it. I see it in her eyes, too. It won't work out. You two are too different."

"Who are you to know that?"

For a sister-in-law, Lena kind of sucked.

"That's what I thought." She winked at him and smiled like she'd won.

What the?

"She might feel the same way, but you're going to have to work harder than the occasional kiss."

With that bomb, she walked off, heading toward the bar. So Lilia really didn't feel the same way, or was she starting to and he needed to tell her how he felt? What if she didn't feel the same and then he still had to be around her for the next eleven months? Tonight wasn't the night to have this discussion. But he also couldn't stay here and be this close to her all night without knowing she was his. Really his.

He started toward her, glancing around to make sure no one else was going to intercept him this time. "My blog is taking off," Lilia was saying to Candace when he was within earshot, "and I'm beginning to get known, so I really don't want to change my last name right now."

That was part of the agreement.

He whispered in her ear, "I can't do this," then set down his drink on the nearest table.

"What?" Lilia whirled around and grabbed his arm.

"I have to go." He tried to keep his voice down and talk over the noise all at once.

"You don't feel good?" Her sincere gaze met his and instead of the warmth he always felt, his stomach squeezed. Tonight was too confusing. The past week had made him a mess.

This entire ordeal had been a mistake. She could keep the money, he'd never dream of taking it away from her, but he couldn't carry on the charade any longer.

"Consequences," Lena said as he passed by her on the way out the door.

Yeah, now he understood completely. He was in love with Lilia, but everything else was a lie and he couldn't take it any longer. He couldn't pretend he was pretending to be her husband. He wanted to be hers, and he wanted her to be his. For real. Only he'd backed himself into a corner with a fake marriage he had no idea how to go about making real.

–

"Vincent." Lilia had to jog to catch up to him.

The streetlights flickered overhead, and the bitter cold of the Christmas night filled her lungs and pricked at her skin.

"What is your problem?" She stopped only inches from him.

Anger coursed through her veins, but she was still in her right mind enough to know that she didn't want too many ears listening in. In fact, tonight was supposed to be fun. It was Christmas. They were celebrating. And it had been fun – right up until the moment he'd pulled her into his arms and kissed her. He hadn't even given her the courtesy of a regular kiss. Nope, his lips on hers had stirred the fire that had burned steadily for a week, fanning flames she had to stamp back down deep if she had any hope of surviving the year and not being utterly, emotionally crushed.

"I can't do this any longer." His hands were shoved deep in his pockets.

"Do what?"

"So our being married isn't even an issue for you any more? It doesn't even register as a problem?"

"It was never a problem." It's not like she hadn't known what she was agreeing to – she just hadn't expected to like him so much.

"Just a deal." His gaze dropped to the ground.

"It is what it is. Why is this a problem all of a sudden?" It was hard enough to deal with her own internal struggle, but if he was going to be outwardly pissy now, she may as well give up. She didn't have it in her to tell him one thing all the time while feeling another.

"I can't live a lie." His blue eyes set firmly on her as his jaw jumped.

She stepped closer to him. "Well, you better figure it out because this *lie* has been sold and I'm not taking it back."

"I won't make you give back the money."

"Are you serious right now?"

"Very."

"And what about your company?"

"I'll figure it out."

"Because although you had no solution for an entire year, now you're just going to come up with a new answer? If we split up now you don't get to keep your company. You have a perfectly good plan in place." Panic found a place firmly in her throat. What was she going to do? He was just leaving her like this? One week in and she wasn't even good enough as a fake wife? "This is just the answer to you? I have lied to my friends and family for you. I've lied to myself." She'd been lying to herself from the first moment she'd seen him. She wanted him for real; she was just better at hiding it when they were strangers. They weren't any more. They were friends. They were confidants. The breath hitched in her lungs. They were nothing now. Everything about them was fake.

"You didn't just get nothing out of this deal." He ran his palm through his thick, brown hair.

"You're right. I sold my soul to do the right thing. Lesson learned."

"I didn't want any of this. All I wanted was to keep my company."

"And you did. Congratulations. Job well done." Her dad had gone through the treatment one time and had enough money to do it again and keep going to improve his health. She wouldn't change a thing.

"It's more complicated than that." His head shook, and his lips tightened.

She had a feeling it wasn't. Their relationship was black and white – and written on a piece of paper.

"I'll stay with my parents tonight and come by tomorrow." For what, she didn't know. She could stay or move out, but either way she needed time to think.

"That's not necessary."

"Then what exactly are you asking for here?" She rubbed her lips together, keeping her mind off what they were really talking about. Because if she thought about it, she'd cry.

"I don't know."

She took one more step closer, until she was as close to him as she was ever going to get again. "The next time you start dropping statements about living a lie and finding another solution, you'd better know the outcome you desire. Or don't bother." She whirled on her heels and walked as fast as she could on the icy sidewalk back into the bar and straight into the bathroom. She didn't want anyone to see her cry. Then she'd have to explain more than the sham that was her marriage.

-

Vincent heard the downstairs door creak. He opened an eye – it was barely light outside. His head pounded as he sat up to find his sweatpants and a hoodie. One too many shots of whiskey had put him in bed after he'd left the pub.

Lilia's face had haunted him – he couldn't stop picturing her angry eyebrows knitted together over big, brown eyes that hated him. There was no way to blame her for that either. One minute he'd been kissing her, and the next he was pushing her out the door.

The Skype call he'd had no business answering had put him over the edge. Lilia had left her laptop on the kitchen table, and as he'd grabbed the whiskey bottle and a short glass, her computer started ringing.

The man's face on his profile picture had looked a little too friendly. Vincent had stupidly clicked the answer button.

"Hello?"

"Where's Lilia?" A tanned man with an Italian accent moved his head to try to see around Vincent.

"She's not here right now. Who are you?"

"I'm her fiancé. Who are you?"

"I'm her husband." The bottle of whiskey slammed down hard on the table, and he glanced at it to make sure he'd not broken it. She was engaged to someone else? How had that not come up at the coffee shop? His body heated and his heart pounded, and he clamped down hard on his teeth.

There was a bunch of Italian he didn't understand coming from the screen, and he took the opportunity to unscrew the top of the whiskey and swig right from the bottle.

Before he could ask questions like *how long have you known each other* and *how long have you been engaged*, the call disconnected.

He watched her from the top of the stairs and stopped himself from retreating and letting her course go unaltered. He had questions. And, if there was still a chance to save this, then he should. Whether she stayed or went, his heart ached. He really hadn't handled last night well. He should've manned up and told her he wanted a future with her. At this point, he wasn't sure which was worse: telling her he had feelings and watching her leave, or not telling her and having her stay.

And then there was the whole fiancé thing – his embattled gut said he'd been cheated.

"It's early." He was off to a stellar start. Maybe next he'd point out her jeans were blue.

"I was trying to be quiet." She slid big, puffy red earmuffs off her head.

"You were. It was the door that gave you away."

He watched her, unsure of his next step. Was she there to move out? Was she coming back home to shower and stay? Her stare did not bring warmth; instead he felt like a stranger.

"About last night..." He'd started the sentence with no idea how to end it. He kind of hoped she'd jump in and assume everything was fine and they could move past their last spat on to the new one brewing in the back of his mind.

She said nothing.

"You don't have to move out." Getting to the point, it was. With a throbbing head and a slew of known mistakes, he wasn't looking forward to knowing what she'd decided.

"If our deal is over then I do."

"It's not over."

"It sure seemed that way last night."

He rubbed his forehead, wishing he'd stayed in bed. These were very good points, and he had no comeback. "You can do whatever you'd like."

"Not according to this." She produced a thick, folded band of papers and shook it in his direction.

Their prenup.

He made quick work of the stairs and came to a stop closer to her than he should have. Her pomegranate smell danced around him, and he refused to let it soothe him. He reached out and took the thick packet out of her hands. He pretended to read as his lips tightened together. She didn't get to take the high road – not today. "I forget, did it say anything in here about not being able to have a fiancé on the side?"

"What?" Her forehead wrinkled, and if he didn't know better he would've thought she was genuine.

"Your Italian fiancé."

"You've got to be kidding me." She rolled her eyes and walked around him, whirling around when she was at the foot of the stairs. "How do you even know about Zenzo?"

"Zenzo?" That was the dumbest name he'd ever heard. "It doesn't matter. So it's true then?" He threw their prenup on the couch as he walked closer to her, this time keeping a foot between them.

"No. I mean, he asked me, but I turned him down."

"When?" Vincent should've been relieved at that news, but now he was too worked up about her being in another relationship.

"Before you and I even met."

"It would have been nice to know you were in love with someone else when you decided to marry me."

"We weren't getting married for love, if you remember." Her eyes narrowed, and she crossed her arms, her balled fists making it clear he'd succeeded in making her mad.

He remembered all right – the one decision in his life he'd ever made on the fly would forever haunt him. "But we still got married."

"And you got exactly what you wanted out of the deal."

Had he? Looking into her brown eyes, he wasn't so sure. "Of all the women I could have made it down the aisle with." He shook his head as his hands moved to his waist.

"What?"

His eyes widened for a second – he had not meant to say that out loud.

"Just exactly how many women did you ask to marry you before me?" She stepped closer, but he refused to back down.

The number wasn't one he wanted to say out loud.

"How many?" Her voice quieted.

"A couple."

"I'm just the girl who happened to need something in return. Perfect." Her gaze didn't meet his, and her demeanor shifted – anger no longer bubbled out of her small frame.

"I'll void the prenup." If he lost the company to his uncle, there was still a chance Barry would keep him on to run things, he just wouldn't have the final say, which was far beyond anything ideal, but it was something. He'd made a very costly mistake last night and again just now. On so many levels.

"Oh no you won't." She jogged up the stairs.

"Lilia—"

"I'm staying. Well, sort of."

His brows rose, and his gut started to rumble. He didn't like where this was going at all.

"People know we're married now; we've made the rounds. I've decided to go back over to Europe for a couple of months to work. It's perfectly understandable that I'd need to get back to what was making the blog successful, so it shouldn't hinder our deal."

"You're leaving." It was hard to breathe as he looked up at her from the first floor. Instead of bending over and trying to gulp to fill his lungs, he slid his hands in his sweatpants pockets and tried not to look devastated. The last twelve hours had been a roller coaster of unwanted emotions, but her leaving wouldn't fix anything. And he wanted to fix what they had – to go back to last night when he'd swayed to the music with her and pressed his lips to hers.

"It's a win-win. We stay married, and when I come back, we can be seen at dinner together so no one gets suspicious. By the time the year mark comes around, no one will think twice about the divorce. They'll chalk it up to my schedule."

"Win" wasn't the word he'd use to describe what he was hearing. She was leaving him without leaving him. She was smart, and this would've been the perfect plan had he not wanted to be around her. But he did. He desperately did.

"When?" He cleared his throat, trying to remove the burning that threatened to take his voice completely. "When are you leaving?"

"The first. I have to line up a couple of jobs, then I'll be out of your way."

Her gaze fell to the carpet before finding his eyes again. The coldness had been replaced. Hurt. Her brown eyes were filled with so much hurt. He'd done that. He'd taken a perfectly innocent deal and complicated it and then managed to hurt the woman he loved.

"I'll talk to Jan about canceling the reception." He could not fake that everything was okay for an entire night when his world had just crashed around him. In fact, some time off and away from Casper was sounding pretty good.

She didn't look back. And he didn't say anything. Her mind was made up, and his pride stopped him from chasing after her. He knew how she felt now; there was no question that she didn't feel for him what he felt for her. He'd been a fool to think she would.

Chapter Ten

Lilia met Lena for coffee at the same fateful spot she'd met Vincent almost two weeks ago – she even picked the same table by the window and same chair where she'd first seen his brilliant blue eyes. Ever since their after-Christmas talk, she'd only passed him while coming or going. There were no more events to hold hands at, no more chances for kissing, no more laughing. There was no more eating dinner with him, talking to him by the fire, and no more of him. He barely looked at her now.

She pulled one knee up to her chest while she waited for her late sister to get her hot chocolate.

Her eyes burned. She'd put makeup on heavily today to mask the redness under her eyes that wouldn't go away. She teared up over the slightest thing – everything in her life was clouded by sadness. She didn't even know Vincent very well – how well could you really know someone in three weeks? And she'd married him only for the money, so she hadn't just broken up with the love of her life. He probably thought she was a gold digger – and why would he honestly be interested in a woman who was only interested in his money?

They were doing exactly what they'd agreed upon. Yet her heart was broken. She'd stupidly fallen in love with Vincent while she posed as his wife. She'd wanted him to ask her to stay when she'd told him she was going to

Europe again. But he hadn't – he hadn't even looked upset about her decision. Vincent didn't care what she did as long as he got to keep his company.

That's unfair. You're not about to give back the money Dad needs. The situation could not be more messed up.

"Hey. Sorry. I forgot what it was like to sleep in and couldn't get out of bed." Lena unzipped her jacket and took off her ridiculously bright, royal-blue knitted hat with a big ball on the end of the point. She'd had that thing since they were kids, and sometimes Lilia thought that was the only way their friends knew who was who. "Are you okay?"

"Yep."

"Talk. I had the same look when Clark and I broke up. Except you look way worse."

"We didn't break up. We weren't ever together."

"Stop it. I'm tired of listening to you two skirt around the issue."

"Us two?"

"Vincent is totally into you. He told me as much in the pub."

"Then why did he try to call this whole thing off that night?"

"I don't know. Men. Maybe he got scared."

"Scared of what?" His deal was done, the company was his. She was the one with the most to lose if it all fell apart.

"You're pretty awesome." Lena set her elbows on the table and moved closer. "Loving all that awesome can be hard."

A breathy chuckle escaped Lilia's lips. "He's not in love."

"But you are in love with him."

"Maybe. I think I got caught up in the situation." And then he'd found out about Zenzo, which made everything worse, and that was dumb – she'd neither said yes to Zenzo nor talked to him since the bank parking lot.

"It'll work out. Give it some time, let things settle down. It's new for both of you."

Lena's words helped to calm the jumbled mess that was Lilia's thoughts. She wasn't going to be the first one to make the move – not after Vincent had backed out and was okay with her leaving. When she returned in two or three months, she'd assess what the situation was then. Maybe after time and distance she'd have her head on better.

"I'm leaving." She took a quick drink, ready to explain herself. "Come with me."

"What?"

"I'm going back to Europe for a couple of months, continue what I was doing."

"I thought you were going to Australia next."

"There's more opportunity in Europe, and it's easier to travel between countries."

"What about Dad?"

"He's getting the treatment. I won't stay away long this time. I just need to get out of here. You should come with me. They always need more English teachers."

"No. I can't. That's crazy. And I like my job." Lena sat back and studied her. "Is he going with you?"

"Nope."

"It would be super romantic."

"I suppose. But it's just me. I didn't even ask him."

"When?"

"I leave in a couple of days." Being thousands of miles away from Vincent was sure to help put this all behind her

– too bad she couldn't just leave her heart here, too. That was the real problem.

"I hate it when you go."

"Me, too."

–

"You've got it all wrong." Vincent tapped a pen on his desk, no longer happy to see his mother, who'd popped in on her way to meet a friend for lunch.

"Everything was fine between you two. What happened?"

"Define 'fine.' We had a deal. You know that, so don't pretend you didn't. That's all it was."

"I don't think so. I saw the way you looked at her at dinner."

"What is it with you and *looks*? There was no look."

"Regardless, make sure you don't mess the business up while you're torching your personal life."

"You and Dad have managed to do that for me."

"It wasn't my idea. You know that. And your father didn't want you to end up alone. Because that is certainly the path you are on." He'd always looked up to his father, in life, in business. This one little clause was causing him to start doubting his memories, and that pissed him off, too.

"I'm not alone. I'm married. For a year." Except Lilia was leaving, and he would be alone. He was already alone. He'd been happy with his life before he'd met her. Now, even the simple things he'd enjoyed before her, like eating ice cream and watching TV, weren't as nice.

She checked her watch and then stood. "Stick out the year, Vincent."

"That won't be hard. She's not staying in the country." The words sickened him. She'd said she hadn't said yes to that other guy, but would she start seeing him again once she was back in Europe? She'd brushed the Italian off like he meant nothing, but the thought of her with anyone else tightened Vincent's throat. Lilia wasn't currently speaking to him, Jan refused to cancel the party and he desperately wanted to go back and change Christmas.

"When is she leaving?"

"Tomorrow."

"Then you'd better make good use of today. Don't let her go without speaking your piece, Vincent."

She left him in his own misery. He knew he needed to tell Lilia. He knew that sooner or later the truth would come out – and if he waited too long he might miss his window. But what if she said no? What if he'd been right, and she didn't want more? Could he live with himself if she turned him down? He didn't know. He sat forward and picked up the phone. He was going to tell her before she left. Tonight. Because he couldn't live the next few months in the unknown. Tonight, he was going to lay it all on the line.

Chapter Eleven

"I thought you wanted to go out tonight." Lilia studied the front of Carrigan's Pub as Lena parked. New Year's Eve had arrived quickly, and she had no resolutions. Maybe something like "be divorced and in another country this time next year" would be the most appropriate at this point.

"This *is* going out. Luke's having a party. We always have a good time here."

Lilia bundled her coat against the cold and snow as they rushed into the pub. The place was packed. The jukebox was going strong, and people danced with full cups.

"It's busy," Lena yelled as she grasped Lilia's hand and led them to the bar.

They managed to angle into a spot and flag down Luke.

"Two, please." Lilia was half tempted to put on an apron and help her brother out. The busy work would keep her mind from forming all sorts of opinions she didn't want to think about.

Luke brought them their whiskey sours, and they faced the crowd to see what kind of drunk dance party they could have before the new year gave them all a clean slate to mess up.

"To new beginnings." Lena held up her glass and clinked it with Lilia's.

New beginnings indeed. Lilia's flight was first thing in the morning, and it couldn't come fast enough. Vincent hadn't been home when Lena had picked her up, and she wasn't sure if he'd be up when she left. She couldn't even remember the last thing she'd said to him. And that made her want to cry.

"There you are." Jan appeared next to her.

"Jan. Hi." She sipped from her drink, trying to drain as much as possible before having whatever conversation she was about to have. "What are you doing here?"

"The party, of course."

"Party?" Her voice was octaves higher. The thought of seeing Vincent again made her hands shake. *Is he here?*

"We're having it here. Vincent said he'd tell you."

She nodded with a small, polite smile as she processed the fact that Vincent was throwing a reception party to celebrate their wedding and hadn't even bothered to tell her about it. He really didn't need her at all.

Her New Year's celebration was officially over.

"Excuse me." She ducked away and got a couple of steps before a hand was on her upper arm.

"Wait," Lena said. "Just wait."

"You did this, didn't you?" She stared into the eyes of a traitor.

"I may have played a small part."

"Unbelievable."

"Hear him out. If it sucks, then you'll know, and you can stop sulking and leave the country in good conscience."

Lilia pulled her arm away and continued to the door. She wasn't going to talk to Vincent, not in front of a bar full of people. She wasn't going to put herself out there only to get shot down.

"Lilia Carrigan," Vincent's booming voice called out over Luke's new karaoke corner. "Where are you?"

She stopped dead in her tracks and faced the faux stage. *This ought to be fun.*

"Can you come up to the front?"

She barely glanced at him as she moved through the crowd to stand by his side.

"I want to thank everyone for coming out to celebrate our marriage." He laced his fingers with hers, and her heartbeat kicked up. She was going to miss holding his hand.

Lilia surveyed the crowd, and familiar faces popped up – her parents were there, and most of the people from the Carrigan Christmas party list. Why couldn't this be real? Why couldn't Vincent be hers forever?

"Now, to my bride." He set the mic down, stepped closer, and held her other hand, too. "I love you," he whispered, his lips so close to hers. "I should've told you weeks ago. I didn't know what to do, and I handled everything so badly, but I can't let you leave without knowing how I feel."

Tears started to stream down her cheeks. She should say something – words like *I love you* would work – but all she could do was gaze into his brilliant blue eyes.

"I know we've only known each other a short while, but in that time I've gotten to know a loving, funny and exceptionally beautiful woman I can't live without." He kissed her. "This world is not without its obstacles, and I am less than perfect. But for you, I'll try every day to be the best man I can be. That'll probably not be enough, but for you I'll give my all."

Her life flashed before her eyes, and Vincent was in every frame. She loved him. So much.

She tried to say the words, "I love you," but ended up mouthing them instead. Judging by the smile on his face, he understood.

He got down on one knee in front of her, his back to the crowd. "Lilia, my love, my one and only. Without you, I am so lonely. Please stay with me, let's build a life. Will you forever be my wife?"

"Yes." She sniffled, and more tears blurred her vision and dampened her cheeks. "Yes." She nodded until he was standing and sliding his arms around her hips and kissing her.

"Did you like my rhymes?" he whispered into her ear, then kissed it.

She laughed, wiping her tears away. "I loved them."

"I figured one of us should really get down on one knee and recite a poem." He kissed her again, and this time, she heard the claps and hoots around them – she'd forgotten it wasn't just them in the room. "Oh no." Her body numbed, and she frowned.

"What?"

"My flight. My trip." She couldn't go now. Not when they were really together. Really married.

"We never took a honeymoon." The sides of his eyes crinkled as his hands rubbed her back. "How about I come with you?"

There was no one else she'd rather have by her side. Christmas was officially her favorite time of the year.

A Heart for the Holidays

To Tapher: for supporting my dreams – even when that means brainstorming a holiday novella at the lake in the middle of summer.

Chapter One

"He doesn't want a new heart?" Silver Morgenstern snapped her head up from her emails, which were piling up by the second.

No one on the National Organ Transplant List ever turned down an organ. Or purposefully removed themselves from the list.

Janae's eyes behind thick, red-rimmed glasses darted to the note on top of a manila file cradled in her arm. "He stopped in, but you were busy."

"Give me the file. What's this guy's name?"

"Fisher." A small smile streaked across her assistant's face.

"Did he say why?"

"He's, ah, one of a kind. I never actually thought he'd go so far as to take his name off the list, though." She pushed her glasses up and refocused her attention on Silver. "No, he didn't give a specific reason."

"We'll see about that." If this guy, a Mr. Fisher Tibbs, really wanted off the list, he could pull his name. But he'd already been on it for… Silver skimmed down… four years. That was a long time to give up on – and right when he was next in line for a viable match in the region. "Thank you, Janae."

Silver leaned back in her oversized cognac-colored office chair and crossed one knee over the other. Prairie

Wind Medical Center in her hometown of Casper, Wyoming, was a far cry from the third-world countries where she'd practiced for years.

She'd had aspirations once. Born of her own childhood, when her grandpa needed a liver transplant. Even at the age of ten, she knew she wanted to bring hope back into people's lives.

That had been dashed with one flick of a wrist and lots of blood.

So now she held the medical director's job rather than a surgeon's position. Her ambition to help had been relegated to a polite, rote greeting every time the phone rang in this new life, the life that was slowly draining her soul.

She rubbed her left thumb and index finger together in a circular motion as she read through Tibbs's chart. Idiopathic pulmonary arterial hypertension. Huh. A rare diagnosis causing the arteries flowing from the heart to the lungs to narrow. Usually people just had PAH. The idiopathic part basically meant there was no known cause for it, hereditary or otherwise. That was a bum hand to be dealt.

Still, what an odd time to call it quits on the list – he definitely needed a heart to live to old age. There wasn't anything in his chart about depression or a reason why he'd be forcibly taken off the list.

She grabbed for the black, fine-tipped pen on her desk to write down the address he'd given for his employer and winced as she gripped the barrel.

It's going to get better. It's not permanent. Your body is healing. She automatically recited the words in her mind with each sting in her right thumb and index finger, and the subsequent burning in her wrist. Stupid, stupid words from a woman who knew better.

As a surgeon, she knew her hope of regaining the full use of her right hand had vanished twelve months ago. But her mind refused to give up on her dream, her accomplishments and the future she'd laid out for herself more than two decades ago.

She couldn't get a hand replacement to make everything in her life great again, but this guy might have an opportunity to receive an organ that could save his.

There had to be more to Mr. Tibbs's story.

She couldn't sit in her office one moment longer or look at another email. Mr. Tibbs needed some sense talked into him. She might not be able to do anything for him in the operating room, but she sure as hell could offer a well-informed conversation.

The medical director position at PWMC came with the distinct pleasure of managing the National Organ Transplant List regionally. It was the only part of her job she actually enjoyed. And today she was going to oversee the hell out of it.

Silver stood, adjusted the hem on her sensible eggplant colored dress that tickled her knees when she walked, and grabbed the forms Mr. Tibbs was going to need to sign if he really wanted to remove his name. Although she intended to talk him out of that particular choice.

Soft holiday music streamed in the newly expanded main lobby as she pulled out her keys, tightened the belt on her black trench coat, and headed into the parking garage.

The office he'd listed on his contact form wasn't far. He'd be frail, probably pale, and wouldn't be able to walk far without losing his breath. The heart affected every part of the body, and this guy had been having problems for a while now.

She found the white building with a colorful sign that clearly stated she'd reached the Combat Children's Hunger office and parked her Jeep Renegade.

A rush of heat blew her scarf into her face when she opened the glass front door. She'd expected to see a warehouse full of food being packed and sent out for delivery or a bunch of offices where people were scurrying to drum up donations. There was none of that. The room before her was basically a large lunchroom like what would be found in an elementary school. It reminded her of some of the smaller, underprivileged towns in Tanzania with one-room schools where the kids did everything, including eating.

Brightly colored artwork hung on the walls – palm prints in paint on construction paper, drawings with colored pencils, and pictures of smiling faces, some young, some not.

Combat Children's Hunger was stenciled onto the wall in black lettering beside a picture of a handsome man in a baby-blue button-up, smiling but showing no teeth. She stepped closer to read the tiny gold nameplate affixed to the wooden frame.

Fisher Tibbs.

Her gaze bounced back to the cheerful, golden-brown eyes forever memorialized in the photo. This was the guy who didn't want to live beyond the next couple of years? The picture had to be recent, because the file said he was thirty.

"Can I help you?" A head popped out of the meager office to her right. The same face, right down to the five o'clock shadow, greeted her.

"Yes, hello. I wanted to—"

“Volunteer? Great.” He stepped completely out of his office, filling the door frame with his tall build – he had to be at least six-foot-four. “We can use all the help we can get this time of year. Lots of food going out to make sure kids are fed for the holidays.”

She swallowed and nodded, the French twist she’d wrangled her long, blond hair into that morning staying perfectly in place. She basically funded Paul Mitchell’s hair thickening and taming product lines.

A slow smile flourished on his strong jawline, adding wrinkles on both sides of his mouth that were nearly invisible through his thick, brown five o’clock shadow that was probably knocking on the door to a thirteen-hour stubble.

“Fisher Tibbs.” He stuck out his palm, and she let her hand slip right in and be consumed by the hard flesh, only pulling back when he did.

“Silver. Rae.” And now she wasn’t giving him her full name. *Because he’ll know who I am.*

What was she doing? She wasn’t here to volunteer. She barely had enough time in her day to do the work that was her day job. Volunteering and do-goodery was a thing of her past, as of twelve months ago. Another lifetime.

She was here to talk the man out of a death sentence.

Only the pink of his cheeks was healthy, his brown eyes sharp and his white smile easy.

The man standing before her had a lot to offer. Especially to children who were hungry and single women who wanted to impress their mothers with a charitable-hearted hottie date for the holidays.

“Nice to meet you.” His gaze fell to her jacket then her nude heels, and he didn’t miss a beat when their eyes connected. "Do you have time now to go over the basics, or do you have to get back to work right away?"

"I'm on my lunch break. I've got some time." Thank goodness the truth was coming out of her mouth again. She'd let him give her the tour and then dive in to a speech about the effectiveness of transplants and the success rate and that surely he had something or someone to live for.

She snuck a glance at his ring finger. Bare. She'd start with his job then.

"This way." He held his palm toward the wide-open space before sliding his hand back into the pocket of his dark jeans as he led the way. And she let him.

She hadn't volunteered, given back to any community, since her accident. Her chest tightened. Helping out a little wouldn't hurt. She could still have a conversation with him about keeping his name on the list. The two actions weren't mutually exclusive.

If she volunteered, got to know him and gained insight into his life, then she could better convince him not to take his name off the list. Of course, there was no guarantee he'd get a heart in time but removing his name solidified the bleakest outcome.

"I expected a plain old warehouse with dried goods. This is quite different." A small, fixed smile touched her lips for a moment.

"Shane," Fisher said, his attention diverted over her shoulder, "you're supposed to be in school."

She spun around to find a slender teen who hadn't grown into his feet yet.

"I have a free period and thought you could use the help." The young male ambled toward them.

Fisher braced his hands on his hips. "Didn't you have a math test today?"

"First period."

"And?"

A smile filled the high schooler's face. "Ninety."

"Good job, bud." Fisher held up his palm, and a grin filled his face.

The kid smacked his hand into Fisher's. Pride filled both of their eyes.

"But now get back to class before they call you in."

The teen strode away with a small hop in his step.

"We aren't a day-care or Boys and Girls Club or anything like that—" Fisher focused back on her, satisfaction still filling his eyes "—but we do try to provide a safe space for kids to do homework and hang out while they wait for their parents to pick them up."

"And help them study?" The program he was describing was a heck of a lot more involved than meals. Good. This was all good, and it was only going to further her argument regarding his transplant.

"Only when it's not over my head." He stopped in the middle of the large room. "Of course, we provide meals, too. There's the kitchen—" he pointed to the left, at the cafeteria-style area "—where they can play games, hang out, and do homework. Our doors close at seven." He smiled.

"Impressive." Her gaze momentarily dropped to his smile. It was an easy, comfortable smile, one that instantly made her chest lighten in return. He was charm personified. His chart had to be a mistake. She cleared her throat in a poor attempt to collect herself. She had half a mind to really flirt with this man and figure out how to have his babies. But that was going too far. Especially for the first meeting. "How close are you to the school?"

He held the door open for her to enter a back room that was more like the warehouse she'd expected. "We're a block away from the elementary and two away from the high school." His almond-shaped eyes crinkled on the sides as he surveyed the expansive stacks of boxes of macaroni and cheese, cans of soup and ravioli and jars of peanut butter.

She couldn't ruin his day with morbid talk about the pros and cons of living. He'd been all smiles since that boy said he'd scored well on his exam. Something must've happened to steal Fisher's spark for life, but you wouldn't know it by his championing of his non-profit. Breaking into their meeting with why she'd really stopped in would be abrupt and probably not go over well.

She didn't have to take his name off the list today anyhow – and he hadn't signed the proper forms yet. The papers she'd tucked into her bag would stay put. For now. Heck, she could even mail them to him, and if he returned them before she had a chance to reverse his decision, then she wouldn't file them. Filing mix-ups were common. Eventually she might lose the battle he didn't even know he was in, but it wouldn't be today.

Or maybe even this week.

–

He tried not to glance at Silver's calves again, but they were just so perfect. Not skinny – there was an actual roundness that was sexy as all get-out, and then with her high heels… Nope,, there was no point. She was here to volunteer, and that was great. They were short on help as it was.

"You have a great… location."

His gaze traveled over her cute, round nose and up to her eyes, where he caught a glimmer of curiosity as she adjusted her shoulders before continuing. Damn right he'd found the perfect spot. He'd had to fight the city for the permit. But it had been an election year, and no candidate wanted to go on the record as being against feeding kids.

"That wasn't by accident." He winked without thinking.

Her eyes were big, round, very blue and intensely focused, as if she were computing everything he was saying for some greater outcome. Was she here to volunteer or to size up his operation? If she was here to spy on him, she was certainly the right person for the job. She was just his type – sexy as hell, eyes that he could stare into for hours and probably the best in her field.

He may not have a long life expectancy, but he wasn't dead. Not yet. He could still appreciate a beautiful woman when he saw one.

Which wasn't a fact he normally had to remind himself of, but there it was. Flashing like a railroad crossing. No good could come from crossing that line. For either of them.

"How many meals do you provide on a daily basis?" Her heels clicked on the polished concrete floor.

"We're open for dinner Monday through Friday and noon to six on Saturdays. We hand out meals for kids at the schools on Fridays to get them through the weekend." There was so much more he wanted to do, but funding was tight and they'd had to cut Sundays out completely last year. "The project I'll have you start on is packing backpacks with food supplies for over the holidays, when school isn't in session. We're still open, but many of the kids won't be able to get here."

How parents could not make sure their child was fed, he'd never know. Although, he knew sometimes the parents were going without food as well. It was a fact of life for many all over the world.

Which was why he'd started CCH in the first place. The thought of a child not having food for a day, or a week, was enough to bring tears to his eyes. He didn't even turn away adults when they needed a meal.

"How do you stay funded?" She cupped her hands in front of her jacket. "Your smile is great and all, but unless it turns into dollars, I'm assuming there are some donations involved."

A chuckle escaped his lips. And here he'd thought she was so proper. What would she do if he randomly started singing his answers?

"More like schmoozing at fundraisers and tons of mind-numbing paperwork – for grants." Some of which were drying up as of late, and the endowment he'd set up wasn't going be able to make up the difference for too many more years.

The last thing he wanted was for his life's work, the work he did in the name of his daughter, to fall apart. He was meeting with his lawyer later this week to come up with a succession plan. If the doctors were to be believed, he had only a couple years left without a new heart.

He led Silver to a long conveyor belt where pallets of dried goods, organized by food, were stacked.

"This is where we stuff the bags, assembly-line style. We'll start packing them tomorrow and pile them up to go to the schools. They'll be given away here as well."

"Efficient." She smiled.

"It's a good operation once it gets going. This is about it." He took a couple steps in a half circle. "The kitchen connects here." He waved his hand to his left. It was a basic commercial kitchen, which he managed to rent out to chefs as an extra income source for the CCH.

"Did you start Combat Children's Hunger?" She walked side by side with him as he held the kitchen door open for her to go first and refused to check her out from behind. His decision to remove his name from the transplant list hadn't been easy, but it was the right call to make. What wouldn't be right was to start a relationship with someone who'd have to bury him soon.

"I was a social worker before I started CCH. The amount of children I saw who regularly went without food…" He shook his head. "It was deplorable. I had to do something about it. I couldn't sit back one more minute. Then the right opportunity arose, and I jumped."

Silver didn't need the full story. He never told anyone – which is why he'd not named the organization after his daughter, Maggie. Megpie's story was private. It wasn't for pity looks. His grief was older than his daughter's age when she passed, but it was present nonetheless.

"When did you start this?"

"About five years ago."

She nodded some more, her lips pressed firmly together. Her forehead wrinkled, and she looked straight into his eyes. "Sometimes people give up too easily or think they can't make a difference, but they can. They shouldn't give up."

"I completely agree. No one should ever give up." His words were more forceful than he'd intended. Conceding to defeat and doing the right thing were on a whole other level. "I appreciate you coming in to help make a difference." Bringing on another volunteer was good, but he had a lot of calls to make. This was one of their busiest times, and he needed 550 more cans of chicken and tuna, individually wrapped peanut-butter crackers and pudding cups by tomorrow. "Do you want to come back to help serve dinner?"

"I can do that."

"I've got a couple forms for information we like to keep on file. Emergency contact and such. Let me grab those for you."

He led the way to his office, not sure what to say next.

He opened his right-hand desk drawer and grabbed stapled sheets from a file marked "volunteers." She reached out and took the paper from him with her left hand.

"I'll bring this back tonight." She opened her black bag and put the papers inside. "What time should I be here?"

"As early as four if you can." He glanced down her nice coat to the pleats at the tip of her skirt then back up to her big eyes barely lined with mascara. The woman was natural and put together. Some ritzy career – or someone – had to be funding her style. He didn't know particulars about woman's shoes, but if the heel height was any indication, this pair was expensive.

"It's a date." Her warm smile was slow to fill her face, but for a moment it lingered.

Then she whirled on her heel, the bell on the front door jingling as she made her way back out into the cold.

Fisher returned to his office and sat down on his threadbare chair, which barely passed as office furniture, and picked up the phone.

"Hale." His best friend answered on the first ring.

"It's Fisher."

"If you're calling to cancel our beer, you could've just texted. Like you normally do." Paper rustled in the background. Henry Hale was a master multitasker. Which came in handy since he'd started his own practice.

"We're still on for later. I was calling because I need to get on your books to discuss my will. I need to update it." He didn't have anyone to leave the non-profit to, but there would always be someone to hire to take over. Henry didn't know it yet, but he was going to be in charge of the hiring committee.

"Always with the will. Buddy, I hate to break it to you, but you know you're not going to be needing one anytime soon. You've got to be pushing top ten of that list these days."

Top name, actually. Or he was. He no longer had to wonder when the call would come. He'd expected to feel a great sense of relief now that the pressure was gone – the pressure of anticipating the call that said a heart was available. But that relief hadn't come. Maybe when he officially signed on the dotted line, the calmness would overtake him.

"I'm taking myself off the list," Fisher said in one quick burst.

"What?" Henry was no longer multitasking.

"I've decided to remove myself from the heart transplant list for good."

"You have got to be kidding me. Why? What happened?" There was a long pause. "Geez, I didn't even look at the date. I know the anniversary of Maggie's surgery is tomorrow, and I'm sorry, man. Let's talk about it tonight, but don't do anything rash. You have a lot to live for."

Henry had been in law school when Fisher was dealing with hospitals and doctors nonstop. His friend had come home to hang out with him and Maggie every chance he could. Henry had been there for Maggie's transplant, and he'd driven all night before she died, making it just in time to say goodbye.

"I don't need this talk again. I got news from my doctor, and a transplant isn't likely to take anyway, so why try? I'm not living for a new heart any more."

He'd been down that dark and gritty road before with Maggie. And it had hollowed him out. He'd barely made it back in one piece, which was largely a credit to Henry. Fisher wasn't about to take a perfectly good donor heart for himself, only to have it wasted, when it could go to Wilson or John, who'd have a better chance of success. Either of those boys could do wonders with their future. They deserved to have that shot.

He wasn't afraid to die. Reuniting with Maggie in heaven when his time on earth was done didn't sound half bad.

"Then pick something else." Henry's words were clipped. "Anything. And live for it."

Fisher's chest tightened. They'd grown up together since the third grade. It didn't seem right to tell the one person who served as family over the phone, but he'd never be able to look Henry in the eye, explain the decision he'd made and watch as sadness crept into his gaze, even though he'd try to disguise it with a long speech.

"That's not what all of this is about."

"We'll see. I'll have my paralegal make a list of hobbies you could take up and things left to experience in life, and we can go through it point by point over my beer and your coke, wings and whatever's on ESPN at the bar."

“See you tonight.” There was no arguing once Henry started talking about his lists and staff – Fisher was ninety percent sure Henry didn’t even have a paralegal at his office yet.

He hung up the phone and looked out the front window just in time to see the sun hide behind a cloud threatening snow. He’d taken the first step – now he just had to convince Henry that he’d made up his mind. Fisher would get the peaceful feeling he was searching for – he just needed to sign those papers.

Chapter Two

Silver cut out early from work to change into olive-green skinny jeans, a brown sweater with a thick band around her waist and boots with a two-inch-thick heel, before heading over to Fisher's to help with dinner.

Her phone buzzed right before she opened her car door in the small parking lot of CCH.

"Hey," she greeted one of her best friends, not shutting off her Renegade yet. Heat was too paramount to her happiness.

"Come have a drink with me." Lorelei Sullivan sounded like she was rubbing her forehead and pressing her cell against her chin. "This day could've gone better."

"Can't. I'm volunteering." Silver let the last word slide through her lips a little slower. She hadn't meant to tell her friend. She didn't want to get Lorelei's hopes up that she was finally coming out of her fog, taking back her life and doing things she used to love.

"You are?" Lorelei's voice raised an octave.

"It's nothing. It's something for work." She hadn't forgotten her mission. "What happened? Your case not going well?"

"We're still prepping, but there are some roadblocks."

"Sorry, Lolo, you'll get it. You're a shark, girl." Silver smiled as three girls walking into CCH with brightly colored backpacks caught her attention. Fisher had built an impressive community center for children.

"I don't feel like it today. The boss is on a rampage."

"Then rampage back." Lorelei was born to be a take-no-prisoners lawyer and defend the innocent. "Use that beautiful brain under all that glossy brown hair."

"Your nice words are working. Keep them coming."

"Go home. Take a long, hot bath with a glass of wine then make popcorn and eat it with those cookies that are still in your freezer from last weekend, while you watch one of those crime dramas that you always solve first."

"I forgot about those frozen chocolate-y mousse balls." Lorelei's voice perked up. Her mom was a master baker and spoiled them during the holidays with a constant flow of treats.

"Eat them all. They're so delicious. You'll feel better with some relaxation, then you can brainstorm the problems of the day. If I get done at a decent time, I'll come over. But I've got an early day tomorrow."

"All right. But brunch for sure this week."

"I'm in. I'm sure Maisy is, too." Silver opened her car door and trudged through the snow to the shoveled sidewalk.

"Yeah. She's so weird lately. I think she's dating someone and not telling us about it."

"Then we'll order her some double mimosas and get it out of her."

"Gotta go. Hale the Conqueror is calling." Lorelei's eye roll was loud and clear over the phone.

Silver pocketed her phone in her big, puffy navy jacket. The temperature had dropped significantly as the sun began to set. Coming back to Wyoming after living abroad in countries where the average temperature was in the nineties was still a shock to the system, and midway through December, Silver was seriously contemplating long johns under her jeans.

The main room was packed with kids laughing, writing in notebooks and playing games. Long lunch tables filled the kitchen half of the room while the other space was left open, although it had been filled in with groups of kids sitting on the floor, standing around talking and playing with a ping-pong table she hadn't noticed earlier in the day.

She peeked her head into Fisher's office. No Fisher.

Bookshelves lined the entire wall behind his desk and were clumsily filled with books and stacks of paperwork. The window on the right wall had a nice view of the front of the building, and he could see who was coming and going for a block. The desk, chair and other furniture were modest.

All of the money must go to the food and operation expenses.

She'd seen her fair share of the flip side of charity work – sometimes the money really did go for what was promised, but other times it paid for lavish items for the people running it. A small smile hung on her lips as she whirled around to find Fisher.

She strode straight to the kitchen, her boots making a softer noise on the hard flooring this time. The kitchen area reminded her of a concession stand, only there weren't candy bars and nachos behind the counter. Instead, metal serving trays were lined up under a glass protector.

The faint smell of potatoes filled her nose as she got closer to the window. Her stomach growled. She should've eaten something before showing up to serve dinner. And then there would be the clean-up. Between all of that volunteer work, she also had to talk to Fisher to find out why he'd called her office in the first place.

"Ms. Rae." His gentle eyes crinkled at the edges just before the sides of his lips rose. "It's nice to see you again."

She stopped just before the counter. He was already in the kitchen, blue plastic gloves on his hands.

"Surprised?" She held up her hands, palms facing the ceiling. She'd bet that a lot of people said they'd come back or sign up for a time, only never to show.

"Grateful." He set a large black crate down on the counter, and then the muscles in his arms flexed as he lifted giant jugs out of it. After that, he hefted up another crate filled with apples. She looked away and pretended to inspect the countertops and machinery behind him as he placed the bin of fruit in the serving line. "The door to your left will get you back here."

This had been a terrible idea. Not the volunteering part – that had spiked her dopamine levels all day. It was the lying and the false pretenses part that was knotting her stomach and tensing her jaw so much she was starting to get a headache behind her ears.

Okay, new plan. She'd try to get to know him, and in the conversation she'd tell him what she did for a living, he'd bring up the list and she'd do her best to sway him away from giving up. Because that's what he was doing – giving up on life. She let her gaze roam down him as he stood beside the line, adjusting the jars and opening loaves of bread. His jeans hung off his broad hips just right, and the sleeves of his flannel red-and-blue button-up were rolled up, exposing thick, brown arm hair. His boots were probably steel-toed, although he didn't need that type of protection to serve food. He was the essence of a working man, and there was nothing she appreciated more than a man who was good with his hands.

"Ms. Rae." His voice was raised, and she flicked her glance up from his corded forearm to find him staring at her with eyes that were such a shade of golden brown it was almost as if they were shining. He kept his mouth closed, probably trying to hide the fact that his chest was rising and falling faster than it should for such a menial task. Heart failure would do that to a person. She'd keep an eye on that symptom, and if the opportunity arose, she'd use it to start a conversation about his condition.

"Please." She smiled, small and controlled. "Call me Silver." *That way I'll know you're actually talking to me.*

"We're short tonight because Gina has a cold. So it'll be you and me serving and cleaning up. The good news is that it's PB&J night. Are you good to stay a while?"

"Sure. What would've happened if I hadn't shown up?"

"I'd get it done anyway. Dinner might've been delayed. I try to serve by five."

"Do you have kids? I don't think it's breaking child labor laws if you have your own kids help."

"I think the rules are fuzzy on that one." A stiffness to his deep voice made her pause. Her joke had hit a nerve. "But no, no kids."

"Is everyone a volunteer?" Her gaze skittered across the sterile environment, not landing on anything in particular.

He cleared his throat. "No. There are two part-time people besides me. It helps when I can count on people to do the tasks at hand rather than hope volunteers show up. Especially when we stuff the backpacks. That's a big job."

"Basically you're a one-man show around here. This place would be nothing without you." She stopped herself from biting her lip or fidgeting – what was one supposed to do to act natural? Where did she usually put her hands when she spoke to other people? She could not remember. She set them on the counter right as he reached in front of her to slide a stack of plates her way. The sides of her palms grazed the top of his hand. Startled by the warmth, she pulled her hands up quickly. He should be colder than most. She could feel her heart beat faster, and a nervous laugh escaped her lips before she glanced his way. Nothing. No reaction. He was simply going about his business, laying out the plates and napkins.

"That's a slippery way to think. Everyone's replaceable," he said matter-of-factly.

Dammit, she was really trying to open up the lines of communication here, but that made twice now that he'd evaded her like everything was fine. Things weren't fine, but geez, he sure liked to act as if they were. She would have had absolutely no idea he wasn't planning on a long future if she hadn't seen it with her own eyes in black and white.

"I'm not so sure about that. You seem to have the magic touch." She turned her head away, feeling heat in her cheeks. She wasn't talking about their touch just a second ago, but was he going to think that's what she'd meant? And that she was trying to be coy about it?

"I'm just a man with a plan is all." He turned and retreated to a back pantry.

She rubbed her forehead. Really, she was going to cool it with the innuendoes for a while. She cleared her throat, making sure her words would carry back to him. "I'll have to check my schedule, but I'd like to help." She made a mental note to send in an anonymous donation, too.

As he returned, his head bobbed, appreciation loosening his square jaw, although he didn't smile this time. Instead he turned away, grabbing something below the counter.

"Put these on." He handed her a set of the plastic gloves. "It's a good thing your hair is back, or you would've had to wear a net."

She slipped her left hand into a glove with no problem and then gingerly tried to get a deceptively tight glove on her right hand without twisting, pinching or snapping any part of her skin. The mere act of scrunching her fingers so they could wriggle in radiated pain from her thumb.

He pushed one giant loaf of bread and a white container toward her. "You can spread the peanut butter."

Silver lined six pieces of bread up on the steel countertop and opened the extra-large jug of peanut butter. She side-eyed Fisher, who was opening grape and strawberry jelly tubs and sticking spoons in each one.

"I'll be the sweet thing tonight." He winked, and had she been holding anything in her hand, she would've dropped it straight to the floor.

A chuckle escaped her lips. "I shall try not to take that title away from you. Tonight anyway."

She palmed the first slice of bread in her right hand and tried her best to shovel out a hunk of peanut butter on the knife with her left hand. Spreading it without cutting into the bread was difficult – she still wasn't as adept at using her left hand as she'd like to be. "Is this much okay?" She offered her covered slice to Fisher. Who knew how far the supplies had to go?

He leaned over, unnecessarily close, and she swore she heard him take a breath before he spoke. "Looks good."

She laid it down in front of him and picked up the next slice, a small smile tugging at the corners of her lips. "What do you do about the kids with allergies? Any of them allergic to peanuts?"

"None that I know of. Or they stay away on Thursdays. It's always PB&J for dinner. Tomorrow is pizza. Rosana's donates every week."

"That's pretty charitable." She'd loved that about the work she'd done in other countries – the people and businesses that were usually so willing to help out their fellow man. Casper was a great community for that, too. *Shoot, don't forget about tomorrow night.* She really needed to put her schedule in her phone; if she forgot about the Ellison party, there'd be hell to pay. The hospital needed to snag a few more major donors if that new trauma center was ever going to get built.

"She's been a lifesaver this year, for sure." Fisher scooped out a blob of purple goo and used the back of the spoon to spread it on the bread, then capped it off with another piece and set it on the top tray beside him. "And the kids love pizza. It's our busiest night, and I think that's why. It also takes a load off, not having to make anything that day."

"What else do you serve throughout the week?" She continued her part in their little assembly line, concentrating on her hand-eye coordination.

"Basic kid fare, although, let's face it: if you were a hungry kid, would you really be picky? I'm not. Mac and cheese, mashed potatoes, corn, chicken when someone donates it or it's on sale at the wholesaler."

"From grocery stores?" Ugh, her questions were not personable at all. How in the world was she supposed to gain insight into this man's life if she just kept asking him about his non-profit?

"Yeah. I've been doing this a while and have built a rapport with the managers of most of the stores in town. They're good about remembering us when they have too much of something that will go bad soon."

There was a scream from the main area, and Silver's head shot up, searching out the sound in the crowd. Kids bustled around the area that was devoid of tables, and another cry sounded over the murmurs.

Silver was out the side door and jogging toward the large group that had gathered. She didn't realize Fisher had followed her until he was by her side, clearing a path.

"What happened?" he asked.

"She was just walking over here and fell," a girl answered.

A girl who wore her hair in a French braid and looked to be around ten years old was lying on the floor. Silver knelt down beside her.

"Where does it hurt?" she asked slowly, in a calm voice. The voice she used to use on a daily basis with patients.

The little girl didn't say anything but instead slowly rolled over onto her left side, gripping her midsection. "My stomach," her words were slow, but the pain was clear in her squished features.

"She's been complaining all day that she didn't feel good." Another little girl with straight brown hair and glasses leaned in, her brow furrowed.

"What's her name?" Silver asked.

"Miranda."

"Miranda, my name is Dr. Silver." *Dammit.* She was sticking to her ruse even in a potential emergency. "Can you show me specifically where it hurts?"

The young girl closed her eyes, perspiration shining her pale face.

"Miranda, where's the pain?" Silver added more insistence to her tone.

Miranda sluggishly rubbed her right side above her hip.

"Okay, I need you to lie on your back. Can you do that for me?"

"I'm going to throw up," Miranda declared between distressed sobs.

Silver found Fisher's eyes in the crowd. "Can you get me a pail?"

He nodded and disappeared.

"I need some room here; you can all go back to what you were doing. Miranda is going to be okay," Silver raised her voice to the crowd of small faces, but no one moved.

"You heard the doctor," Fisher's voice carried. "Give them space."

All signs pointed to Miranda's appendix. She needed a hospital now. Silver felt around in her back pocket for her phone, not finding it. Ah, dammit, she'd left it in her coat. She didn't want to yell, "Call 911!" in a room full of kids, most of whom looked terribly upset that their friend hadn't stood up yet.

She pressed the back of her hand to Miranda's neck, checking for a fever. Yep, she was hot all right. Thank goodness the group had listened to Fisher and only her friend remained. Silver lifted the bright yellow shirt on the girl's right side and started to press down with her index and middle finger very lightly. CCH was a five-minute drive to the hospital, but it was faster by ambulance.

"Ouch, no, stop, that hurts." Miranda scrunched up in pain and gingerly tried to roll back onto her left side.

Fisher was back with a bowl.

"Call 911." She lowered her voice as she swiveled her head to look up at him, all the while keeping her palm placed tenderly on Miranda's right side. "I'm fairly certain it's her appendix and it needs to come out now."

He knelt beside her and pulled his phone from his jeans pocket, his lips pressed together as he kept his gaze on Silver and waited for 911 to answer.

"I'm over at Combat Children's Hunger on A Street. We need an ambulance. Possible appendix issue with a girl." His sentences were choppy as he answered the operator's questions. "Eleven. I'm not her dad. She's not in good shape. Lots of pain. Despondent."

Silver wanted to ride with the little girl. Hell, once upon a time she'd have followed her all the way to get a CT scan then into the operating room and removed the appendix herself. Full service. That's what she'd been trained to do.

But she couldn't do that any more.

"Where's her phone?" Fisher asked Miranda's friend, who ran full speed to a backpack fifteen feet away and then back again. "Her mom works at a dentist's office right near the hospital. She'll meet her there."

"They're probably going to rush her right into a CT scan then surgery." Silver turned her attention back to her patient. "It's going to be okay. We're going to get you to the hospital, and you'll be in good hands there."

The sirens wailed closer, and Fisher rushed to the front door, ushering in two EMTs a few seconds later.

Ronald and Jane, dressed in standard blue EMT uniforms from PWMC, rushed through the doors, one with a kit and the other holding a yellow board.

"Hey, Doc," Ronald greeted Silver as his partner checked the young girl's vitals.

Please don't call me by my last name. Dammit, this thing with Fisher had gone too far, and it was only the first day. "Her name is Miranda. She's complaining of pain in her abdomen. I'd say appendix. Her friend said it's been at least a day. Her stomach is swollen on the right side and tender to the touch. She's pale, lethargic and diaphoretic. I'm worried about sepsis."

The EMTs loaded Miranda onto the transport board. "Will do. Are you coming?" Jane asked.

"No." Silver glanced at Fisher, who was focused on the little girl, his lips turned down and his eyes dull.

Oh, how she wanted to be back in control and doing what she absolutely loved most in the world. But Miranda would receive excellent care with the surgeon on duty. Silver hired only the best and made sure the staff she'd kept on after she took over was top-notch. "Her mother's been notified and will be there when you arrive. Can you make sure she gets to her daughter? The release forms will need to be signed quickly."

Jane nodded.

"It's going to be okay," Silver told the little girl. She briskly walked with them to the back of the bus, holding the girl's hand and making sure a genuine, reassuring smile reinforced her words.

"Where's my mommy?" Miranda squeaked out.

"She'll be there. Jane is going to take care of you in the ambulance, and you'll see your mom shortly. You're going to be okay."

Lights flashed and sirens whirred as Miranda and the EMTs pulled away. Silver watched as the ambulance rushed down the street and disappeared with a right turn.

A chill finally reached her core, and she wrapped her arms around her chest.

She wanted Miranda to be okay, and she didn't wish that pain on anyone. But wow. What a high. She hadn't felt that rush, that surge of adrenaline taking over, in a long time. She smiled to herself. It was nice to know she could still assess under pressure. Still help without doing the actual surgery. Being stuck behind a desk with paperwork was not as satisfying as she'd hoped it would be. She needed more. Something different. Her last ten minutes had proved that beyond a shadow of a doubt.

It had been a year since the accident, though; it might be time to regroup and really figure her life out. Live again, instead of letting life happen to her. Lorelei and Maisy could help her with options – the three of them brainstormed the hell out of all kinds of problems together.

She cradled her right thumb between her left thumb and index finger, rubbing absently.

"That was something." Fisher's deep, gravelly tone almost made her jump, so deep was she in her thought hole.

"She'll be fine." Silver squeezed her arms tighter, the brown fabric of her sweater not stopping the freezing temperature surrounding her. "Appendicitis is common, and the surgery is routine. There shouldn't be any complications. It's a good thing she was here and not home alone."

"So, you're a doctor. A damn fine one, at that." He shoved his hands in his pockets, standing so close his spicy scent cut through the cold and filled her lungs.

Fisher couldn't have been any more perfect if he tried. Too bad they hadn't met under different circumstances – one where she wasn't lying.

"I am." She turned to the door, the biting air getting the better of her.

"That sure came in handy." He chuckled as he walked beside her and opened the door for her.

And a gentleman. Her insides heated a bit; hopefully, he'd attribute the pink on her cheeks to the dipping temperature.

"I think you could've figured out she needed 911 if I hadn't been around."

He shrugged. "You never know."

Yeah, he would've been just fine.

All eyes were on them; the big room filled with children was silent, minus a couple of whispers.

"Miranda is going to be okay. She's on her way to the hospital and will get the care she needs." Fisher's reassurance rang out loudly, sure to reach the kids in the back. "Dinner will be ready soon."

Groups huddled up, and the silence was replaced with chatter as Silver and Fisher made their way back to the kitchen.

She never would've predicted all this when she ate her Cheerios this morning.

"Do you work over at Prairie Wind?" Fisher asked, taking his station in the kitchen.

She started up their little assembly line of sandwich-making again, grasping the knife with her right hand and quickly switching to her left when the pain started after the first swipe of peanut butter.

"I do." *Now's my chance.* She should just tell him all in one sentence and be done with the incognito act that she never had meant to happen in the first place. Her heartbeat thudded, one quick pulse after the next, and she gripped the handle of the knife harder. This was it.

"Good place."

"It is. I've only been back for a year. I was abroad before that."

"Which country?"

Why? Why had she changed the subject? She hadn't even given him the chance to ask what exactly she did – which area she worked in or her job duties.

She pressed a little too hard on the knife, and an impression of the edge sank into the bread. "Different areas in Africa mostly." She spread more peanut butter than she should have to cover up her mistake.

"I bet they appreciated your skills."

"I like to think so." They sure hadn't needed her when her ability to practice surgery had been ripped from her. The program she'd worked for had offered her a position, administrative in nature, but the thought of watching other people do what she longed for had been too much. When the CEO of PWMC had reached out and offered her the medical director position, it seemed like her only option to keep money coming in while licking her wounds back in her hometown. So far a year of licking her wounds had only made them worse. She was done with that. She had to move forward.

Fisher was moving forward – kind of. At least he'd decided he didn't want to be healed or get better. How could he come to such a serious decision and still be spreading jelly on a piece of bread, acting like nothing in the world was wrong?

She had to find a way to tell Fisher the truth and talk to him about his options. She'd keep coming back until she did.

Chapter Three

Fisher watched the kids settle in to dinner, his lips turning down at the lack of excited chatter he was used to hearing. They had to be still affected by Miranda's impromptu trip to the hospital. After all, it had happened less than an hour ago.

He set the last sandwich on Wallace's plate and turned to put the metal serving tray in the sink. Silver was squatting and moving things around on the bottom shelf of the pantry.

"You can just set the bins in there." He folded his arms across his chest and leaned back on the stainless-steel countertop. "You don't have to move all that stuff."

"I'm putting all the like items together." She stood and brushed off her hands. "All done. What's next?"

Silver had been a natural, talking to the kids like they were real people. Oddly enough, he'd come across more adults who wanted to help out but froze up when it came to talking *to* the kids, not at them. He glanced at the students again. Sending them home in somber moods wasn't an option. Most of these kids had a lot to deal with without piling on distress from a place that was supposed to be safe.

"Follow me," he told Silver, holding open the door to the kitchen. "Grab your jacket."

Her brows knitted together before she slung her jacket over her arm. He headed straight for the front door. Snow was everywhere, and, thanks to the cold temperature, it was still soft. He bent over, balled a fist of snow in his bare hands and spun to face Silver. Whoa. His vision blurred for a few too many seconds, and he blinked, clamping his jaw tightly. He never got used to these symptoms, which seemed to be happening more frequently.

"Get ready. You might want to start making a pile." He hid the snowball behind his back and walked into the room like he wasn't planning on starting a war. He bounced the ball in his right hand a couple of times, cold liquid running down his hot palm. "Snowball fight!" he yelled then lobbed the ball in the direction of the closest table before jogging back outside. Hoots and hollers followed him.

He took aim as they came rushing out. He should've taken a moment to make his own pile of snow bombs before declaring war, but oh well.

He spied Silver to his left. She'd set up by the row of evergreens that had a wall of blown over snow beside the building to form a barrier, and she had a dozen or so snowballs made at her feet. Smart woman. He hustled to her side, throwing one at the first kid trying to form a ball in his hand.

She picked up two from her stockpile and handed him one. She bounced it a couple of times in her right hand but threw it with her left, hitting Chelsea in the shoulder. He picked up more from her stash and handed two to her. She threw a ball the size of her palm right before one smacked her square on the cheek. She erupted with laughter – a strong laugh, followed by a wide grin that brightened her blue eyes.

He chuckled, ducked at an incoming ball and tossed one back in the same general direction.

They balled snow as fast as they could. It was them against the kids.

Damn, he should've grabbed his own jacket.

Suddenly, she was smearing snow all over his face and laughter completely surrounded him.

"Gotcha," Silver managed between gasps of laughter.

"I see how it is." He hunched down and swiped up snow as he whirled around, intending to splash snow in her face. But his estimation of her proximity was off, and instead of throwing snow at her, he caught her in his arms and they tumbled to the ground. He tried to break his fall so as not to land completely on her. He failed, only managing to get one hand on the ground to brace his weight.

It was a good thing there was a fair amount of snow to pad the fall; he was practically twice her size. Their legs were intertwined, his body pressed down on hers and his heart pumped harder.

His nose was inches from hers; he could feel the heat coming off her body. She smelled sweet even through the cold. He took in her pink cheeks and lips, which parted as her chest rose. His gaze flicked up to her wide eyes that watched him; no panic or rush to move filled her gaze, only an easiness.

His chest tightened when he tried to take a breath. He didn't break eye contact but concentrated on his breathing. In. Out. He wasn't running out of air anytime soon.

Her gaze traveled over his face and down to his lips.

Kiss her.

No. Kissing Silver wasn't in his plans. Or a part of his future. Starting anything with her wasn't an option. He shifted to one side so that she wasn't trapped any longer. He had to. Before he did something stupid and reckless and fueled by a desire nagging deep in his gut.

Without missing a beat, she smushed more snow into the back of his head as she rolled away from him. He scooped up snow with the hand he wasn't using to brace himself on the ground and looked up just in time to see her take off after Ashley and Kendra, who'd been pelting them nonstop. He threw an unformed snowball in her direction, watching it dissipate high in the evening sky.

The parking lot lights kicked on. He'd have to shut down the fun just as fast as he'd started it.

Silver disappeared around a tree, and Fisher wiped both palms down his face, the melted ice running down his neck before he stood up.

"What's all this?" Henry adjusted his leather gloves, tramping through the snow.

"Every man for himself." The kids were screaming and running around laughing. *Job well done today.* This part is what gave him satisfaction – happy kids who didn't have to worry about anything other than being a child while they were at CCH. The events like the one tomorrow night hosted by the Ellisons, where he'd have to wear his real leather shoes and a tie, were only a means to an end. Hobnobbing with current and potential donors was crucial. The future of CCH, his legacy, depended on it.

Henry didn't miss a beat, rolling two snowballs quickly and pitching them at two boys on the outskirts of the fight.

Silver ran in a zigzag pattern away from the girls on the front lawn and circled Fisher and Henry.

"Just stand right there." She pulled on Fisher's shirt, forcing him to take two steps to his left, effectively making him and Henry her shield as she crouched behind them. She tossed a ball over their heads, and it crashed to the ground. Kendra and Ashley laughed, and then three boys whaling snow at them diverted their attention.

Fisher side-eyed Henry. He knew what his best friend was already thinking. But, no, Henry was wrong. He was not interested in Silver beyond her capacity to volunteer.

"Whew." She stood.

He and Henry turned to face her as she put her hands on her hips. "They have great aim."

"It's the apps and video games. Gives them great hand-eye coordination." Henry stuck out his arm. "Henry." She shook his hand, and her gaze dropped to his gloves.

"Silver." Her eyes widened, and she shoved her hands in her coat pocket, producing red gloves. "I knew I was forgetting something." She jammed them over her hands and rubbed her palms together.

"You've got quite the party going on out here." Henry glanced quickly at Fisher before settling back on Silver.

"And you saw it from downtown and decided you'd had enough of your boring day?" Fisher raised a brow. Henry had come to check up on him. He'd worried his friend. It wasn't how he'd wanted the news to sit, but Henry was going to have to come to terms with it.

Henry's jaw moved side to side before he wiped all concern from his face and replaced it with a fake-as-hell grin Fisher had seen him use too many times to count. "Got off work early and thought I'd stop in."

Liar, liar, pants on fire. Henry hadn't left work early or taken a full weekend in years. He was worried and didn't need to be. Fisher had come to grips with his situation already. There was nothing anyone could say to change his mind now. Not even Henry.

-

Silver brushed the snow off her jacket and pants, stomping her boots on the entry carpet. She took a deep breath in through her nose and out through her mouth, wiping a couple drops of perspiration from her forehead. Snowball fights were hard work.

"What do you do, Henry?" she asked, sizing up the two men. There hadn't been a mention of any siblings in Fisher's file.

"Attorney."

"He left out the cutthroat part." Fisher wiped his red hands on his jeans. He wasn't even wearing a jacket. And he was breathing hard again. She bit back a chastising comment about wearing a jacket and not overexerting himself… but he didn't know she knew about his health. And she wasn't exactly upset about their close contact on the ground, in the snow, like a dang movie.

Why hadn't Henry been able to convince Fisher to stay on the transplant list? Was he okay with him dying? She got the lawyer thing; he looked like a charmer with his dark hair, good posture and that presence about him. A real talker. If he couldn't persuade Fisher, how was she supposed to?

"We're done for the night." The abruptness of Fisher's voice brought her back to the moment. "I'll give them a few more minutes then close it down. You can go."

She smiled tightly. Today she'd failed. Good thing she was coming back to help stuff backpacks. She had to regroup and come up with a better plan. There was no denying now that Fisher should stay on the list. He had way too much to give. He couldn't die.

Chapter Four

Fisher ordered another coke from the counter at the fundraiser. The only reason he was here, the only reason he ever wanted to be any place there were fancy people, was to get his organization out there. He was the face of it. If he didn't show up and remind people that CCH still existed, they forgot and so did their pocketbooks come donation time. And Thanksgiving and Christmas was a big time for him.

This was the seventh event he'd been to in a month. There were five more on his schedule before the new year.

"Should I be surprised you're here?" A silky voice caused him to spin halfway around.

He was met with a smile lined in red, lashes flush with mascara and a grin. A pull deep in his gut volunteered a smile in return. "Doctors have to be at fundraisers now?"

"When they work for a hospital that wants to expand its infrastructure, they sure do."

When she leaned in to order a ginger ale from the bartender, the tight black dress that cut off at her knees rounded against her butt. The woman had a great body, and the modest yet sexy-as-hell dress she wore did nothing to cover her curves. Not to mention it was complete with red heels that matched her lipstick.

"And you're not even drinking. You really are a saint." He took a sip of pop from his green glass to stop himself from continuing to compliment her. At this rate he was going to be waxing poetic by the time she got her glass.

Not to generalize, but he'd always had good experiences with doctors, even if the situation didn't turn out well.

"Not yet. Pacing is crucial at these events." She winked and sipped from her red glass, a curl behind her ear escaping her up-do and resting on her collarbone.

"Miranda is doing well, by the way. Her mom called to give an update. She'll be back next week. She wanted me to thank you."

"That's great news." Silver turned to the crowd, scanning faces.

The Ellisons were the hosts for the evening. There was no particular business or non-profit benefiting tonight, but for a number of years now the family had offered a holiday party that was the who's who of Casper. It was a night not to be missed if networking was your goal. Fisher had already spoken to his major contributors and secured their continued support. The only foundation left to get face-to-face time with was the Ellisons themselves. He'd yet to get them onboard, and it would help out substantially with rising costs if he could get his foot in the door. Not to mention the sustainability of the place once he was gone. The more money he could secure now, the better chance CCH had at being something that didn't die with him.

"I bet this is a gold mine for you." She took a step forward, inviting him into the crowd.

His feet moved without a second thought. He'd worn dark jeans, a black button-up shirt instead of his preferred flannel and black loafers for the occasion. This was as dressed up as he got.

But since when did doctors fundraise?

Job security in tough times, perhaps. Although he couldn't imagine her not being sought after if yesterday's performance was any indication of how good she was with patients.

Most of the guests were dressed like Silver, very put together in holiday colors, and the venue, a historical home a few blocks from CCH, was decorated in golds and silvers to complete the festive atmosphere. Perfection. Nothing out of place, no homemade drawings or ornaments all on one side of the tree.

"So, what do you do for fun?" Silver took a drink, and he followed her lips to a cherry lying on top of the ice cubes.

"Fun? What's that?" He wrinkled his forehead to go along with the sarcasm. "I believe one has to have free time for that."

"There's got to be something."

"CCH is my fun. Not a lot of time for anything else. What's the saying… love what you do, and it won't be work." He raised his glass to his lips but didn't drink. "Henry usually talks me into softball intramurals in the summer and a bowling league in the winter." Sharing information with her was easy. Too easy.

He didn't need to be getting into any sort of friendship. He was just about to excuse himself when a man came up on Silver's side and hugged her.

"Blake." She smiled warmly, and a pull deep in Fisher's chest wanted her to focus her happiness on him. "It's so nice to see you again. This is Fisher Tibbs. He runs Combat Children's Hunger."

"Nice to meet you." Fisher shook Blake Ellison's hand.

"I haven't seen you and Halle in forever." Silver didn't miss a beat. "Are you coming to the Christmas party at Carrigan's Pub this year?"

"Yeah, it's on the calendar," Blake said. "It'll be nice to finally go to a holiday party and bring the kiddo. Two hasn't been as bad as everyone said it would be." Blake took a swig from his beer.

"It's not the twos you have to watch out for but the threes." Fisher raised his brows. "They're mobile and have no fear." Megpie may have been sick, but she'd still been a toddler testing boundaries. But he'd take Maggie at any age if it meant she was still alive.

"Let's hope it's none of the above. Especially since we're expecting." The proud dad put his hands in his pockets, thumbs out, and rocked back on his heels. "Which is why Halle isn't here tonight. That morning sickness is rough this go-round. All food smells seem to trigger her in the evening. She's tried everything."

"There's an herbal store downtown. They've got an anise tea that's usually pretty effective." Dammit, he needed to shut his trap. Why in the world was he giving advice on morning sickness to someone he didn't know? It was Silver – he spoke freely around her for some dumb reason. He sipped his drink and glanced around the room, shutting down his involvement.

"I'll pass that along."

"Congratulations." Silver squeezed Blake's arm. "I'm sure her OB is giving her excellent care, but if she needs anything or has questions, have her give me a call."

"Will do."

"Speaking of help—" Silver's gaze volleyed between them "—who does Fisher need to talk to in order to submit a request for funding?"

This gal had some gumption. He liked it. His jaw tightened. No, he didn't like it, he just needed her boldness to help his organization.

"That would be Melissa." Blake reached into his back pocket, pulling a card from his leather wallet. "Here's her card. Tell her I told you to call and set up a meeting."

"Slick." Silver glanced down at his wallet. "I see someone prepared for the season."

"I don't make those decisions, nor do I remember all the phone numbers," Blake said. "The cards are necessary to get people where they need to go."

"Speaking of which, we better snag the mayor before he leaves." She gazed at Fisher and smiled. Her "we" meant him and her. "It was so nice to see you."

"Thanks." Fisher held up the business card and nodded at Blake and followed Silver through the groups gathered throughout the room.

"You go back with Blake Ellison?" Oh, good, he did know how to use his voice without volunteering personal information. He could've piped up more back there, but he was too in awe of how she worked, how effortlessly she chatted up Blake and made a contact for him in the process. What other skills did the woman have?

"My sister-in-law's brother is married to Blake's sister." Her eyes danced around as she connected the dots, their arms nearly touching. "Yeah, I think that's right. Anyway, we all went to high school around the same time. Small town."

If it were such a small town, he would've met Silver years ago. When he was in a better place. Nah, it wouldn't have mattered. His heart condition had been around since high school; a lasting relationship wasn't meant to be in his world.

"Thanks for introducing us. You didn't have to bring up CCH."

"Oh." Her eyes widened. "I'm sorry. I get carried away when something is on my mind."

"It's okay." Even when she was unsure, her features were stunning. Her cute round nose was in perfect proportion to her creamy face. "I appreciate the in." A smile escaped his lips. "Can't get CCH off your mind, huh?" Fisher glanced around but didn't see the mayor.

"Something like that. You have a good thing going on over there." She stood close to him, no doubt so they could hear each other over the noise, and when she turned, her red lips caught his attention for a moment. His lips tingled to capture hers.

One stolen glance.

Except it wasn't stolen. She'd witnessed him watch her lips. Her expression was unreadable.

He resisted the urge to clear his throat. "I don't see the mayor." In fact, he hadn't seen the mayor all night. *What is your game, Silver?*

"Short and sweet. That's the secret to winning at these things."

"I'll have to remember that." Except she hadn't left *him* behind or kept their conversation brief.

"Finally." A woman in a white, knee-length dress linked her arm with Silver's. "I've been looking for you."

"I wasn't hiding. Lorelei, this is Fisher. Fisher, Lorelei." She bounced her cup between the two, and Fisher shook the brown-haired woman's hand. "Fisher runs Combat Children's Hunger."

"Oh." Lorelei's voice raised along with her brows, amusement skittering across her features. "I get it now."

Silver jabbed her in the side, and he held back a chuckle.

"I'm so glad Silver is getting involved again. It's good for her." Lorelei's attention was diverted. "Gotta go." She walked straight past him, not looking back.

Okay then, that was a drive-by conversation full of meaning. Why did Silver need to get involved again?

"Best friend." Silver took a breath. "Whaddaya do?" She drank from her glass and glanced around the room.

"What prompted you to volunteer at CCH?" Fisher asked. "There are other places in town that need help, some even medical. You certainly have a lot to do with your time, I'm sure."

She raised her glass to her lips and kept her gaze on his. Panic seemed to flit across her face. Had she not wanted to volunteer?

"I miss helping out. I've been back for a year now and wanted to dive back in." She glanced away, rubbing her lips together and swaying on her feet. If there'd been music playing, he'd have had half a mind to ask her to dance. It was a good thing the other half of his brain would totally prohibit that. No good could come out of him wanting to dance with her or flirt with her or kiss her.

That was it. He scanned the room for a place to set his glass for the waitstaff. He had to get out of here. Fantasies were starting. A connection was forming, and there was no room in his life for any of this. Second-guessing himself now wouldn't bring him happiness or peace – it would just stir up a decade of frustration.

He'd made his decision, and he was good with it. End of story.

"You know the tree-lighting ceremony is next week," she said. "I haven't been in forever."

He stopped looking for an exit and locked eyes with her. "A bunch of the kids from CCH are singing and have been insistent I come see them." He set his glass on a tray by a table covered in gold decorations and sweets. It was past his time to say good-bye to Silver. His body started to tense.

"Do you want to go together? I make the best hot chocolate."

His heart started pumping faster, and his breathing wasn't as easy, but he didn't take a deep breath or make a big deal out of it. He never did. Usually, though, when he had trouble with oxygen it was because of overexertion. Not a question from a stunning woman.

He told his feet to move and his tongue to utter, "No, thank you," but nothing happened. "Sounds good" came out of his mouth instead. His brain just didn't know how to listen when it came to Silver. He ground his teeth together. He'd agreed only because he was a gentleman and was planning on going regardless. If he'd said no and then bumped into her there, it would have been awkward. "I'm going to call it a night. I have some things to do at CCH."

After next week, he'd make sure to only see her when she volunteered.

–

Something was off with Fisher. She let her gaze roam over him – looking for what, she didn't know. Wait. Was there a little perspiration on his forehead? She grabbed for his right palm. Yep. Clammy. She started to raise her eyes to his chest to watch his breathing when his body jerked. His face whipped toward the exit, his eyebrows knitted together.

"You're headed to CCH this late?" Silver wrinkled her nose. She didn't have to dig her phone out of her clutch to know it was past ten.

"There's a truck that needs to be unloaded by morning. If I do it now, then I can sleep in a little." He slowly gazed down at her hand holding his.

Whoops. Doctor mode was automatic, and she couldn't tell him why. She dropped his palm and crossed her arms over her chest, looking around the room. "I'll go with you." She raised her brows, pressed her lips together and headed to the coat check. He wasn't getting a chance to say no. She couldn't leave him alone. Her insides started to twist; that last piece of cheesecake she'd indulged in at Lorelei's for dinner before coming to the party hadn't been such a good idea.

She found him by the door just as she buttoned the top button on her black trench coat, slipping her gloves on as the brisk night air hit her face.

"I can follow you," she said. That was dumb; they both knew where CCH was, and there was no traffic this time of night.

"I walked here." He put his hands in the pockets of his black Carhartt jacket. She hadn't seen him at the coat check – where had he stashed it?

"I'll walk with you. It's a nice night." And the lies just rolled off her tongue at this point. An ice cream cone was nice, celebrating Christmas in July was nice, walking three blocks in freezing temperatures in a dress and heels was definitely not nice.

He swiveled in her direction and raised an eyebrow. "I'll drive you back to your car when we're done."

"Deal."

Now what was she going to do? Point out all the symptoms that anyone with any medical knowledge should be concerned about? No. She bit her lower lip. She couldn't, because those symptoms were only symptoms if she knew his full background. And he hadn't told her that. Yet.

She sniffled. They were not even halfway down the block, and the cold had already made quick work of a jacket that was probably intended only for forty degrees and above. She was not going to make it two and a half more blocks. She could make an excuse to leave, but then she'd just worry all night. She certainly wasn't staying with him because she liked the prickly sensation covering her skin every time she was around him.

Clip-clopping noises drew louder behind her. She turned to see a horse-drawn carriage coming toward them in the dark night. Fisher stepped into the street and raised his hand, catching the attention of the older man clutching the reins with thick leather gloves.

Fisher shoved his hands in his pockets. "We may as well." He shrugged and stepped closer to the driver as the two giant horses halted. "Hey, Richard. Out for a night ride?"

"I take the girls out to give people rides downtown during the holidays." Richard was bundled up, complete with a scarf over most of his face. "They get a kick out of it. So do I."

"We need to go up a couple blocks to Combat Children's Hunger. Mind giving us a ride?"

"Sure thing, Fisher. Hop in."

"Thanks." He swiveled her way, offering a hand for the tiny steps, glancing down at her heels. Right. Not the safest attire to climb in. She grasped his hand tightly, a chill zooming down her spine as his fingers wrapped around the edges of her palm and supported her all the way up. There were blankets on the bench seat, thank goodness. She sat and spread the blankets out on her lap, leaving half for Fisher. He surely had to be cold, and being out in this weather wasn't good for him or his lungs. His thigh grazed hers as he sat. Then settled. They were leg to leg, and she didn't move a muscle.

The horses took off with a start, and she threw her hands out for balance, grabbing the first thing her palm landed on. Fisher's leg. His head tilted toward her, and his gaze dropped to her hand as she slowly removed it, tucking it under the blanket. She rubbed her lips together and looked anywhere but at him. This was not the time to blush. Or maybe it was. Her cheeks were already touched by the cold.

A shiver rose from her shoulders, but it didn't completely have to do with the temperature. They were alone. In a horse-drawn carriage on a beautiful, albeit freezing, winter night. The setting was romance personified. Too bad it was going to be wasted on them.

-

He'd thought a ride would be a faster way to get to CCH and be done with the night. That was before they were sitting in a fancy damn wagon under a blanket, and – he tilted his head to the sky – little snowflakes were started to fall. Yeah, this had been a great idea.

He shifted his gaze to Silver. She never would've made it in that thin coat and dress. "Warming up?"

"A little." She bit into her bottom lip, not looking directly into his eyes.

Richard went past the street he should've turned on. Great, he'd decided to take the scenic route. Fisher pushed his back into his seat and crossed his arms.

"This is the first time I've ever ridden in a carriage or been this close to horses."

"Aren't you from here?" His brow arched as he inhaled, but the cold stopped a full breath. He concentrated on getting enough oxygen and not freaking out. *Easy. Slow breaths.* There were down sides to his heart condition, the stress on his breathing being the most notable. And annoying.

"Yes, but that doesn't mean I grew up around animals."

"What did you grow up around?"

"More socialite activities than outdoor ones. You?"

"My dad was a ranch foreman. I think I took my first steps to get to a horse." He chuckled, picturing riding next to his dad for countless hours and years. *When was the last time I rode?*

"I've always wanted to…" Her words trailed off as she watched the horses move along the deserted road.

"I'm still in good with a couple of ranch owners. I could arrange a ride when the weather is nicer." His face fell at the calculation of time between now and good weather in Wyoming. "Or just on a day that's over forty degrees and sunny." He probably had years left, but it could only be months, and he wanted to ride a horse again before his health really started to decline and he didn't have the strength to pull himself into the saddle. But now was not the time to think of what might be. He'd made his choice, and nothing would be changed by his worrying.

"You'd do that?" She tilted up her chin, her big blue eyes searching his.

Hope. That's what Silver reminded him of – someone who was constantly hopeful. How nice it would be to have that type of worldview.

"Of course." The way she looked at him, so caring, he'd do anything to make her happy. "It'd be nice to ride again. There are some great trails if we go up on the mountain."

"I'm going to have to mentally psych myself up to get this checked off my bucket list." A smile filled her round face. "Horses can smell fear, right?"

"They're pretty good judges of character. But I like to think I am, too, and you'll be just fine."

"I have been in some dicey situations in third-world countries, and I don't remember being as nervous as this about doing anything."

"Relax, we aren't riding them in five minutes."

She nodded and bit her lip again. "Right." She chuckled. "I'm a planner."

"You don't say." He gave her fake surprised eyes to make sure his sarcasm was clear.

"Oh, like you aren't?"

"Hey, we are in a horse-drawn carriage after a party in fancy duds. I make things happen."

"Duly noted." She rubbed her hands together under the blankets.

"Where are your gloves?"

"I have, like, ten pairs and can never seem to remember them."

"Let me see." He uncrossed his arms, cupped her hands in his, and rubbed. It wasn't just for her benefit – he was freezing, too. Warmth started at his palm and crept up his arms and down his chest, like someone was slowly soaking him in hot candle wax.

"Thanks, that takes the edge off." She pulled her hands back, and a long scar on her right hand caught his attention. He'd seen it before, when they were serving food, but up close it looked, and felt, like a deeper wound than he'd originally assessed.

"What happened?" He nodded to her hand.

"A stupid accident." She shrugged and turned in her seat to face the front, quickly slipping her hands back under the blanket.

"Looks painful."

"It was." A small frown tugged her lips down momentarily.

"Then I guess it's good you're tough."

"You think so?"

"Good judge of character, remember?"

She side-eyed him and rubbed her lips together. "Sometimes you just have to buck up and deal with what life dishes out."

"Words easily said when things are good."

Her head snapped to face him. "Who said things are good?" Her brows rose.

"Are you going to die right now?"

"Chances are slim."

"Do you have a roof over your head?"

"I will soon." She winked.

"Are you starving?"

"Definitely not."

"Do you know you're going to get past the problem?"

She was silent.

And then still silent. He was about to put his arm around her or something to offer comfort, but she spoke before he moved.

"I'm headed that way." Her lashes fluttered as she sucked in a deep breath. "I think I'm about to make some big changes in my life."

"There's no time like the present."

Richard pulled back on the reins, and the horses stopped in front of CCH, just in time to prevent Fisher from telling Silver about his own permanent problem. She was a doctor. She'd understand better than most. He hadn't even realized they were so close to CCH. The world had a habit of falling away when Silver was around.

He hopped out of the carriage and gripped her hand as she stepped down. A smile tugged at his lips. Their ride was probably one of the most ambiguously honest conversations he'd had in a long time. Silver was good company. Good company, indeed.

Chapter Five

"I haven't been to one of these in forever." Silver inhaled the scent of the evergreen trees covered in the freshly fallen snow.

"A tree lighting?" Fisher was in step beside her. She could smell his cologne through the frosty air trying to numb the insides of her nose with every breath. His scent was sleek and sexy and burned in her memory forever.

"Yup." The sun had nearly set, and the park was lit with the occasional streetlight and multicolored bulbs guiding the way to the seating area. There wasn't a cloud in the sky despite the eighty percent chance of snow she'd heard on the radio on her way home. "We used to come every year when I was little. It feels like the start of the holiday season when I see the park lit up, hear the choir singing and get hot cocoa." She hugged the Thermos she'd filled with her grandma's recipe, complete with Bailey's, Kahlua, three different types of chocolate and a tap of whiskey because, according to Grandma Betty, the act of hot chocolate was worthless unless it made you tipsy, and tipsy when hot chocolate was involved was never a crime.

Silver had debated whether to bring it, because, really, he shouldn't drink with any sort of organ condition, but she'd felt nostalgic this afternoon while taste-testing her batch. Fisher didn't have to have any, but she sure as crap was going to have more. Being home this last year had been rough, but she might finally be ready to accept the hand life had dealt her and move on. Be happy. She had no idea what that path was. But, still, new things were on her horizon.

"How about here?" Fisher pointed to the seats in the back row and pressed his palm to her back to escort her.

A comforting heat sank deep into her gut. Ever since they'd met, life seemed a little easier. And she hadn't lied to him directly any more, except for her name and occupation and what she was really doing a week ago at CCH. There'd just not been a good opportunity to come clean yet.

"How long has it been since you've been to one?" He sat on the very outside seat, and she next to him, thankful her coat covered her butt. The chairs were plastic, but still.

They had a great view of the choir that would sing the traditional holiday melody and the trees that would light up one by one in concert with the melody.

"Years. I don't think I've seen one since I started college, and then with my internships and overseas work…" She smoothed out the king-sized blanket she'd grabbed just in case the snow started to fall.

"Which country in Africa did you say before?"

"Tanzania. For a year." Until she'd made a mistake by accidentally slicing into her own hand. If she hadn't gone to school with the head surgeon at the nearby military base, she probably would've lost the use of it completely.

"Wyoming is great and all, but why did you come back?" His eyes twinkled back at her in the glow of the holiday lights; her breath caught in anticipation as his gaze roamed over her face. "You seem better suited to giving orders and saving lives instead of sitting behind a desk."

Why didn't I just tell the truth that first day? She could tell herself that this sinking feeling was because she thought he was handsome and nice and she wouldn't mind pressing her lips against his, but she knew. It was lying. The not-complete-truth telling. Then she'd lied again on his forms; she'd told Janae that she'd take care of his paperwork, but she hadn't even sent it to him. And she'd purposely dodged people at the fundraiser so they wouldn't ask her about the transplant portion of her work while she was around Fisher.

She couldn't bring herself to let this man give up. He didn't really want to die – he just hadn't realized it yet. She'd get him there. The Christmas festivities would help, and maybe he'd change his mind on his own. Then she could come clean. Tell him who she was, what her job truly involved and that it was all okay because his paperwork hadn't been filed yet.

No one should give up on life.

Least of all a man who had so much to live for.

A man she hoped might want to live for her.

She sucked in the cold air a little too hard and blinked as she coughed. She was losing her mind. There was no way she should be thinking like this. Too many variables were in play that made a relationship between them unknown. Would he live even if he were lucky enough to get a heart? Did she want to stay in Casper or take a job traveling, finding a way to help others without a scalpel? She was leaning more toward teaching these days – showing people how to help others was starting to sound like a fulfilling next step.

"I was doing what I always dreamed of." She started to unscrew the lid of the Thermos. Suddenly she needed the spiked hot chocolate. "I loved the mechanics of the hea—" She stopped herself dead cold from finishing that sentence. She'd never said that she was well-versed in surgery, including the heart procedure he needed. Just that she was a doctor. "Healing ailments to give people a better life," she corrected quickly.

He leaned in, his mouth slightly open to ask a question, when the sound system cut in. "Welcome, Casper, to the annual tree-lighting ceremony of Central Park." Claps and shouts of glee came from the crowd as the announcer introduced the choir from the high school and thanked the sponsors who'd made the ceremony possible.

Silver poured a couple sips of hot chocolate into the lid and offered it to Fisher, raising her eyebrows in question. He shook his head, like she'd expected him to, and she sat back a little farther into her chair. Heat rushed down her throat with each sip. The smell of rich cocoa brought her back to Christmastime in the Morgenstern household – Mother directing the people she'd hired to bring in an outrageously big tree, adorn the outside of their mansion with festive lights and hang wreaths on every available surface.

The choir started to sing "We Wish You a Merry Christmas" in joyful harmony as the three aspens behind the choir racks lit up in red, green, and yellow.

Nostalgia settled on top of Silver's shoulders, and she slumped closer to Fisher. The strength of his body was hard against her insulated, puffy coat. Neither of them moved an inch the rest of the ceremony.

By the time it was over, the entire park was lit up like the North Pole, and neither of them made a move to leave. There was no hurry. She could sit here all night.

In fact, she didn't want to leave. Leaving meant everything moved forward. Fisher would eventually find out she'd met him under false pretenses, and while she hoped they could laugh about it, she had a sinking feeling that he wouldn't be smiling. Their relationship, or whatever had started, wasn't going to end well, which was a shame. Then there was the little thing about her life and her future, letting her dream career go for good. She'd never had to try to find a purpose; she'd always known what she wanted to be when she grew up and had thrown herself completely into it.

Chilled air filled her lungs, and when she exhaled, she said goodbye. Goodbye to her past. She wasn't going to waste any more of her life pining for something that was over and done. There was no use.

Now she had to figure out what she wanted to do next. Who she wanted to be.

She screwed the cap back on the Thermos and tucked it between their chairs. She searched her pockets for gloves, and then her purse. Rats. She'd forgotten them. Fisher grabbed her hand as she was about to set it in her lap under the blanket.

His hand dwarfed hers, yet his touch was tender. His thumb caressed the scarred, sensitive flesh that marred the top of her hand between her index finger and thumb and ran all the way down to her wrist bone – the original cut jagged and messy and the subsequent cuts precise from the surgeons who'd done their best to repair the damage.

"What actually happened?"

"A wrong place at the wrong time sort of thing." She didn't like to talk about it. Ever.

"Ahhh." His gaze searched hers, silently pleading with her to continue. "You can do better than that."

She watched his gentle touch rub over her scar. She hadn't even winced when he'd touched her hand. "I studied for years to become a surgeon." Her quick smile faded just as swiftly. "It was all I ever wanted to do. Save people. And the body is so fascinating." Hell, she'd purchased her own human anatomy doll with the babysitting money she'd saved by not going to the movies every weekend with her friends. She'd painted every single piece, learning about it in the process, and then assembled the hard plastic man only to take him apart through the years as her classes progressed.

When her head rose she was met with golden brown eyes that were warm. Inviting. *Damn sexy.*

"I studied hard, was at the top of my class, landed prestigious internships and traveled abroad helping those in less fortunate countries. I lived my dream for a while."

She could see it in his eyes. He knew there was a "but" coming. Obviously. The scar took up half of her hand.

"Slipping on a wet floor with a very sharp blade. That's what caused this." She pulled her palm from his. She was sharing, and he was caressing, and it was all adding up to make her chest tighten.

"You cut yourself?" His brows knitted together.

"Yup. I was getting ready for surgery, arranging the tools, and I stumbled, tried to brace myself but fell and never let go of the blade." She'd slashed her own dreams in three seconds.

"Wow. I don't know what to say to that."

His honesty was nice. There really wasn't much to say that other people hadn't already said. And nothing, not any word, ever made her feel better.

"It's just a fact at this point." She hid her hand back under the blanket, squeezed her palm, then relaxed.

"How long ago?"

"About a year."

"That's is why you came back?"

"My options were pretty limited after my second surgery, and I couldn't hold a scalpel." Actually, she could hold the metal instrument, she just didn't trust herself. And since she couldn't fully control the shaking and the cramping she experienced even when writing, no one else trusted her skills either.

"You're still in the medical field." The hopefulness in his tone nearly brought tears to her eyes.

He wanted her to find peace. Why didn't he want it for himself? Why didn't he want to heal if given the chance? In his shoes, she wouldn't have to think it over or pull her name off a list.

"You know, seeing what I can't be every day almost makes it worse." She'd never admitted that truth out loud before. The antiseptic smell of the hospital reminded her of the anticipation of the challenge she used to feel walking through the sliding doors. The men and women in white coats, with pens in their pockets, reminded her of rounds, when she'd meet her patients, get to know them, watch them recover.

Holy crap. She'd gone about this all wrong. She'd never considered doing something outside the walls of a hospital. This could be the answer though. She needed a whole new start.

A smile she couldn't contain spread across her lips, and she leaned in, kissing Fisher smack dab on the mouth. "Thank you." She pulled back, letting the enjoyment of her impulsive reaction to her epiphany sink into her bones.

"For?"

"I think the reason I've been wallowing this entire year is because I didn't take myself out of that space. Every day I'm reminded of what I can't have. I need to find something new."

"Sounds like something I'd say." Fisher chuckled, reached his arm around and laid it on the back of her chair. He touched her shoulder with his thumb ever so slightly. Technically, he was only touching her fluffy jacket, and the only reason she knew was because she'd heard the swish of the fabric. But still. The gesture was endearing. And made her want to start stripping some layers off – outside, in a park, in the middle of winter.

Snow started to fall whimsically, each flake melting before the next came along. Tonight was more than she had bargained for – both sharing and caring. Fisher was more than she'd thought she'd ever find.

–

He rubbed his thumb over her puffy jacket. The dark navy color matched her eyes, and the gold of her scarf accentuated the pink of her cheeks. Her blond hair flowed over her coat – he hadn't realized it was so long. She'd always had it pinned up.

"How many of these lightings have you been to?" she asked.

"None."

"What?" Her eyes brightened as her cheeks plumped up in a grin. "This is your first time?"

"And it was perfect." He winked automatically, clearly unable to help himself around her. He knew he was headed down a path he shouldn't walk. Didn't want to walk. But there was no stopping the words that wanted to come out of his mouth around Silver.

Silver was a lady who was put together. Calculated. Precise. One he liked to be around.

"I'd hate for your first time to be anything less than." Her chin turned up, the Christmas lights making her face glow. Little snowflakes fell around them, and his chest warmed. He'd not felt this strongly even with Maggie's mother. Which might've had something to do with their being so young and quick to fight. And then there was her whole "leaving when things got hard" bit that he'd allowed to jade him toward all relationships for the past ten years. *Ten years.* Damn, he'd let that woman ruin a good chunk of his life.

But he couldn't blame it all on her. There was Maggie's diagnosis. Then his. Then the transplant and the subsequent failure. It didn't seem fitting now to take a perfectly good heart away from the good guys on the list below him just so it could fuel the shell of a man he'd become. Pearly gates and streets of gold sounded like an upgrade.

His quick, curt smile stung – how cold the night had become. He didn't much feel like socializing any more.

"If you didn't come here for lights, what did you do to find your holiday spirit?" Silver continued.

"What makes you think I don't have this holiday spirit you speak of all year round?"

He should live in the moment. That's what he'd vowed to do when he decided to take his name off the list – not take any of his days for granted, because they were numbered.

But living them fully didn't mean he had to drag someone into his numbered days, take them down with him. And certainly not Silver, who already had enough to deal with in her own life. He never should've allowed himself to be around her so much in such a short amount of time.

"You are quite the do-gooder year-round, but there is a special spark that only this specific time of year can bring." Her gaze wandered to the cheer blinking all around them. Most of the people were gone – it was just them, surrounded by twinkling lights and snow.

"Maybe it's just you. Your natural spark." He couldn't help himself; he dropped his gaze to her lips and lingered too long. He wanted to kiss her, too. Kiss her glossy lips, trail his lips and the tip of his tongue down her creamy neck and slip his arms around her hips.

Damn his warring mind and body. He knew this was wrong, but he did nothing, absolutely nothing, to stop it. Her lips kept distracting him. Her small peck on his lips hadn't been enough. *What would they taste like?* The answer to that question contradicted everything he'd set his mind to. Everything. He wanted to be in a bad mood and storm off, but he couldn't. Not when she was practically in his arms.

He swore he saw a nano-smile on her full lips. Her gaze fixed on his, silently prompting him to… what? Kiss her?

He glanced behind her to break the moment. They shouldn't even be having a moment. "Holiday parade. That usually kicked off the season. Then driving around to look at the lights on houses. There used to be this place up on the east side, a Santa funhouse." The multicolored glow of lights around them was a good distraction from her beautiful eyes – ones that didn't look on him with pity, because she had no idea he was dying. The decorations on the trees, and the lit Santas and reindeer speckled about were cheery. And calming. "This guy and his wife would decorate their two-story top to bottom, even open the side fence, because their yard was decked out, too. That's when the spirit caught me, seeing Christmas through Mag—"

His throat felt like a snake was slowly choking him to death. *Megpie's eyes.* Her sassy brown eyes that matched his had always brought him happiness.

Christmas through a child's observation was pure joy. A whole different perspective. One long forgotten by the time adulthood was in full swing. Those four years Maggie was alive were the best he'd ever had. Probably ever would.

"Through?" Silver turned in her seat, her lips not much farther than a small crane of his neck.

Dammit, he needed to get it together. He couldn't do this. He didn't have enough energy to love someone else, to let them in only to have them shut out in the worst way possible. There was no coming back from death.

"My daughter," he said in a rushed breath as the snake continued to constrict.

"I didn't know you have a daughter." She tucked her blond hair, curled at the ends, behind her ear. "How old is she?"

The hopefulness in her eyes was almost enough to bring him to his knees – if Maggie had still been alive, would Silver have wanted to join their little family? Maggie would've adored Silver with her "princess hair," to use a term Megpie was so fond of.

He shook his head and felt his body completely deflate. "She died five years ago. When she was four."

Her hand jutted out and clenched the top of his thigh. "I'm so sorry."

"She loved Christmas and all of the decorations."

"What was her name?"

"Maggie Elaine."

"As in Margaret?"

"No." A quick chuckle escaped his lips. "Just Maggie. My little Megpie. She was my ball of joy and always on the move."

"What happened? If you don't mind me asking." Her gaze left his for the ground.

"She was a preemie. Lung problems from the get-go, but everything seemed fine at first. It wasn't until she was about one that things took a turn. Soon after that we found out she'd need a double lung transplant, and that took years."

He could practically see Silver's mind at work, sorting it out from a doctor's viewpoint. She remained silent, slightly bobbing her head as she took in the information.

"I finally got word that she was a match. Things were looking good." He'd finally, *finally* started to see a future with no hospitals, only raising his little girl doing normal, everyday activities. "Then they weren't. Her body rejected the lungs, and it all happened so quickly. Felt like one day she was sitting up, asking for her dolly, the next day she was gone."

He didn't even know if she'd heard him say goodbye.

Tears threatened, because they always did when talking about his little girl and how she'd died – hooked up to all of those machines in a sterile hospital room. Awful. All awful. He wasn't about to go out the same way. He was going to die on his own terms.

"No one should ever have to go through what you did."

"No, they shouldn't." On either side of the equation. "The anniversary of her death is coming up, just after the new year. I bring her flowers. Pink carnations. She called them princess flowers."

"It sounds like you were a great dad."

"I like to think so," he said, his voice barely above a whisper.

Neither of them moved as silence settled over them, and suddenly he wasn't so cold any more. Talking about Maggie, telling Silver about his daughter, had warmed him inside and out.

"What about your wife?" Her question nearly startled him out of a trance.

"Wife?"

"Maggie's mother?"

"We were never married. She left us when Megpie was diagnosed with chronic lung disease."

There one day, gone the next. Luckily for Maggie, Sharon came from a wealthy family, and her dad offered a substantial sum for him and Maggie to basically go away. He'd had no choice but to take the money; Maggie needed the surgeries, and the care was expensive. There'd been a small amount left over when Megpie died, and he'd used that to create the endowment that was sustaining CCH.

"That's horrible."

"I have no regrets. I don't know what Sharon has." He stood. He didn't know how else to get away from all of the emotions clouding his mind, tightening his chest and numbing his body. It was time to go home.

Chapter Six

"You know what sounds good right about now?" Silver turned in the passenger seat to face Fisher.

His eyebrows rose in question as he pulled up to her home and put his SUV in park. She'd get her car in the morning – Lorelei could pick her up for Sunday brunch. Her parking garage was a considerable distance farther than where Fisher had parked, and his vehicle had heated seats.

"Pumpkin pie," she answered her own question.

He turned his head away from her; silence filled the cab. She was pushing too hard. She needed to pull back. She just couldn't with him. Not until she was able to tell him what she knew. Not until he decided to live.

He turned back to her, rubbing the whole of his index finger over his bottom lip. "It just so happens that pumpkin is my favorite pie." He cut the engine, halting the steady stream of heat, leaving her skin to feel the sting of the night as she opened her door.

"I happen to have one sitting in my fridge. Homemade. Would you like to come in?"

She was going with it. She didn't want the night to end.

This whole thing had started with her wanting to show Fisher that he still had a life to live, but now she was starting to find hers again. The future, her future, seemed brighter when he was around.

"It's never too late for pie. I think that's a holiday rule." He followed her up the stoop to the wraparound porch.

She opened her front door and flipped on the light in the entryway. "It's written in a book in the North Pole, I'm pretty sure. The living room is through there." She pointed down the hall. "I'll get us the pie. Do you like whipped cream?"

"Definitely." The silkiness in his answer drew warm lines down her back that swirled around her waist. She walked into the kitchen quickly, before he saw her cheeks redden. She scooped out the pie and plopped it onto paper plates in a jiffy, then she grabbed the whipped cream can and forks on her way out.

"I thought you'd have a tree up and your place decorated to the ceiling with Christmas," he said as he took a plate and fork from her.

She sat on the couch next to him, handing him the whipped cream before folding her legs on the cushion. "I didn't feel like it this year."

"Maybe now that you've been to the tree lighting, you'll get out your stuff."

"I wouldn't even know where to start looking for it. I've only unpacked what I've needed since moving back, and the rest is in poorly marked boxes in the garage."

She took a bite of pie then set her fork down on her plate. It had been a long day, and the familiar ache was returning. She'd have to remember her meds before bed.

"Have you done all that you can for your hand – physical therapy, that sort of thing – or are you out of options?"

"That last one."

"You must have been scared."

"Sometimes I still am." She picked up her fork again, suddenly needing the comfort of the sugar high. He nodded and shoved pie – well, mostly a fork full of whipped cream – into his mouth.

"I'm starting to realize that there is more out there than surgery." She sighed and nestled further into her plush couch cushions. "Maybe I can find something else to love."

A flash of heat flitted across his eyes, and she set down her fork.

He glanced down at his plate. "Any ideas?"

"No clue." She chuckled, but more out of nervousness than anything else.

"Do you like cooking? This pie is great, by the way."

"I didn't make it."

"You said it was homemade."

"I didn't say by me. My mother picked it up at a bake sale today."

He laughed, a full-throated, belly laugh that made her smile. "Baking's out. Okay. What about teaching? Could you teach in your field?"

"I have been thinking about that more and more lately." She did enjoy helping at the research hospital.

"Good. Now we're on a roll. And if you wanted away completely, there's always things with makeup and hair and nails and all that stuff you beautiful women like to do."

Her neck warmed at his compliment. "Those things are more like hobbies for me." She laughed. "Did you always want to do non-profit work?"

"Social work is right in that gray area. I never had an opinion either way."

"I can see little Fisher Tibbs helping families and kids cope with issues. Out to save the world."

"Nah, when I was a kid I wanted to be a fireman."

"It was the outfit, wasn't it?"

"The gear?" He winked. "It is pretty cool."

"What swayed you to go for social work?"

"There are so many people who don't have a voice. I wanted to be an advocate for them."

"Why children's hunger?"

"We have a lot of good non-profits in the area that cover issues for kids and adults, but there was a gap for keeping kids fed at dinnertime and over the holidays. I wanted Maggie's life to make a difference."

"Why didn't you name it after her?"

A darkness crossed his eyes. "I don't usually talk about her."

"Why not?" Keeping that bottled up wasn't healthy – she should know, she was well versed in the matter. But she really needed to settle down. If she pushed him too hard, he was going to stop being so open with her. "Whoa, sorry, that was forward."

"It's difficult—" he blew out a breath of air "—and there aren't a lot of people in my life I willingly spill my guts to." Yet he'd told her about his Megpie – he could've sidestepped the details, but he hadn't.

"I'm the same. I have two close friends, and that's about it for me. Well, Lorelei, Maisy, and Vincent, my brother. I respect keeping it close to the vest."

"I'm not sure if it makes each day easier or not, but that's the route I've gone."

"Well, one day, when you're ready, I'd love to hear more about her." Silver shook the whipped cream container and sprayed on more so that she wouldn't stare at him until he kept going. She wanted him to keep sharing. She wanted to know everything about Fisher Tibbs. And not because of her mission, but because he was a thoughtful, kind man with a killer smile that made her insides warm.

"She had blond hair that bounced when she walked." He smiled proudly. "And she loved yellow."

He leaned in, glancing down at her lips, which parted. The air grew thicker between them. "You have whipped cream..." He pointed to her cheek, then reached out and ever so gently wiped his thumb over the side of her lips.

She leaned in, hot tingles spreading over her body and swirling around her. He moved a couple of inches, and she pressed her lips to his. The smoothness of her lips brushing against his turned the tingles to white-hot waves of need. She swept her lips over his again, and he opened his mouth to her, their tongues swirling together. She breathed in his scent, desperate to be consumed by him.

Suddenly, he pulled back, his gaze laced with regret. Her chest tightened. Now she'd done it.

"I have to go." His brows wrinkled together, and he stood quickly, not touching her once.

"Uh, okay." She blinked and rubbed her lips together. "Sure."

"I have an early morning." He was halfway to the door.

"I guess I misread the situation." *Oh my goodness.* Tears pulled at her eyes. *Don't cry. Don't cry.*

"I don't want to get close to you. I can't."

"Why not?" She knew why. It was a dumb question. But maybe his answer wouldn't be medical. She was up and on his heels.

She'd started to fall for him. She'd known it from day one. But he was keeping her at arm's length. He was nice and friendly and flirty, but he was holding back.

"Because I can't give you what you want. I'm not future material."

"What does that even mean?" Now was the chance for everything unsaid between them to be out in the open.

"Even though I want it to, this – you and me – will never work out."

"You're ending it before it's even begun?"

"I'm thinking only of you." He turned, the wide expanse of his back to her.

She couldn't say anything. She knew why, and she wanted to tell him, lay out why that reasoning was dumb, remind him that if he stayed on the list he'd probably get a transplant in time and they could be together. For a very long time.

"Wait." She closed her eyes. He wasn't going to like any of what was about to tumble from her mouth. "I—"

Without any warning his hands were cupping her face, and his lips were on hers, hard and wanting. She leaned in, opening her mouth to him.

"Silver. There's nothing you can say. I'm sorry. This is all on me."

Before she could say anything more, he was gone. Just like that. She walked to her living room window in time to hear his SUV door slam and the engine turn over. She braced her foot on her other leg and leaned against the wall, tears silently falling to the carpet.

It all went wrong so fast. She shouldn't have lied. She shouldn't have rushed things. She shouldn't have started to trust a man who refused to open his heart.

Chapter Seven

Fisher dialed the regional transplant office on Monday – for the second time. It was harder to get off the list than on.

"Prairie Wind Medical Center. How can I help you?"

"I'm calling about the transplant list. I need to sign a release to take my name off the list."

"Okay. Your name?"

"Fisher Tibbs."

"Hey, Fisher. It's Janae. I thought that was sent out to you already."

"I haven't seen it. Do you need me to come in?"

"No. I'll make sure Dr. Morgenstern takes care of it." There was a long pause, and he felt it coming. The question. "Is there anything I can say to change your mind?"

"No, Janae. There isn't. How's Whitney?" Janae had a daughter Maggie's age. They'd been friends because, as a nurse, Janae had brought her daughter to play with Megpie while she was in the hospital.

"She's doing good. Her birthday is next month. You should come by the party. We're going to have it at the park by you."

"Let me know, and I'll swing by."

Maggie and Whitney would've been lifelong friends. They were both sweet girls with hearts of gold. It would be a hard day, but he should go wish Whitney a happy birthday at least.

–

Silver had been going through her pile of mail and hospital information and other items on her to-do list when Fisher's name appeared on the stationery Janae favored.

He wanted his paperwork.

He hadn't let it go.

She grabbed the forms out of the bag she'd been carrying around since she'd gone to see him that first day. If he wanted them, she was going to give them to him. He could ink his death certificate if he wanted – that didn't mean she had to mail it in and make it a reality.

She filled out a return envelope, addressing it to her office, specifically Dr. Morgenstern. If her cover hadn't been blown at the fundraiser, the chances of him finding out now were slim, unless she told him. And she had no intention of telling him now.

She cradled her head in her hands. She needed to tell him. It was stupid, really. Not even a big deal.

But if it wasn't such a big deal, why couldn't she just tell him that she was in charge of the local transplant list? Instead, every time she saw him they moved further from the truth and further from any kind of real chance at a relationship.

She rocked her head onto the hand she had braced on the desk. She did want a relationship with him.

Someone who still didn't want a heart.

Was it dumb to want him to change his mind now that they'd met? Now that he knew her? Cared for her enough to think about his future? Because if she were really being honest, that's what she wanted. And wouldn't that be romantic?

She sucked in a deep breath of stale hospital air. If – basically, *when* – he returned the papers, she'd call him and come clean. She'd lay everything out: who she was, what her job really entailed and why he shouldn't want her to make his request final. Then, after he had a couple of days to absorb the information she was sure to spew in one breath, she'd go to CCH, make him really hear her, really process that he wasn't alone in life and had a bright future that could be filled with whatever he wanted. She shoved the papers in a manila envelope.

The feelings were currently one-sided. She knew that.

Still, she could hope he'd eventually come around and fall in love with her. And maybe, just maybe, it wouldn't be too late to save his life.

Chapter Eight

He shouldn't be at work on Christmas Eve, but sitting at home only left him alone with his thoughts about Silver. At least here he could go through the stacks of mail that had piled up before he had to be at Henry's for dinner.

If he'd met Silver last month or a year ago, would he have made the same decision to pull his name from the transplant list? Was it still his best move even now? He hadn't read the fine print when he'd returned the paperwork, but he was sure he couldn't change his mind and reclaim the same spot on the list. He'd be moved to the bottom and that wouldn't give him a heart in time. So the decision was a done deal, no matter who came into his life or how they made him feel.

Silver had called a couple of times, but each time he let it go to voicemail and hadn't brought himself to listen to the messages yet.

He might've been able to have a future if he would've waited just another day to request the paperwork.

He'd shaved, put on a black button-up shirt and told himself all morning that he wasn't going to go see Silver. Wasn't going to apologize for the other night and his behavior.

Sharing with her, laughing with her, caring about her. It had, all of a sudden, become too much. He couldn't be what she needed no matter how much he wanted to.

And, damn it, he did. He wished he was in perfect health, looking into his bright future, and could ask her to be by his side.

But it was better that things ended now and that it was all on him. With his luck, she'd probably refuse to leave him and stay by his side until death did them part – in about twenty-four months. He couldn't do that to her. He wouldn't.

Everything was better this way.

He picked up his phone to call Henry as he stretched his sore back. He really needed to get a new mattress.

"Yes to beer," Henry answered on the first ring. "Don't cheap out."

"I'll be just a bit longer." Fisher rubbed his clean-shaven jaw. Man, he was getting old. His body was sure sore today.

"You went in to work, didn't you? You've got to step back and enjoy your days off. Hell, even I don't work on Christmas Eve."

"Just catching up while there's no one here."

"What about Silver? Don't couples like to spend holidays together?"

"We were never a couple. And, anyway, I ended things."

"Fisher." Henry's lawyer voice was automatic when he was about to lecture. "You have got to stop living like you are dying. You like her. Don't shut her out. And get your ass back on that list."

A humorless chuckle filled Fisher's small office. "When will you acknowledge that I actually *am* dying?"

"Not going to happen. I will acknowledge that you have choices you keep running away from."

"I'm not running away from anything."

"Fisher, you are running away from happiness and sadness and the act of living life. You can't control everything."

If I could, my daughter would still be alive.

"Go to her," Henry continued. "Get back on the list. And trust that you deserve happiness. As your best friend, that's all I ask." Henry clicked off, and Fisher leaned back in his chair before he made the effort to hang up his phone.

That was a real conversation.

They hadn't talked about Maggie in a while, and Henry hadn't been that straightforward about his condition in just as long. The call about the will was the first in years when they'd had an open dialogue.

There were merits to Henry's reasoning. Stupid points that, even if Fisher believed them, he couldn't do anything about.

If he came clean to Silver, if he laid it all out in the open, would she reject him or want to spend as much time with him as possible?

There was only one way to find out.

He grabbed the top three envelopes sitting in his mail bin, tearing open the side of the first one.

An updated information request from the National Organ Transplant List.

He pressed his lips together, throwing the letter on the desk and sitting up so fast the back of his chair snapped up with his momentum. Great, just what he needed – a reminder of his decision that John or Wilson or any of the countless deserving people under his name on the list needed help more than he did. Now he could add bad timing to his list of grievances about his lot in life.

They shouldn't need anything from me now. He didn't ever want to hear from the registry again. It was chipping away at the surety of his decision slowly but surely, and what was left didn't make him smile. It flipped his gut. He dialed the 800 number on his cell and grabbed his jacket. He was going to get double the beer and set them straight all at the same time.

"National Organ Transplant List. How many I help you?" a cheery voice greeted him as he left the building.

"My name is Fisher Tibbs, and I have removed myself from the list yet I just got a form asking to confirm my contact and medical information."

"Okay, Mr. Tibbs, thank you for calling. Let's check into the issue." A keyboard clicked on her end as he started his SUV and pointed it toward the only liquor store open on Christmas Eve.

"Can you confirm your birthdate and social security number?"

He rattled off the information. Maybe he'd get a bottle of whiskey, too. He wasn't supposed to be drinking, let alone the harder stuff. But if he was ever going to make an exception, today was it.

"I see here that you are still on the list, quite high up in your region I might add, and… Nope, there's been no request submitted to remove your name."

"I filled out the paperwork last week. Would you not have received it yet?" A small bit of hope started to spark – maybe he could void the paperwork if they hadn't made his request official yet.

Would he be doing that for Silver or for himself? He gripped his phone and steering wheel tighter and stopped at a red light.

"All paperwork sent to us is overnighted. We should've received it from your local office." Her words were spread out as if she was searching for something else while she spoke. "Our regional office is run out of the Prairie Wind Medical Center by a Dr. Silver Morgenstern."

Silver Morgenstern? How many Silvers were in this town? Who worked at the same place?

There was only one answer.

She'd known the entire time about his condition. And had sent him the form to remove himself from the list as he'd requested. But never actually filed it.

Could that be right?

"I'll, um, call them to get this straightened out then." He disconnected before he could do something stupid like remove his name out of spite. Dammit, he was going with the plan he'd established a month ago. A plan he'd been completely at peace with until he'd met Silver. It was not a decision he'd come to lightly, yet she'd chosen to totally disregard it.

His entire body tensed, his face hot. His stomach turned, and vomit threatened his throat.

He was the only person at the stoplight when it turned green, so he flipped the car around, pointing his SUV toward Silver's house.

She didn't get to make this big decision for him.

He ignored the relief his mind was trying to push at him. He didn't want to even try to think of her reasons for not carrying out his wishes. They were *his* wishes, dammit. Not hers. They weren't a team.

They weren't in this life together.

They weren't anything.

–

Silver bundled up in her black jacket, wrapping the gold scarf around her neck and digging around her purse and then the closet for the matching gloves. She was already late for Christmas Eve dinner. Her brother had called twice already to confirm. Something was up – Lilia was probably expecting, which would be outstanding.

Good thing I never told Mom about Fisher. Silver absolutely wouldn't have been able to handle today if she'd had to explain over holiday dinner that Fisher, who she was not dating, didn't want anything to do with her any more. She hadn't called him this week from her work number to explain her role in the transplant list though, a part of her didn't want him to answer and really find out who she was. That hadn't stopped her from obsessing every time her phone dinged, pinged or made any sort of noise, or from being completely let down when it wasn't him calling to apologize and tell her he wanted them to be together.

Finally, her gloves were already stuffed in her black jacket pockets. She grabbed them and opened her door, looking for her keys to lock up.

"Silver." A stern male voice caught her by surprise, and she screamed, jumping back into the doorway.

Her head whipped up, and the panic surging through her veins was replaced with happiness. Until the stern set of Fisher's face registered.

"What's wrong?" She glanced over his body. Nothing seemed to be out of the ordinary. Except for the beads of sweat on his forehead. It had to be in the single digits outside.

"Why don't you look for yourself?" He thrust a white paper at her and put his hands on his hips.

She recognized the red logo first, and her gut started to churn acid. Judging by his curled lip and the cold eyes staring down into the depths of her soul, he'd figured it out.

"Fisher, I—"

"Do you lie to all patients, or just to me, Dr. Morgenstern?"

Her purse dropped to the snow on her porch. "I didn't intend to lie. I wasn't trying to deceive you." All of the time she'd spent over the past couple of weeks fantasizing about Fisher and the different conversations they could have, needed to have, and all of those words completely eluded her now. But she needed to explain herself before she lost him for good.

"So you were just going against my direct wishes. Is this a habit of yours?"

"No—"

"You don't get to make decisions for me." His voice rose, but he wasn't shouting yet. That was probably coming though, given the hard set to his face. "Why did you even show up at CCH?"

"To meet you. To talk to you about your decision and the ramifications." Tears filled her eyes. His eyes weren't giving. He hated her. "To show you there's more to life. More to live for."

"So I'm your personal charity mission now? Or are there others?" His cheeks reddened, and she could see white knuckles by his sides.

"You need to calm down. This isn't good for your heart." She shook her head as tears streamed down her face.

"You don't get to doctor me. I'm not your patient. All of this. Since the day we met. It was all because of the stupid list? What, you can't fix your own life so you wiggle your way into others' under the guise of *saving them*?" His words were thicker, harder with each sentence.

"That's why I met you, but our friendship hasn't been because you're a project of any sort."

"The next time I hear from you, it better be because you are confirming my name isn't anywhere near that list." He turned on her porch to leave.

"Why do you want to die so badly?" she spat out, heat flushing through her body. How the events had unfolded in their relationship were regrettable, but her actions didn't absolve him of choosing to give up his future.

He froze on the steps, his head hanging for a moment before he turned back to her, the tightness in his brown eyes not relenting, not letting her in at all. She wanted to slap him senseless so he'd get off his high horse. How was it that she was the only one battling for his life? She gritted her teeth. She was on the edge of giving him both barrels, because what did it matter now? He was pissed, and anything that had started between them clearly didn't matter to him.

"I don't have to explain myself to you."

"No," she crossed her arms over her chest, "you don't, and I know that you don't want to believe me, but I regret the way I handled this. I made mistakes." She took a breath, trying to steady her voice.

"You did." He raised his hands to his sides, the anger in his eyes replaced with the broken resolution that usually surfaced when she gave a patient bad news. "You knew this whole time and still let me care about you." The smallness of his voice broke her heart as he headed for his truck down her un-shoveled path.

No, this day, this conversation, wasn't supposed to go like this. She cared about him, too. So much. "Fisher, I—"

"Save it."

Like hell. This was probably the last time she'd ever have his attention to speak her peace. "Your giving up on any sort of future you may or may not have doesn't bring Maggie back. This won't give her death meaning."

"Don't you dare presume to know why I made my choice."

She opened her mouth to tell him that everybody had crap in life to deal with so suck it up like everyone else, when he suddenly fell to his knees, one hand reaching for the ground, the other to his chest. She dashed down the steps as he landed on his side in the snow.

"Fisher!" She crashed to her knees beside him and gripped his waist, rolling him onto his back. She pressed two fingers to his wrist as she pulled her phone out of her pocket with her free hand and called 911. He was alive, but his pulse was weak. She lived three minutes from the hospital, but there was no way she'd be able to get him in her car.

His chest rose and fell, his pulse weaker as he took a breath and stronger when he exhaled. Not a good sign. Idiopathic pulmonary arterial hypertension caused a higher risk of blood clots. The list of things that could be going wrong right now was too long to narrow it down to one. He needed a hospital.

The ambulance arrived wailing, but it didn't seem as loud as usual. All she could see was Fisher's pale skin; all she could hear was his shallow breathing. She reached over, wrapping her palms around his left hand as she reported his IPAH condition. "I'm riding with you." She hopped in the back before Jane could disagree, never letting go of his hand.

They couldn't end on this note; the last time she spoke to him couldn't be a fight. He couldn't just die like this. Alone.

She wiped her cheek on her shoulder, her eyes so full of tears she could barely see him.

His continued unconsciousness wasn't a good sign.

She'd never understand his pain, but if it was anything like how broken and heavy her heart felt in her chest right now, making it hard to breathe and sucking all hope out of the air, he was going to have to fight to come back. Fight to heal.

They hurried him out of the ambulance, and she rushed to keep up, ready to order the tests she knew he needed so she could figure out exactly what was going on and how bad it was. He was supposed to have years left, not minutes.

"Dr. Morgenstern. I've got this." Dr. Wilmington stepped in front of her, blocking her path to the room.

"I know him. He's got IPAH."

"I've been briefed on his chart. I'll handle this and let you know as soon as I do." She pointed to the waiting area, and as badly as Silver wanted to call rank on her, Wilmington was a damn fine doctor and could, in fact, handle Fisher's case.

"Don't let him die," she whispered to her colleague, her arms falling to her sides as curtains closed around Fisher. She'd studied how to fix most problems in the body, but healing the hurt she'd caused him, caused herself, was beyond her schooling.

Her feet wouldn't move. The muffled voices and commands almost soothed her. There were no codes being called out; they were working to save him. People rushed around her and she stood there. She had no idea how long.

"Silver." Lorelei jogged up, hugged her and led her to the waiting area. "What happened?"

"How'd you know I was here?"

"Nurse Robert called. Said you were upset."

"It's Fisher. We were talking. Well, fighting—" she sniffed back tears "—because he found out what I did and he was so mad. I don't blame him." Lorelei hugged her sideways, and the pain in her chest lessened. "I still don't regret it. Especially now. What if he doesn't wake up?"

"Mr. Hale?" Lorelei gave Silver a sideways glance before letting go and walking over to the man talking to Robert at the nurse's station.

"Ms. Sullivan. What are you doing here?" The man rotated toward Lorelei.

"I'm with my friend." Lorelei turned to Silver, who recognized Fisher's friend from the snowball fight. *Henry is Lorelei's boss?*

"Dr. Silver Morgenstern, this is my boss, Mr. Hale." Lorelei stood straight, a serene, blank expression gracing her high cheekbones. She'd gone into work mode: show no emotion.

Silver stretched out her hand to the gorgeous lawyer Lorelei rarely talked about. Which would be something she and her best friend would be discussing later, because he looked like exactly Lorelei's type – smart, sexy, and rich.

"We've met." His handshake was firm. "What's going on? The call was cryptic. Where is he?" Henry's gaze frantically searched the area, panic taking over.

"He's here. They're checking him out now." Silver used her calming, slow doctor voice to make sure he was hearing her.

Worry wrinkled his forehead.

"How do you know Fisher?" Lorelei asked Henry, her work persona faltering.

"I'm his best friend. And emergency contact. What's going on?"

"He passed out. I had the ambulance bring him here, and they've been working on him ever since."

Henry rubbed his hand down his face. "Dammit. Did they say anything else? Can I see him? Is he going to make it?"

"I don't know." That was the truth. She didn't know why he would pass out all of a sudden and what other conditions were impeding his heart, or if he was even pumping it on his own right now. Dr. Wilmington hadn't been out to give an update yet.

"You were with him when this happened?" Henry stopped pacing and ran his hand through his hair.

"Yes."

"I should've just let him do his own thing, but no, I had to stick my nose in and pressure him to tell you how he felt. Stress isn't good for his heart."

"What?" How he felt? Yeah, she'd gotten that message loud and clear all right. She took a deep breath and tried to put on a blank face of her own. She couldn't blame Henry. She'd hurt his friend, and if someone did that to Lorelei or Maisy, she'd act the same way.

Henry kept talking. "He was supposed to be grabbing beer for me to have while my brother's kids battled each other in video games and my parents argued over who's cooking what." He shrugged. "Family tradition."

"He did come to see me, but it wasn't to make up." She was so confused. Not about what Fisher had said to her – that was playing on repeat in the recesses of her mind. But what Henry was saying didn't make any sense.

They were ushered into the ER waiting room by Nurse Robert. Henry sat down in the seat across from them, and the focused lawyer who was used to hearing all sides of a story emerged. The worry in his gaze was only secondary.

"We were actually arguing because I, um, sort of got in the way of his paperwork, and he was never taken off the recipient list. He'd just found out. And was *not* happy." It was one thing to finally be honest about what she'd done and another to cover her ass to a lawyer.

"I see."

"I know why he was mad, and I don't blame him." Words tumbled out as if she might drown if she didn't say them. "I just, I just couldn't. I couldn't – I can't – watch him throw any chance he has of living out the window. Nothing in this life is guaranteed." Henry wasn't Fisher, but she might never get to state her case to him, so she had to get it out. All of it. "I care way too much about him to let that happen."

"Am I to understand that, against my client's wishes, you, a doctor, did not file paperwork he was expressly within his right to have executed?" Henry sat forward, resting his elbows on his knees, and didn't look away.

"That sums it up pretty good. Am I to understand that you are his best friend and condone him throwing in the towel on his life?" A flare of anger shot through her voice. She had nothing to lose at this point. If this guy wanted to go after her entire license, she'd happily save him the trouble and throw it in his face.

Especially if it meant Fisher would be all right.

But what she'd done had only kept him from being taken off the list – it didn't mean he was going to get a heart that was a match or that he'd get one in time.

Time was the enemy.

"One accusation does not befit the other, Doctor." Henry's head dipped, and she couldn't see his expression until moments had passed and he gazed first at Lorelei then back to her. "I've tried to talk him out of it so many times since I found out. I never thought to interfere with the paperwork. Well done. Well done, indeed."

A big breath filled her chest, and she let it out quickly. That made one less person to convince. There was still hope that with this scare, Fisher would see the merits of staying on the list, of living his life. Of spending it with her.

Silver could feel Lorelei's tension level drop significantly too with Henry's side smile. Interesting.

Minutes ticked by on the clock on the wall. No answers came. Nothing made sense, nothing made the situation better. Fisher was in a room hanging on for dear life, and she was stuck in a glass room.

The only facts she'd learned were that this side of the waiting room sucked royally and Lorelei was hot for her boss. That was a conversation she'd save for later, after Henry was gone and she needed a distraction from her own heartache.

"Dr. Morgenstern," Dr. Wilmington called out.

Silver stood on legs she could barely feel. Her entire body was mostly numb, yet her tear ducts where working perfectly. She joined her colleague in the hall, trying to read the expression on the older woman's face. The thin line of her lips and her furrowed brow behind rimless glasses said nothing. The doctor had been trained in not giving too much hope.

"He's stable. For now." The cautious words brought little solace.

Technically, Silver shouldn't be privy to a patient's status. Having a position at PWMC hospital finally had its perks. But Henry was Fisher's emergency contact, the person he chose to make decisions on his behalf. Silver popped her head back into the waiting room and waved him over.

"He's breathing on his own. It's his heart we're most concerned about." Dr. Wilmington glanced between the two of them and said gently, "We're seeing signs of heart failure, and with his condition, there isn't much we can do."

"Is he conscious?" Silver asked, one arm wrapped around her midsection, the other rubbing her neck. This was worst-case scenario. If Fisher didn't get a heart soon, he'd spend the rest of his time in the hospital. From what she knew of him, the hospital wouldn't be able to hold him. He'd check out and be dead within a day. *Dead. Gone forever.*

"No. We're running tests to answer that riddle. His heart condition shouldn't be keeping him in a comatose state."

"Coma?" Henry rubbed his forehead and started to pace.

The only time Lorelei had talked about her boss was to rave about how good he was under pressure and how his intuition had saved the day on many cases. And then there were the days when Lorelei couldn't stand him because he was never satisfied until they won the case. Of course, that was his professional life; personally, he was starting to lose it. Silver could see it in his eyes. Or maybe she was witnessing her own failings as an impartial thinker under stress. She'd always prided herself on staying calm and rational in all contexts. Not any more.

"It is coma-*like*," Dr. Wilmington emphasized. "We don't expect him to stay unconscious for long, but until we know why, we're running tests starting with the most likely."

"Which is?"

"I'll come back when I know more." Her tender smile was small and shut down the conversation without being hasty or giving false hope or undue agitation since Fisher's diagnosis was in question. The PWMC legal team would be proud. She eyed Silver before she returned through the double doors to the ER, her blue-covered shoes silent.

Dr. Wilmington hadn't wanted to say terms like "internal bleeding" and "pressure on the brain" and frighten the daylights out of Henry, and frankly Silver was glad she didn't have to hear them said out loud.

In this case, not knowing specifically might turn out to be better. If she knew, she'd play out every scenario of what could be happening to Fisher right now – losing brain function, heart tissue dying, an overall weakened state – and then she'd curl up in the corner and sob like a baby because there was nothing she could do.

Chapter Nine

Beeping noises roused Fisher. *Where am I?* He tried to open his eyes but couldn't, at least not much. Only enough to see a lot of white and blue. *How long have I been like this?*

What was the last thing he remembered? Talking to Silver. No, fighting with her. Watching a tear roll down her cheek and cussing himself out for being the one who put it there. She hadn't deserved his bitterness. He wasn't even angry *at* her. Not really. He was frustrated with himself for being a stubborn fool who hadn't changed his mind sooner. Hadn't had the balls to admit he was wrong and that he wanted to live.

I want to live. I want a new heart.

She'd lied about her real identity. He had lied by omission about his heart condition. She'd not filed his paperwork. Then he'd collapsed, and his world had gone dark.

His head ached, and his body was weak, drained. He couldn't move anything, couldn't open his eyes. *Work, dammit.*

This was it. This was how it all ended. He would've taken a deep breath and cried a little if he could. If his body were working right.

At least he got to see one truth before he died.

He loved Silver.

He would've wanted to build a life with her. Have a family with her. Now he'd not get the chance.

There was no reason other than his faulty heart that he'd have passed out the way he did, that his body wasn't strong enough to open his damn eyelids.

Heal, dammit.

Drowsiness crept over him, pressing his body harder against the bed. His eyelids closed tightly.

He was going to get his wish after all.

He wasn't going to be on the transplant list any longer.

-

The four glass walls were closing in on her. Silver's phone vibrated in her pocket. Janae's name flashed on her screen.

"Hello?" she answered, unsure if Janae was calling about work or for personal reasons. It was Christmas Eve after all.

"Silver, good, I'm glad I reached you." Janae breathed hard into the phone.

"Are you running?"

"Rushing, actually. I'm on call for the National Organ Transplant List. We got one."

"What?"

"I'm hurrying into the office because I need to double-check a record."

"Are you here?" Silver's heart started to pump quicker.

"Yeah."

"I'll see you up there." She turned to Lorelei, who was sitting crossed-legged, leaning back in her chair, and watching her boss like she was stalking prey. "I'll be back. I need to go take care of something."

She hurried to the elevator bank, grateful for the distraction.

A part of her hoped Fisher matched the donor. If it was a heart. The ER had been crazy busy, but she hadn't overheard anyone talking about a donor.

She stepped off the elevator in time to see Janae unlocking their outer-office door. "You got here quick."

"I was downstairs. A friend of mine is in the ER."

"I'm so sorry. Everything going to be all right?"

Silver stared at the blond. No, everything probably wasn't going to be all right. She did a half shrug, half head bobble thing as she made a beeline for the laptop on her desk. "Which organs are we dealing with and which questions have been posed?"

In the back of Silver's office, Janae unlocked a separate door that housed the medical records of transplant-specific patients. Being a regional supervisor required that she have direct access to the files at all times, for situations such as this when a file and tests were called into question. The hard copy data always won.

Janae reappeared with five files in her hands as Silver logged on to the National Organ Transplant List system.

"There was a two-car crash on the interstate. One male died at the scene, the other two victims were taken to the hospital and died on the operating tables. Both donors. So we have a couple of organs."

Silver squeezed her thighs together in her chair and curled her toes. Was one of the victims able to donate their heart?

"The first potential match they had was a kidney from the female. The other kidney was damaged in the crash." Janae looked up from her email on her phone. "And the reason she died." Her frown was out of place – Silver had never seen anything but a smile on the girl's face.

"They matched it to another female in Casper but needed her latest PRA results. She'd been too high in the past but was working on bringing them down. Everything else makes her compatible for the kidney." Janae rattled off the name, and Silver checked the in-house electronic medical record to verify it against the data in her file.

"Her PRA is lower now, and she's within the range." Silver sighed in relief as Janae emailed their first finding. Time was of the essence, so they had to let the official National Organ Transplant List people know to okay everything in the proper way. Looked like Dr. Silas, one of the best surgeons on staff, would have a full schedule for the next twenty-four hours. "Next?" She could feel her heart pumping in her ears.

"They've assigned most of the others already. The next question is about a liver. That's why I had to grab these files." Janae pointed to the three files in the stack.

Fisher didn't need a liver. Silver's heartbeat slowed, and her arms went numb. She slid the manila folders out of the way to the last name and closed her eyes, saying a little prayer, before focusing on the name. Thomas Rizzoli. Not Fisher.

Breathe. Keep breathing. You don't know he needs a heart tonight. By the time she got back downstairs, he could be awake and fine. Best-case scenarios did happen.

But a heart for the holiday would be the best present.

Chapter Ten

Silver picked up three cups of coffee on her way to the waiting room. If Lorelei had left, then she'd drink the extra cup. She had no intention of leaving until Fisher woke up. Even that might not be enough. She wanted to talk to him. How they'd left things sucked, and now that all the truths were on the table, maybe they could talk it out. And he could get better.

But, holy crap, there was no reason he would've actually changed his mind. She had still lied; she still hadn't performed his written wishes. She still wasn't someone he wanted to be around.

A problem for a different time. She'd deal with all of that once he woke up. When she could look into his golden eyes and see the life in him. Once he smiled at her again.

Probably Fisher smiling at Henry was the closest she was going to get, but, hey, a girl could dream.

"Hey." Silver distributed the cups and took a seat near her friend. She'd expected to interrupt a conversation, but Lorelei and Henry were both on their phones.

"I tried Maisy, but she's not picking up. I'm sure she'd be here if she could."

"Thank you." Silver crossed her leg toward her friend. "Any news?"

"No. We haven't heard anything."

"I tried to go see him, but they wouldn't let me." Henry pocketed his phone, leaning back in the semi-padded chair, resting his ankle over his knee.

"He must still be unconscious then." Her gaze dropped to the black liquid that was only making her stomach hurt worse.

Henry's phone buzzed and drew her attention from the caffeine that was allowing her mind to run too freely. Fisher should've been awake by now. The longer he was under, the worse the prognosis.

"Excuse me." Henry stood with eyebrows knitted together. "This is Hale," he said as he hurried out of the area.

"How are you doing?" Lorelei leaned in and nudged Silver with her shoulder.

"We were fighting." She took a deep breath. "I wish we hadn't been fighting."

"It's going to be okay." Her friend squeezed her knee and gave her the best cheery nod and comforting smile she probably thought Silver would believe.

Silver knew too much about what was at stake to be that optimistic. Not *everything* was going to be okay even if Fisher was, but her first priority was to make sure he was alive to make that choice.

Henry rushed back into the room, grabbing Silver's shoulder as he stopped in front of her.

"They matched him with a heart."

"What?" Silver and Lorelei both stood. "Who did?"

Adrenaline blurred her vision for a second. Fisher hadn't been on the list upstairs. Unless his match hadn't been in question. Then they wouldn't have needed her assistance.

"The people." Henry held up his phone. "That transplant list. There was a car accident, and one of the people who died was a donor and a good match for Fisher."

"Oh my God." Silver's face heated, and she felt the tears well. "When?" She cleared her throat to speak at her normal volume. "When can they do it?"

"They said that since Fisher can't sign off, I have to. They're already talking to the doctor." Henry's features were heavy, uncertainty clouding his eyes.

"Are you going to sign?" she asked carefully as Lorelei wrapped her arm around her side and squeezed.

Henry didn't say anything. He just stared.

"Henry. It's not good that he still hasn't regained consciousness. He needs that heart. I've seen his file. He won't live long without it. Even shorter now."

"Do you know why he made the decision he did?"

It was the one thing she'd set out to do when she showed up at CCH that day. "No."

"At his last doctor's appointment, he was told that the chances a transplant would be successful were a little lower."

"Statistics and doctors can be wrong." There were no guarantees, but physicians also needed the patient to believe they were going to pull through and get better. Mindset was always important. She could cold-cock the doctor who told Fisher his chances of rejection were a couple points lower.

"Did he tell you about Maggie?"

"Yes, she had a lung transplant, and acute rejection occurred."

"That's a very doctorly way of saying she died. They'd finally been handed hope, and everything was going well, and then in an instant she was gone."

Silver nodded. She'd been attempting not to be crass. Or lose her temper over the fact that Henry wasn't chomping at the bit to get Fisher that heart. Hearts didn't live outside of the body and stay viable for long. Minutes counted.

"Nothing with transplants is guaranteed." The color was draining from her face, her entire body, she just knew it. All hope she held, every little morsel, Henry was stomping on with his size-twelve loafers.

What was up with his best friend? Shouldn't he want to save Fisher the most?

"I think he's known he was going to die young for so long that he just stopped living. Actually living." A smile crooked to one side of Henry's face, causing a dimple. "That was until you showed up."

"I want him to live, Henry." Her voice started to shake, and she paused, regaining her composure. She wanted to make the decision. Give her the form, she'd sign it. It took all of her willpower not to scream, "Sign the damn paper and get Fisher that heart!" But she couldn't make that decision. Henry knew him best. Fisher had given the decision to Henry. Not her.

"If you truly believe that Fisher doesn't want a heart," she continued, "that he really is happy and at peace with his decision, then I'm not going to try to change your mind or get in your way."

Chapter Eleven

Fisher lay flat on the gurney as the nurses rolled it slowly. Silver reached for his hand and laced her fingers with his. She didn't want to let go.

He hadn't regained consciousness yet, and the tests hadn't shown anything concrete or a reason not to go ahead with the surgery.

Henry had stared at her for what felt like an eternity before finally reaching out, taking the paperwork, and, without even reading it, signing by the X with a shiny fountain pen from his pocket. He handed the papers back to the doctor, nodded toward her, their gazes not meeting, and walked away. She hadn't seen him again for thirty minutes. Not until Nurse Robert said they were ready for Fisher.

They reached the double doors to the OR, which she'd passed through so many times before, but this time she wasn't allowed. She was going to be relegated to the waiting room. Again. There was a possibility she could strong-arm her way in and watch in the corner. But she couldn't. She couldn't watch him be operated on and not be able to do it herself, not know that everything would be done properly.

She was completely helpless.

"Just a moment." She found Nurse Robert's eyes, and he stopped the gurney.

She leaned down and whispered in Fisher's ear, "You are a fighter. I know you want this heart. I know you want to live. You're going to come out of this, and then we can argue if you still want to. I believe in you. I'm on team Fisher, and nothing is going to change that. Fight, Fisher, fight." She kissed his cheek, gently untwined her hand from his, and wrapped her arms around her chest as he disappeared into the OR.

–

It had been five hours since she'd watched Fisher roll away. The surgery should've only lasted four. Why weren't they back yet? She paced the row of windowed walls in the blasted waiting room, which she never wanted to see again.

It was one in the morning, but the caffeine had wired her.

She'd long since insisted that Lorelei go home. Henry had made a bed, a very uncomfortable-looking situation between three chairs, and had fallen asleep in what had to be an excruciating crouching position an hour ago. His back was going to regret that tomorrow. Or today, since it was past midnight.

"Dr. Morgenstern." A male voice stopped her in her tracks.

"Dr. Isaacs. How did the transplant go?"

"Really well. He just got out of recovery and has been put up in ICU."

Shuffling drew her attention over her shoulder. Henry had roused and high-tailed it over to them in record time, wiping a hand down his face.

"We are going to monitor him closely, and we need to make sure he wakes up soon," Dr. Isaacs said. "I'll give him twelve hours before we start more tests and run some scans. His vitals were strong during the surgery."

"That's a good sign." Fisher's new heart was beating strongly. She couldn't help but smile.

"It's still too early to tell."

"I realize that."

"Can we see him?" Henry piped up.

"Not yet. But later today I'll approve him for visitors."

She pushed her shoulders back. "Dr. Isaacs, we're going in there."

He started to protest then nodded and stepped aside. Make that two perks for being the hospital's medical director.

She pushed the elevator button for the third floor. She and Henry rode in silence. She opened the door to Fisher's semi-lit room, holding it open for Henry and hanging back.

Fisher had been put in a single room right next to the nurse's station in the ICU.

Henry stood by Fisher's bed, his back to her. She was the outsider. Fisher probably wouldn't even want her there. If Henry knew the fury Fisher had displayed right before his trip to the hospital, he'd probably not let her stay.

"The things you do to have a beer with your best friend." Henry chuckled faintly and rocked back on his heels. Silence stretched as Henry looked over Fisher and the equipment he was hooked up to. "We all believe in you, man." He patted Fisher's shoulder and hung his head. "Keep me posted." His gaze briefly met hers, and he was out the door.

Fisher's five-o'clock shadow was officially a beard now, and she smiled as she scooted a chair up to his bedside.

The man barely fit in the bed. The nurses had packed him with blankets and laid out his IV – her eyes trailed over the tubes to the machine. The doctor had been right – Fisher's vitals were looking good, and that new heart of his was pumping like a champ.

In the quiet, with only the two of them, she finally felt a shred of peace. She reached for his hand, wrapping it with her palms, and closed her eyes. She more imagined than actually smelled his scent. How she wished it was there.

The tension in her back and neck started to dissolve into sleepiness. Finally, they were on the other side of the situation. Recovery. Fisher might see this part as the worst, but she didn't. There was hope in healing.

He'd come this far. He was going to make it the rest of the way. The couple of weeks he'd need to stay in the hospital to be monitored might make him feel better about rejection as well.

Rejection wasn't happening to Fisher.

She leaned in, setting her elbows on the white sheets. "Merry Christmas," she whispered, watching his chest rise and fall with a new heart. His new heart. *Beat, baby, beat.*

"You're the best present of all. I'm sorry I didn't tell you who I was. After I met you, it all happened so quickly, and I didn't want you to push me away. I didn't want you to reject me because of my profession, to make meeting you about my job. I only wanted to enjoy you. And I did. I loved the time we spent together, and I'll cherish it forever. No matter what happens." She sniffled because saying things out loud, even to a man who wasn't going to remember any of it when he woke up, was still hard and emotional and dammit, she really wanted him to wake up.

"But you know what? When you wake up and I can finally look into your beautiful brown eyes again, I want you to pick me. I want you to see that your condition doesn't define you. Or us. You, Fisher Tibbs, are an amazing man with a heart of gold who just got a second chance at life whether he wanted it or not. And I hope you choose to live it."

She sat with him, hearing the nurses changing shifts outside the door. She mindlessly talked about anything and everything she could think of in a low, soothing voice: the storm with nine inches of snow predicted; how Lorelei had the hots for Henry; how she was going to start looking at new jobs that would be fulfilling, the Red Cross was an organization she'd long admired, although she didn't know what else she'd be good at; how she was going to have to make it up to her family for missing Christmas Eve dinner and that next year she hoped he was a part of that tradition.

The last thing she remembered before drifting off as the sun rose in the clear blue sky was telling him she loved him.

Chapter Twelve

Pain hit him instantly. His eyes popped open, and he took in the space before moving a muscle. Mostly because his body ached.

He was in the hospital. In a room. Hooked up to a bunch of stuff. His chest burned something horrible.

There was a blond mess of hair on his arm.

Silver.

Her butt was planted in a gray chair, and one hand held his while the other rested on his arm, which also braced her head. He gingerly reached over and moved a few curls out of her face so he could have an unhindered view.

Her lips weren't glossy, her mascara was smeared, and her cheeks were bare. She was the most beautiful woman he'd ever seen.

He didn't know why exactly he'd landed in the hospital, but she was there with him. Holding his hand. Falling asleep by his side.

By the looks of it he hadn't been out too long – she had on the same pants as when he'd gone to see her on Christmas Eve. Some holiday. Hopefully, she could salvage Christmas with her family.

He took another breath but couldn't make it a deep one. Why in the hell did his chest hurt so damn much? Not wanting to break the grasp Silver had on him, with his free hand, he shuffled around the gown he'd been dressed in and opened it up to see white gauze on his chest. He peeled back a side to find a long, red line stapled closed. It stopped about five inches from his belly button. It suspiciously looked a lot like his chest had been cracked open.

His entire body tensed, and he tried like hell to remember anything since he'd gone over to Silver's house pissed. He couldn't.

Somehow he'd had surgery. But for what?

She'd never taken him off that list.

He'd passed out and probably needed a heart.

Then he'd received one.

Whether he wanted it or not. Apparently.

Getting a new heart when he was out cold would've been a great-timed miracle.

He squashed any hope rising in his gut. He didn't know what happened. Maybe they decided a temporary pacemaker would do the trick, or he needed stents put in, or they had to do something else to his heart and crack his chest open in the process.

He rubbed his thumb over Silver's temple. Her skin was so soft. She looked like an angel.

He sucked in air, and the radiating pain made him hold it in for a moment and release it slowly. He was going to have to remember that deep breathing was off the table for now.

Silver started to move, rolling her head on his arm before squeezing his hand and letting go. Then rubbing his arm.

He wanted to be relieved, happy, that she was here with him. But not knowing what had happened to him was keeping any joy at bay.

Especially if it involved the whole heart transplant possibility that was against his direct wishes.

"Please be awake," Silver whispered into his arm, and his entire body heated with the need to hold her in his arms. Drag her up into the bed with him, pain be dammed.

"Hey there." His voice came out raspy, his entire mouth was dry.

Her head shot up, her eyes wide. "You're awake." She grinned, pushed herself up and kissed his cheek before sitting back down.

"From what, is the question." He raised his eyebrows. She knew what he was referring to. Pleasantries were nice and all, and he'd like more of her lips on his skin, but why exactly did he have a scar on his chest?

She glanced down to the exposed bandage, every trace of her grin leaving her creamy, round face. He knew the answer before she spoke.

"You were unconscious. Things weren't looking good." Her gaze met his, her blue eyes darker than normal. "They stabilized you and were running tests—" her shoulders slumped, and she shook her head "—but it wasn't looking like things were going to get better. After a number of hours, a call came in that you were a good match for a heart available in the area. They needed to move quickly, and you were already here." She paused, biting her plump bottom lip and scraping her teeth over the flesh. "And you needed that heart to survive."

He'd undergone a heart transplant. Without even knowing it.

He'd also *lived* through the transplant. *For now.* He needed to talk to the doctor. Find out what chances of survival they were giving him. Find out if there were any signs of rejection yet.

He broke eye contact, looking out the bank of windows to the park they'd sat in only last week and watched it light up. Last week he'd known it might be his last Christmas. Now, he might have dozens of Christmases left. A smile twitched at the edges of his lips, but he squashed it.

It's all too good to be true.

"How long ago?" he asked.

She glanced at the clock on the wall. "You got out of surgery eight hours ago. It's Christmas Day."

His life had completely changed in less than twenty-four hours.

"Obviously you never did file my paperwork." Dammit, he was an asshole, but what else could he do other than fall back on his original anger? Anger that didn't pull at his gut or tighten his sore chest or weigh on him. No, it definitely wasn't gone, but something had started to replace it, something that made his body twitchy and uneasy.

"I did not." Her chin jutted out, and she tucked her blond hair behind her ear. "And I wouldn't change what I did."

"It's not what I wanted."

She stood, taking her warmth with her. "This is a lot to take in, and you probably need more rest. The doctor will be making rounds soon, so he can answer any questions you have."

She grabbed her purse and jacket and headed for the door.

"That's it?" He tried to sit up but was hit with a wave of pain that forced him to rest back against the bed.

She whirled around, red blotches climbing up her neck. "What's it?"

"You get me in here, wheel me into surgery, take my heart out, put a new one in, and that's it. You're just going to tell me that the doctor will be by soon?"

"Well, I'm not going to sit here and argue with you. I am not sorry for any of those steps, except the one where you collapsed in my front yard and weren't conscious to make the decision for yourself when your name came up."

"I had made a decision, and you chose to ignore it," he gritted out. His heart rate was kicking up, and he wasn't sure that was a good thing right now. Now that he had a new organ to protect and the future to think about.

She stomped toward him, no apology on her face as her eyes narrowed on him. "You'd made the decision to ignore your own life, to be content with dying. I refuse to watch you die, not when you have the option to live. The only thing I'm sorry for is not trying to talk you out of that mindset before yesterday. You will never hear me apologize for your new chance at life. Ever." This time when she turned around her blond curls bounced all the way out the door, until he could no longer see her down the hallway.

He didn't know whether he wanted to kiss her and hold her in his arms, or if he never wanted to see her again.

-

"Knock, knock." Henry entered the hospital room just as Fisher finished dinner. If he wanted to call Jell-O, ginger ale, and cranberry juice with ice chips on the side dinner.

Because he didn't. He wanted a fat steak the size of a cow. "Merry Christmas."

Henry had get-well balloons and a red-and-white bouquet of flowers in his hands.

"Flowers and balloons, really?"

"The nurses confiscated the six-pack."

"Figures." Fisher laid his head back down. He'd been in and out of sleep all day thanks to the pain meds. If his mind had its way, he'd be rehashing both fights he'd had with Silver in the last day. "What took you so long?"

"I was here through your surgery and had to make up the sleep somehow. Plus, your girlfriend's stress level wore me out."

"Oh, she told you what to do, too?"

"You're lucky you were with her. She saved your life." Henry's matter-of-fact tone left no room for retort. He sat in the same chair Silver had slept in by Fisher's side. "You scared us, my man. If the transplant people hadn't called when they did, I don't know how many more tests you would've had to go through. You were out, and the doctors didn't know why."

"So I've heard."

"Speaking of, where is Silver? I thought she'd be glued to your side."

"She was here when I woke up. Then we started to fight about the transplant. She thinks she can make any choice she wants to. She had no right."

"What are you talking about?"

"She didn't file my paperwork to be taken off the list. Then, she made sure they put a new ticker in me when I was out cold."

"Being mad at her for saving your life is messed up. Even for you."

"She overstepped big time."

"You don't even have your information straight. She didn't get the call about a heart. I did. You remember when you signed all that paperwork? And again when you revised your will a couple weeks ago? I'm your emergency contact and power of attorney. I was here at the hospital. When I got here, she was already in the waiting room and worried sick. I'm the one who had to make the decision."

"She didn't force the transplant?"

"No. She was stressed and terrified and scared she was going to lose you. I know, because I was in that same boat with her. She said she didn't want you to die but that I knew you best, and if I really thought you didn't want the heart then I shouldn't sign. But if there was any shred of doubt, I should okay the transplant because you might not get the chance again. It was a perfect storm. I didn't know if you were ever going to wake up. You're a brother to me. I don't think you really want to die. If I made a bad judgment call, I'm sorry. Be mad at me. But it's over and done, and you don't have to worry about dying on the table. So instead of dying on your own terms, how about you start living by them?"

"That's the only choice I have now."

"The other thing you need to do is make sure you make things right with that woman. She's a good person who only wants the best for you. Don't screw it up. You have a longer life expectancy now, and you don't want to spend all those years completely alone because you're stubborn."

"It's too late."

"I doubt it. I watched her. She cares about you."

But he had pushed her away one too many times. He had no idea where to even begin to make things right.

And there were still too many unknowns in his future. Silver didn't deserve to be strung along while he sorted out his new life.

Chapter Thirteen

Silver walked out of the hospital. She was starting the new year off right. Giving her notice hadn't been nearly as hard as she'd thought. Today was the first step to her next best life. There was something out there, and she was going to find it. Until then she wasn't going the office route. Her savings would feel the hit, but she'd done the math. She had six months to get her act together and take a position that would make her happy. She'd already put in an application for a teaching job.

If only she could add being with Fisher to her new life plan.

He'd been released two weeks after his surgery, having no problem with his recovery so far. Or so she'd heard from Lorelei, who'd overheard it from Henry.

"Silver," a male voice called out, and she stopped, turning to her left. Henry, in a dark-gray jacket, came to a stop at her side. "I'm glad I caught you." A bouquet of pink flowers in his hand swayed toward her.

"What can I help you with?" Her gut started to knot – was Fisher having problems? What were the flowers for?

She'd thought about Fisher every single day since his surgery. She knew he needed space. His arms wouldn't be wide open to her until he came around and forgave her. If he ever did.

"It's about Fisher."

She held her breath. *No, no. Please let him be okay.* She crossed her arms around her midsection and dug her nails into her coat. "What about him?" she asked slowly. *Please don't be bad news.*

"He's pig-headed."

Her brows narrowed. "Come again?" Her gaze dropped back to the flowers. Pink carnations. That was familiar. Why?

"I'm probably out of line, but that's a best friend's job, right?"

A chuckle escaped her lips as she tried to smile. Where was this going? "This should be good." She smiled. She missed Henry. She missed being in Fisher's world.

"Listen. Don't write him off just yet, that's all I'm saying. I know you two haven't talked since he woke up, and going to CCH for a big conversation probably isn't the best setting. But I know you'll think of something." Henry checked his watch, the flowers bouncing in their plastic wrapping. "I've got to run. It was nice to see you."

"You, too, Henry. Happy New Year."

She stood in the middle of the entryway for a couple beats as people maneuvered around her to get inside and out of the brisk winter air, before heading for her car. *Pink carnations.* Those were the flowers Fisher always took to Maggie's grave on the anniversary of her death. It must be today. He'd be at the cemetery.

She was out to lunch. Totally crazy. She was just going to show up at Maggie's gravesite, a very personal place for Fisher, and… what? Declare her love for him? He'd rejected her the last time they'd spoken. Yeah, not going to happen.

She couldn't.

She wouldn't.

She blew air through her lips as she buckled her seat belt. She was not going to go chasing after someone who didn't want anything to do with her. That would be pathetic or embarrassing.

Or liberating.

-

Fisher clenched the bouquet of pink carnations in his hand and took the seven steps from the road to Maggie's grave.

"Hey there, baby girl," he whispered as he bent down and set the fresh flowers in the vase to the right of the headstone.

Every year it was harder. Every year the sorrow clenched at his chest, his soul, and an emptiness took over. Dragged him down into a black pit. If he didn't come, would it get easier? No. He thought about her every day. He knew the nooks and crannies of her gravesite like he knew the back of his hand. Being there, not being there, this day was hard to get through no matter what. At least when he was here, there was a stronger connection to her life.

"I got a new heart."

The scar that ran down half of his torso was healing. It wasn't his shell he was so worried about these days. The ache he felt went deeper than his chest, and the only way he was going to restore his heart fully was to talk to Silver. But he didn't know the right words to tell her he was sorry for his assumptions, and the anger, and not communicating with her and instead pushing her away. He really just wanted a fresh start with her. Only her.

"I'm gonna grow up and marry you, Daddy," Maggie'd said and twirled.

Megpie had been obsessed with princesses, couldn't get enough of Cinderella, Belle and Jasmine, making him watch the movies nonstop. He could see her now with her curly blond pigtails, wearing plastic heels and a crown with pink gems. "Baby girl, you're going to marry someone much better than me," he'd replied and picked her up to dance around the room.

"Then you can find a princess, too. She'll have hair like me, and we'll be a family." Her head leaned back, a big grin on her cute, perfectly round face, as he spun them around.

She'd never lost that big, larger-than-life smile. Even when it was hard for her to breathe and her little body was hooked up to so many machines, she had still wanted her princess dress and movies and crown.

A car door shut in the distance, taking him from the past.

He'd found a princess with blond hair like hers, all right. "You were right, baby girl."

He stood and looked into the distance, blinking away tears before they started. The sun was high in the sky, but clouds were rolling in.

The ground crinkled underneath feet behind him. He never knew whether to make eye contact with other grieving people or to greet them at all. He turned to head back to his car, keeping his gaze on the ground in front of him.

"Hi."

His head shot up, and he stared into Silver's blue eyes. Her hands were hidden in her jacket pockets as she walked toward him, stopping a good three feet away.

"What are you doing here?" he asked.

Her head bobbed twice, and she started to swivel back in the direction she'd just come. "This was a bad idea."

"No," he blurted. "You don't have to leave. I just…" He ran his palm down his scruffy beard. "How did you know I was here?" Had he willed her to the cemetery?

"Henry."

"Ah, I see." Henry was sticking his nose into Fisher's business a lot lately. Okaying the heart transplant had been only the beginning – Henry had also talked to Fisher's doctors to line up physical therapy, taken care of CCH in Fisher's absence and scheduled a dietary consultant for his post-hospital stay. Now he'd somehow convinced Silver to come to Maggie's grave. Damn, he was a good brother from another mother.

He took one step toward her. She didn't move back. That was a good sign. "I know it was Henry's decision. About the heart."

She bit her lower lip, his gaze dropped to her mouth and he took another step closer.

"I'm sorry for not being forthcoming about who I was and why I showed up at CCH," she said.

"Apology accepted." Whew, that took a load off. "How have you been?"

"I think I'm supposed to ask you that." The sides of her eyes crinkled as she searched his.

"Recovery is going well. I got out earlier than expected. Numbers are good. Breathing is getting better with each day."

"A cracked rib is one thing, but to have your entire chest opened is a whole other story."

"You're telling me." He took one more step, her perfume filling his lungs. He could reach out and wrap her into his arms if he wanted. If she'd let him. "I'm sorry for the last time we spoke. I was in a bit of shock, I think."

"As is to be expected. I'm sure it was a lot to take in."

"I should've called you. Or stopped by."

"That would've been nice."

He clenched the little jewelry box in his pocket. It was stupid really, a small piece of jewelry he'd had made to leave at Maggie's grave. A part of him was always thinking about her, it seemed like a natural step to literally leave a chunk of him with her permanently. He'd put a lot of thought into the necklace that held his heart. This whole living thing was going to take some getting used to – no more planning for the day or week. He had years to think about.

Silver was here now. Alive and breathing. She'd captured his heart from the first time she'd walked through the CCH doors in her high heels and knowing stare. There was no time like the present to let her know that.

"I want you to have this." He handed her the little red box.

"What is it?" she asked even though she was already taking off the white bow.

"Just open it."

She flipped open the lid to a silver outline of a heart with a second, solid heart dangling in the middle. She tenderly took it from the case and held it up between them.

"My heart is yours," she said, reading the inscription on the middle heart. Her gaze flicked up to his and searched.

"I had my heart, the original model, cremated." He gestured to the piece of his heart she now cradled in her palm. "The only logical place for it to be, though, is with you."

"I don't know what to say."

His throat tightened, and he swallowed down a wave of nausea. He was trying to tell her that he loved her. He reached out and palmed the sides of her arms. "You'll always have it. The original one with all its bumps and bruises and sorrow and death and joy and miracles, because you're my angel. You've been looking out for me since before we met."

A tear ran down her cheek. Did that mean she loved him back? He was literally offering her his heart.

"You had the first version, and you have this one, too," he continued because she hadn't even tried to speak and if he kept going maybe he'd talk her into loving him. "If you'll give me the chance I want to love you wholeheartedly."

He slid his palms down to grasp her hips. "You made my heart whole again." He pressed his lips to hers. "Life is better with you in it, and the only time I can see a future, my future, is when I picture it with you. I don't want a future if you aren't in it. You're the only one since Maggie who allows me to see a life, a full life, one with love and family and joy."

Tears were freely running down her cheeks now. "That's some speech. And this is some token." She put the necklace on then wrapped her arms around his neck. "I'm in love with you." She kissed him then pulled back. "But there's something you should know."

"What?"

"I just quit my job."

A nervous chuckle escaped his lips at her news – news they could deal with together. "That doesn't matter. We'll figure it out."

"I want to join the Red Cross and be a health and safety instructor."

"That's perfect. You'll be great at it." He kissed her again. "I love you." A moan escaped his throat. "That feels so good to say out loud. To you."

A grin brightened her gaze. "I love you, too." She pressed her lips to his, and the entire world fell away as pleasure rolled through his body. He held her tightly. He wasn't ever letting go.

His heart had never been so strong.

The December Deception

Chapter One

Lorelei Sullivan sat statue still, waiting for the verdict. The file folders were neatly stacked on the wooden table in the high-ceilinged courtroom and her navy leather-bound notebook was closed. She'd argued Shelia Monroe's case of wrongful termination well, and she lacked only the words "we side with the plaintiff" from the jury foreperson followed by a hefty dollar figure for the win to be recorded legally.

Not that Hale Law would see a dime. This was the seventh pro-bono case Mr. Hale had brought to the firm this quarter. Of course, it was his firm so he could do as he pleased. She was going to give each one her all. She wanted to be partner so badly she could practically feel the fine white cashmere sweater from Nordstrom she'd been lusting over all fall – the purchase would be an official reward for her victory.

The brunette lady in all black who'd worn a gaudy necklace every day of the two-week trial stood in the jury box and read from a sheet – the words danced to the tune of *Eye of the Tiger* in Lorelei's mind.

Another win.

Mrs. Monroe teared as she reached for Lorelei, putting her shaking arms around Lorelei's favorite black jacket that went perfectly with her fitted black skirt that cut off at her knees.

"Thank you," the middle-aged woman squeaked between silent sobs.

"You're welcome." Lorelei tapped her back and pulled away the first chance she got. She never had any idea how to handle clients when they wanted to invade her personal space. She hadn't grown up with parents who were overly affectionate when it came to professional accomplishments, but she was trying to get better at not acting so awkwardly. It was a work in progress.

"I'll file the necessary paperwork. It will take a little time with the holidays to get your full payment." She reached out and rubbed Mrs. Monroe's shoulder.

Lorelei collected her folders and clicked in her red pumps out of the five-floor building, across the street in the sleet, and into a staunchly square, cream-colored building lined with brown window shutters. Hale Law took up half of the first floor. She swung the glass door with block font wide open and strode for her office three doors down on the left.

"I know that look." Diana passed her in the hall, holding her black coffee cup with the scales of justice prominent.

"Nailed it." Lorelei smiled as she whirled around before continuing to her office.

"Good job, girl," Diana called over her shoulder as she slipped into the kitchen.

Lorelei's high would, of course, eventually fade, and she wasn't going to get another until after the new year. She had one more case before her holiday that was a mediation, but the courtroom wins were what really got her blood pumping.

She pressed her finger to the twist in her hair – the tightness was bugging her today. The pins were dug in a little too much.

"How'd the Monroe case end?" Mr. Hale was in her doorway, donning a pinstriped navy suit jacket.

"We won." She unloaded her MacBook Pro and files from her bag and set them on her oak desktop. "Actual lost wages, lost benefits plus compensation for potential lost wages."

"Good work. Danielle can start the paperwork; she just finished up with my Sheryl filings."

"Perfect. I'll get her the court paperwork when it arrives." The clerk for Judge Tabbs was usually fast. Considering everyone was in holiday-readiness mode, she expected it by tomorrow. Christmas was in just over a week, and no one wanted to work on Christmas. She wanted to tell herself that she wouldn't be working on the holiday, either, but she and her mother always ended up discussing cases, and this year no doubt would not be any different.

"How was the mediation on the O'Hara case?" Mr. Hale asked, still standing with his feet shoulder width apart in the crest of her door like a statue. He was always like bronze – didn't matter if they were at work or not, he rarely let loose. She squelched a smirk; she was one to talk. She had no idea how to talk to him outside of work, and after the first dinner with their best friends, she hadn't made much of an effort. It was easier to maintain a polite rapport between them.

"That is set for tomorrow. It was postponed." There'd been a mix-up in the judge's schedule and a trial case had taken precedence.

"You feel good about your approach?" The side of his jaw rolled as his lips pressed together.

The man hated to lose. Even the thought of it made him tense.

"Yes." She wasn't going to elaborate. She didn't need his input. "Are you going to take time off for the holidays?" she asked, but she already knew the answer. He hadn't taken time off for fun or even had the nerve to get sick since she'd met him more than two years ago.

"I have some potential cases to look over." He slipped his hands in his pants pockets.

She had a couple of files to take home herself.

"I did want to talk to you before you left." She stood so that wouldn't be at a height disadvantage, then quickly grabbed her turquoise coffee cup so it wouldn't look like she stood just to challenge him. She wanted him to say yes, after all. "Are you off to an appointment now?"

"No. What's going on?"

"It's about the partner track." She paused for his reaction but there wasn't one. "When will you be making a decision?"

She'd had this conversation with him twelve months ago. Only then it had been about her starting down the road to partnership. He'd said he'd make a decision in the coming year. That time was now.

"I'll consider it over the holidays to implement in the new year." He broke eye contact.

He took a step back from her doorway before nodding once and continuing down the hall toward his office that capped the end of the hallway. She sat and set the coffee cup in front of her, her body numb. How exactly was she supposed to read that reaction? She had to believe that she was a main contender for partner – he'd not said she was unfit. Now he knew where she stood, so that was good. As long as it was next in line.

-

Henry Hale dialed the conference call number and entered the code he used once every quarter. This was the last official meeting of the year for the branches of Hale Law.

His father, Dwight, and his older brother, Trent, were both in the Buffalo, Wyoming, office. After college, Henry hadn't wanted to practice under his family's thumb. He wanted to get away, be his own person. And having two branches had landed the Hales a couple of retainer clients that did business all over Wyoming.

"Who's on?" Trent asked.

"It's me," Henry replied. "Are you not with Dad?"

"No. I'm home with Arthur. Alicia had court today and the day care is closed for the holiday already."

Trent's boys were adorable hellions, but Henry hadn't quite mastered how to be an uncle yet. It didn't help that he wasn't around them often.

"I'm on." Dwight's voice always boomed no matter how close he was to a speaker. "The main item I want to discuss is bringing on a new partner."

"In Buffalo?" Henry pushed the decrease volume arrow on his phone.

"Either office."

The question was more of a formality. True, his firm technically was a division of the family business, but he retained all control of his Casper office. His father and Trent were partners in name only, a legal move to help them form a stronger presence spanning two towns. He was in complete control of his destiny. And Lorelei's, for the moment.

"Do you have anyone in mind for the Buffalo office?" Henry asked.

"Yes. Alicia is thinking about leaving her firm." Trent's voice was like his father's, just not as strong.

Henry nodded but didn't say anything. His sister-in-law was good people; he had nothing against her joining the ranks.

"Do you have anyone for Casper?" Dwight asked.

"Lorelei Sullivan is interested." There was no harm in being honest. "But I'm not ready to bring anyone up to partner yet."

"Isn't she your top biller?" Dwight pressed. Subtlety was not his strong suit.

"Yes."

That fact didn't matter. Henry was still finding his path, seeing what he wanted the firm to become. If he opened the door to Lorelei just a little, he'd no longer control what he'd worked so hard to create.

There was a long pause building on the line. Oh, fine. Anything to keep the meeting going. "I'll consider it, but not for this year."

He'd fought hard to gain his own independence. He was not about to hand over the reins to his future to someone else.

The problem wasn't with her. It was him. He didn't want to confer with someone about his firm. He didn't want to put his trust in someone only to have them let him down. Except for his friendship with Fisher, whom he was closer to than his own brother, his trust circle didn't include anyone else.

He only hoped Lorelei stuck around for many more years before she figured out he wasn't going to be adding her last name to the sign.

Chapter Two

Henry watched his American Bar Association award fall from his bookcase in slow motion, bouncing not once but twice on the dark hardwood floors in his office. One day. His brother, wife and their three boys had only been in Henry's home for twenty-four hours and already he was willing to call off Christmas. Not that he had much spirit in the first place. But any ounce he'd mustered had been sucked away by his prized possession smashing to pieces. His mentor, who'd died two years ago, had made the introductory speech to present that Nelson Award.

"You know you're not supposed to be in my office." He took a stern tone, although he already knew it wouldn't stop the rascals.

"Sorry Uncle H," the youngest lisped as he ran after his older brothers.

Henry desperately wanted to look forward to trimming a tree and indulging in desserts that people gave out only once a year. Last year had been monumental – Fisher, his best friend, had received a heart transplant and fallen in love. Henry's fourteen-hour days at the firm had paid off as he made inroads in the market and gained more retainer clients.

So why was it, when Christmas rolled around again, he was more inclined to set fire to the tinsel rather than dance with it? Probably because of the two-grand bill his sweet nephews had caused two years ago for new downstairs carpet. This year's damage total promised to be higher.

His phone started singing a wooden percussion tune in his pocket. Lorelei Sullivan's name lit up on his screen.

"Hello?"

"I just finished the O'Hara case." Lorelei's naturally velvety voice dove right into work. No pretense needed. Yes, the holiday time-off wouldn't last forever and soon he'd be able to get back to work.

"Good or bad?" he asked.

"Good."

He expected nothing less than a win from his star lawyer. Besides himself, she was the best he had at his firm.

"Probation," she continued, "set to start January first. After 233 hours of community service, the sentence will be sealed in his juvenile record."

"Nicely done." He closed the door to his office, taking in the silence that was not found anywhere else in his home, and sat in his reddish-brown leather chair.

The seventeen-year-old kid she'd been defending had graffitied a couple of alleys downtown, with impressive skill actually, and the DA had pressed for jail time. A gross overreach. Fighting for the case to be protected in juvenile records had been Lorelei's idea

"The thirty-three is an odd choice." He leaned back and closed his eyes. How in the world was he going to get through one entire week with his family? He'd specifically not taken on any more cases so that his staff could have a well-deserved break. He needed a vacation, that was for sure, just not the kind this week was going to provide. Between now and December 25, he expected to constantly guess which item in his home would be broken next and be on guard for his father to pit him and his brother against each other.

"Something about his son's birthday being today. I don't know… I think he turned thirty-three." She seemed distracted. She was probably ready for a break, too.

"Oh, that's right. I'll have to tell Trent that Gill's probably in town then."

"Your brother is in town?" she asked with a perk in her voice. He imagined her sitting at her desk, wearing a pressed suit with her auburn hair pulled back in one of those French twists.

"Yes. He, Alicia and the boys are all here." He tried not to physically cringe. He should be thankful he had family that wanted to be around each other. Not everyone had that. Still, he preferred the years where he went to their home and could stay in a hotel. "Mom and Dad arrive tomorrow," he continued.

"A full Hale law firm Christmas."

"And all at my house." He tried not to sound sardonic, but he did to his own ears. "We're going to Brahman's tomorrow night."

"That place has the best food." There was a leading pregnant pause on her side. "I've never met the other partners."

Hmm. Lorelei had been the life of her area at a backpack packing party at Fisher's Combat Children's Hunger facility last week. She'd commanded her line of volunteers, laughed most of the time and dealt with the children like a pro.

He rubbed a circle into his temple. "You should come." *Be my buffer.*

"Yes." Her answer was quick. "I'd love to."

He sat forward with a jolt. "To dinner?" he clarified just in case.

"I don't have plans for tomorrow. It would be great to get to know the other Hales. You know me and my work, but they don't necessarily. What time?"

"Six o'clock."

"I'll see you there." She hung up.

He slid his cell onto his desk. Lorelei really would help him out on the whole family holiday front. If she wanted to use the opportunity to try and network, he wasn't going to stop her. He hadn't promised her partner status by inviting her to dinner. She wasn't going to be named partner in his law firm because she met his brother and father.

-

Lorelei Sullivan wiped her palms down her black, skinny pair of pants. Should she have worn jeans? Or something dressier? She rubbed her red glossed lips together. She wasn't going into a courtroom, but she was going into an interview of sorts. She'd finally settled on a sleeveless red satin blouse with a bow that swooped around her neck and tied to the side, three-inch black heels with a pointed toe and her shoulder-length hair waved and pinned to the same side of the bow.

You got this, girl. Seize the day. She was sick of dropping hints. Last New Year's Day she'd written down "become partner" and worked her ass off. This year's resolution would be "become partner or leave." She was darn good at being a lawyer. But she was never prepared to be stagnant.

She spotted Henry at a table in the left dining room at Brahman's Steakhouse. She strutted over with her head held high and her "going out" sequined little black purse under her arm.

Henry stood when they locked eyes.

"Lorelei." He pulled out the chair next to his.

He rarely called her anything but Ms. Sullivan these days.

"Henry." The ends of her lips turned up. She wasn't going to let the awkwardness of having him in her personal space show. She only saw him out of the office occasionally when Fisher and Silver invited them somewhere. And that hadn't happened in a while due to the workload and Henry insisting they take on more pro bono cases this time of year.

He sat next to her in jeans that were perfectly tailored to his thick lines, a blue plaid button-up collar showing under a navy sweater, and shined coffee-colored loafers. The man had a style about him she ate up. He was a classic preppy in casual settings and looked good in a suit at the office.

Yet tonight he didn't slouch in his chair or seem in any way relaxed. Usually when they joined Fisher and Silver, Henry seemed looser and more into his surroundings. Tonight he looked strained. If they weren't in a restaurant, she'd think they were in court.

There might've been a time she'd had a crush on him, but that was short-lived. She was too old to act like a lovesick teenager. He was her boss. She was an adult. And adults wanted things like making partner at a law firm. She respected Henry. He was a hell of a lawyer. And she was going to be the first partner he brought on. Her billable hours, her wins, her everything went into proving as much. Nothing else mattered.

"This is my father, Dwight, and my mother, Viola." Henry motioned to the respective adults sitting at the head and on the other side of the table. "And my brother Trent and his wife, Alicia." They were across the table. "Then there's my nephews, Alex, Anders and Arthur."

"Hello. It's nice to meet all of you." She would've preferred to shake everyone's hands – show them she wasn't weak in any way – but that ship had sailed.

"Uncle H." The oldest boy, who couldn't be more than eight, had a big-toothed, sweet grin on his little round face. "Your girlfriend is pretty." The child snickered to his next oldest brother.

"We're colleagues, Alex." Henry didn't bat an eye or turn red as he stated the fact.

"The pleasure is all ours to meet our top-billing lawyer in Casper." Dwight chuckled once. "Besides my son." Dwight was a smooth talker, with slicked back white hair and a chunky silver class ring from the University of Wyoming on his pinkie.

"I love what I do and it shows." She was going to have to dial down the cheesy.

"How long have you been with us?" Trent asked. He wore a black button-up and a green vest over the top. His wife matched in an all-black dress.

"More than two years now. I clerked for Judge Sydney in Cheyenne on an internship while in college. Before that I did office work for a local lawyer." She always *always* left out the name of said lawyer. Once people found out who she was associated with, not only professionally but by blood, things went one of two ways. Neither she cared for.

"Judge Sydney is respected in more than just Wyoming." Dwight was back in the conversation as he opened his menu. "You must know someone with pull to get a position there."

She shrugged off this last statement. "I learned a lot from him. He's a great mentor." In fact, she still spoke with him, but only at her parents' parties now.

"Alicia, didn't you work for Judge Sydney?" Dwight asked his daughter-in-law.

"No. Judge Mackey in Gillette, before he went down to the Wyoming Supreme Court." Alicia's pronunciation sounded unexpectedly prissy. Lorelei studied the woman. Near black, very straight hair was layered around Alicia's face before falling to mid-breast. She wasn't someone Lorelei would've been naturally drawn to in a social setting – her look screamed high maintenance. "I was going to follow him, but then Trent and I decided to start a family."

"Where are you now?" Lorelei asked. The woman was clearly still very much dialed into the legal world.

"I'm with the DA's office in Buffalo."

"The enemy." Trent flashed a football team captain's smile and lightly kissed his wife's cheek.

"At least Trent has a wife who is very successful." Dwight locked eyes with Henry and the entire table seemed to busy themselves all of a sudden.

She hadn't expected this family dynamic. Henry was the most alpha man she'd ever met – sure of himself, persistent, calm under pressure and a risk taker. Henry was strategic in his decisions. She witnessed it a hundred times. She'd love to stop time and pick his brain without him remembering someday.

"We'll be announcing exciting growth news for Hale Law come Christmas Eve," Dwight continued, although no one around the table was making eye contact with the others.

Her stomach flipped. News? Dwight slid his gaze from Henry and connected with her stare.

"I can't wait to hear." She picked up her water glass and sipped. If she said anything more she was going to smile too much and start talking about how she liked working at Hale Law and was ready for the next step. The man hadn't said specifically what the news was, so it was best she didn't make presumptions. Outwardly. Inwardly, this was a good sign.

The waiter appeared to take their drink orders. She ordered red wine. She wanted to be as calm on the inside as she acted on the outside. She wasn't fidgeting. She wasn't bouncing her knee or pulling her brows together. *Let the night go where it may.* But that wasn't in her DNA, and not taking control was nearly making her mind go a hundred miles an hour, and her need to squirm was strong. She scratched her arm instead.

"Do you have family in town?" Viola asked after setting her menu down in front of her and resting her hands in her lap.

"My parents are here, and then my Aunt Tilly has a dude ranch outside of Buffalo about forty miles. My cousins live in others states though," Lorelei replied.

"What's the name?" Dwight asked.

"Bristow Dude Ranch. She's had it for as long as I can remember. Beautiful place right by the Big Horns."

The waiter came back with hot rolls and took their orders. Everyone picked at the bread, and Lorelei patiently waited for her turn at the butter.

"We've been to your family's ranch." Alicia drank her water without leaving one smudge of her dark reddish-purple lipstick on the glass. "The boys got to feed the horses and ride them."

"Fantastic time." Trent bobbed his head. "We rented a cabin over spring break. A staycation when Arthur was still young and we didn't want to have to fly anywhere."

"I knew your uncle." Dwight didn't look so high and mighty now. "Helluva guy." He tipped his whiskey glass toward her and nodded like people do when they want to express condolences.

The sharp memory of her uncle pinched at the corners of her eyes. Her uncle had been a great man. His sudden heart attack fourteen months ago had taken them all by storm. He'd died in the barn when he and Jack, the ranch foreman, were putting up the horses for the night.

She raised her own glass to toast him. "I'll drink to that."

Viola and Alicia started a private conversation about the boys, and Lorelei just sat there, the wind knocked out of her sails. She hated when she was caught off guard about topics that still stung so deeply.

But Henry's blue eyes held sympathy. "I'm sorry."

"Thanks."

"I haven't been up to the ranch, but I'll have to check it out next time I'm in town."

He was close to her – if she moved just right their arms would brush. He hadn't shifted his seat, but there was warmth radiating from him in this moment that she'd not noticed before.

She crossed her legs away from him, aware not to touch him by accident. "The holidays are the best because Aunt Tilly decorates everything she can reach with years and years of holiday cheer. It's a sight."

"Maybe for New Year's then." His eyes seemed to smile back at her – and not the happiness he usually exhibited when one of them had done well on a case. This was different. It felt different, too, holding some type of familiarity she'd never thought she and Henry had.

The ranch was great any time of the year and New Year's would be a perfect getaway. Especially if he was looking for the cozy, romantic type of vacation.

A plate of steak appeared between them and broke the moment. If it was even a moment.

"You're holding out on us," Dwight accused as he pointed his fork in her direction.

"Excuse me?" She was sure doing a bang-up job of showing how intelligent and partner-worthy she was.

"Your uncle was Tim Bristow, so that means your mother is Francis Bristow."

Two years. She's gone a whopping two years in Casper on her own and without people associating the two. Which was a feat, considering Casper wasn't all that large and people loved to gossip.

"Yes. She is." All eyes were on her now and she felt the weight. All of the assumed judgments of her mother's legacy burned into her skin.

"Well then, ladies and gentlemen, we're in the presence of greatness." Dwight's gaze pulled from her and settled on Henry. "Did you know?"

"I did not. No." A muscle flexed on the side of his jaw.

She tried to catch Henry's stare to give him an apology face, but he only glanced at her briefly. She wasn't sorry she hadn't told him – she wished it were still a secret – but she hated that his father was using it against him.

"She doesn't practice any more," she tried to correct this situation.

"I thought she worked on the big Laskey case last year," Dwight pressed. "Wasn't there a settlement of two billion against the Braleband Company in a case no one thought was even going to go to trial?"

"She consulted. She takes a select few clients a year." The clients usually had to induce some sort of emotional connection, because when Francis Bristow Sullivan worked a case, she gave it her all. In the Braleband case, Francis had glommed onto to the part where children were getting sick as a second-hand consequence of the lack of control over their manufacturing plant. Lorelei had paid only half attention to the case in the news. If she wanted information, she just asked her mother.

One of the kids at the table, or rather under it, started crying. Thank God for small miracles. The focus was no longer on her or her mother.

"Why didn't you tell me?" Henry lowered his voice and asked before taking a bite of his steak.

"For exactly why you'd imagine," she deadpanned.

"Any advantage is a chance to win."

Did he seriously believe that? Because while he said Hale Law was his firm, it was really a branch of the main office in Buffalo. He'd used his family's name and quite frankly didn't seem happy about that choice all of the time.

She opened her mouth to come back with a quip like "Then I guess I'll just sit back and stop billing so many hours because my mother is Francis Bristow" or "Maybe I should just change my name to Francis Bristow Jr. and really lap it up." Instead, Lorelei took a bite of her wedge side salad. Angering him would put her way behind on the vote count. Although, from the shiny dollar signs she saw flashing in Dwight's and Trent's eyes, she might not need Henry on her side.

She wanted things in life because of her abilities, not her mother's. They weren't the same person. She let out a deep breath. Except in her case, they actually were. They both loved the law, and Lorelei prided herself on being really good at what she did. It didn't hurt that if she was stuck or had to work out a problem she could call her mother.

Dinner wrapped up with polite smiles and nodding as she tried to follow their inside stories and jokes. Henry even loosened a little; she thought she saw him smile again when she and his mother started talking about likelihood that most Pinterest pictures had to be Photoshopped because the projects were impossible to replicate. There was never another opportunity to talk about the firm, which might've been for the best given the tension around the table before. Now that they knew who her mother was, she'd never know if any promotion on the horizon was because she was a hard worker or because her mother was.

But she'd have an answer to one of her questions soon – Christmas Eve was only a couple days away.

"Thanks for having me tonight." Lorelei walked with Viola out of the restaurant.

"What are you doing tomorrow?" Viola asked.

"I haven't had a day off in a while, so I'm not sure yet." Today was the closest full day off Lorelei had come, and she'd basically spent it cleaning up her inbox.

"I'll be baking and starting a batch of my famous holiday Kahlúa. You should come by. Maybe bring a favorite holiday recipe of your own and we'll make it."

Henry didn't acknowledge his mom's invitation, though he was right in front of them. Surely he'd heard. He didn't turn around to protest. More face time with Dwight and Trent would be good.

"I don't want to intrude on your family time."

"Nonsense. We'd love to have you. I'm starting at two o'clock. Who knows what the men will be doing." She caught Henry's arm and entwined their arms. "Although I can usually count on this one to help me." She patted Henry's chest, pride beaming through her gaze.

All of the hours she'd been putting in had taken their toll on her ability to keep up on household chores, her friends and, well, herself. When was the last time she'd read a book for fun and not research? Recharging during this vacation was a must. Tonight had been easy, but she wasn't sure she'd made the right impression. Henry didn't talk much about his family. Now that she'd met them, maybe she could do better tomorrow.

Henry's gaze met hers, a smile lighting his eyes.

"All right. You got me. I rarely say no to sweets."

It would be her second cookie day of the season, but this round could bring something sweeter than sugar. It could bring victory.

Chapter Three

Henry answered the door in his rubber-soled house shoes. "Welcome." He stepped to the side to let Lorelei enter his home.

It was two o'clock exactly. No shock she was on time. But this wasn't the buttoned-up Lorelei he'd expected. She took off her red fluffy coat and matching knitted scarf to unveil a navy vest over a green and yellow plaid button-up with jeans and brown boots. And her hair was down. Wavy and auburn and luscious.

She started to take off her shoes by his front doormat.

"No, don't worry about taking off your boots. You'd be the only one." He shook his head. His floors were visibly dirty.

"It's been that rough, huh?"

He'd hoped he could keep his weariness in check. Too late. "The holidays are always a bag of fun." He led her down the hall to the left where his kitchen and dining room connected. The living room was to the right. It was more like a sitting room – no television.

"I heard from Silver. They got to the hotel in Reykjavik okay," he said. She stopped beside him near the granite-topped island in the kitchen. Her perfume, a nice subtle blend of white flowers, cedar and honey, snuck through the remnants of the chili lunch he'd made.

"I still think they are not right in the head to go from one cold climate to another for vacation."

Fisher had snapped Henry a picture of him and Silver in fluffy coats and smiles surrounded by iced buildings earlier. Picturesque, yes. Crazy, also yes.

"I guess Iceland is the place to be these days."

Every continent was on his bucket list. So far he'd crossed off one.

"Nice place you have here." She looked around, and suddenly he was very conscious of what his place said about him and what she'd think.

He'd really never put effort into decorating, hence a lot of blank wall space. He had some pictures, trinkets and mementos he'd collected over the years, but the place was far from having a look or design. Definitely the bachelor pad of a guy who worked too much. His home office, on the other hand, was where he kept anything that meant something – collectibles from his childhood, pictures of his family.

"Where's the rest of the family?" she asked.

"Out chopping down a Christmas tree."

"I see." She nodded her head slowly and diverted her gaze to his empty walls again.

Was that disappointment? Ah, yah, how could he be so daft – she'd said yes to cookies to get more of the face time she thought she needed.

"Lorelei!" His mother rounded the corner from the stairs. "I'm glad you're here. I'm ready to get my hands in some dough."

"We better get started then." Lorelei set her red bag on the island, opened it and swiftly pulled out a card and handed it to his mother. "My mother's recipe for the best sugar cookies you'll ever have."

Viola held the card out and down to read it. "I think we have all of these things." She glanced at Henry. "Did you get everything on the grocery list I gave you?"

"I never knew there were so many types of milk." And his cupboards had never been so full of ingredients that couldn't be made into dinner in three easy steps.

"We'll make your sugar cookies, and then I have killer fudge and ginger snaps we'll do."

"You are speaking my language." Lorelei started to roll up her sleeves.

He could've been wrong before. She seemed genuinely into making cookies with his mother.

"I'm willing to taste test anything you need." He started down toward his office. "Call me when the oven timer dings." With his mom and Lorelei baking and Trent's family out getting a tree with his father, Henry could finally get some peace and quiet in his office.

"Don't you sneak off, young man. You're helping, too." His mother used the stern tone that meant she was never going to budge. Being married to a lawyer and producing two herself, the woman could hold her own in an argument. He and his brother knew when there was room for negotiation and when the ruling had already been made.

He eyed her innocent smile as she laid the three recipe cards on the counter. Maybe not so innocent after all. One would think Trent's kids would be enough in the grandchild department. Apparently not.

"Henry, here's the ingredients list. Put everything out on the counter so we have it. I'm going to go find my candy thermometer I brought especially for the fudge." She disappeared down the hall to the left.

There was a fifty-fifty chance the woman wasn't coming back and all of this had been a ruse to set him up with his own employee. Terrific. Lorelei wasn't a random person or an acquaintance of a friend that he could date. She was off limits.

"Call them out to me, will you?" He handed Lorelei the recipe cards and went over to the cupboards to start pulling.

She named each item on the list and then started rearranging them on the counter in groups of powders and liquids. "If I weren't a lawyer, I'd open a bakery."

"Feel free to bring your goods into the office anytime."

A nervous sort of laugh left her lips as he felt his cheeks warm. What a great job he was doing of putting words together.

"Where's your bathroom?" she asked.

He pointed to the left hallway. "Second door on your right."

She was here as a buffer, nothing more. She'd done a great job last night – he'd almost had a good time even.

Lorelei's phone vibrated on the counter, face up by the recipe cards. The screen read "Always Answer." He glanced down the hall, but she'd already disappeared into the bathroom.

He picked up the phone in its red case with gold flecks. This probably wasn't a great idea, but he had to know. Was she dating someone? He hadn't heard if she was. Was she an emergency contact and it meant life or death if he didn't answer the call right now?

"Lorelei's phone," he answered.

"Who's this?" an older woman's voice questioned.

"Depends. Who's this?"

"Lorelei's mother, Francis. Now you talk."

Whoops. Now he had to keep going so he didn't look like a moron to her mother. "Henry Hale. I work with your daughter."

"I've heard about you."

"Oh, you can't believe everything you hear." He put his free hand low on his hip.

"That's usually said by people trying to be falsely modest or cute. Which one is it, Mr. Henry Hale?"

"Is there a third option?" Crash and burn. He could see the flames now.

A musical laugh burst out from the other side of the line. "I'm just messing with you. By the sound of your voice, I'd say you're as handsome as my daughter described."

Heat flushed his cheeks and radiated through his chest. He put his free hand in his pocket and rocked back on his heels, barely containing a grin. "Lorelei will be back shortly. My family is in town, and my mother talked Lorelei into coming over and helping her bake. We getting ready to start with your sugar cookie recipe, actually." Okay, wow, he needed to shut his trap. Who'd have thought he'd be talking to Francis Bristow? She was someone he'd looked up to in college, especially after studying some of her cases for classes. And she was Lorelei's mother, who he knew she held in high regard.

"My daughter is making sugar cookies for your family?"

When it was put like that, it did sound more intimate than it really was. "She's quite the baker, I'm told."

"She gets that from me. What are you two doing tonight?"

"I'm not sure." He was living one day at a time this week.

"You're going to come over here and have dinner." The statement didn't leave any room for arguing.

"Oh, uh, I'm not sure that's such a great idea." It was an epic idea, and his pulse was starting to race at the possibility.

"So you can spend time with your family but not hers? I don't think so."

"It's not like that—" The professional and personal lines between him and Lorelei were starting to blur.

"I should hope not. Six-thirty. Bring your appetite."

The line was dead.

Lorelei strode into the kitchen, giving him a smile when he caught her gaze. He started to smile back. It had been a long time since he wanted to spend time with another person who he wasn't billing. And even longer since he'd met the parents.

What was he thinking? They weren't dating. They couldn't. He was her boss and that wasn't changing any time soon.

He needed to get out of this dinner invitation. On the other hand, meeting Francis would be a boon… so would spending more outside of work time with Lorelei. It wouldn't be so bad to gain more knowledge of his employee and mutual friend. He took in a long breath. It was a classic win-win-lose situation.

"Why's my phone in your hand?" Lorelei's brows rose and she crossed her arms.

"Funny story." He set the phone down. "Your phone rang while you were in the bathroom, and it said 'Always Answer.'".

"You didn't." She reached for it, calling up the "recent calls" screen. Her eyes were wide when she finally looked up.

"I did." He shrugged his shoulders in an attempt to show the little bit of remorse he did have for his actions. He also made a mental note not to leave his phone alone.

Lorelei sighed. "My mom thought it was hilarious to save that as her name and I just never changed it."

"It worked."

"Apparently." She grabbed a metal mixing bowl and started adding shortening from little wrapped packages.

"There's more."

She stopped reaching for the vanilla and faced him, a line forming between her brows. "What did you agree to?"

"That we'd go to dinner tonight at her house." He watched Lorelei closely for any sign she was okay with this news. "And bring our appetites."

"You didn't." This time the phrase was a lot more exaggerated.

There was his answer – she was not a willing participant. He wasn't going to get to meet Francis after all.

"In my defense, I don't actually think it was ever put up for debate in the two minutes we spoke."

"Yeah, well, welcome to my world." She started measuring vanilla in a teaspoon.

"I totally get it." He had his own set of nosy parents in an involved family.

"You're not obligated, don't worry." She shook her head, focusing on adding eggs into the bowl.

His chest deflated. It was more than missing an opportunity to meet Francis that caused him to slump his shoulders momentarily. This new side of Lorelei was nice. At dinner last night, in a very vague sense, it almost seemed as if they were a couple.

The holidays were becoming a lot more complicated this year than even he could've predicted. And that was saying something, because he'd loosely calculated the chances of his nephews burning down the house at 100 percent.

"I would hate for your mother to think I'm not a man of my word." Was he really doing this? Was he really trying to keep the invitation?

He freaking knew better. This was the moment. When things were falling apart around him, this was the point in time that he was going to analyze his compulsions until it drove him crazy.

She'd stopped adding flour to the bowl and faced him, a smudge of powder on her chin next to her reddish lips. He'd always thought Lorelei was beautiful and smart, but she had so many more layers he'd never even once considered.

She was studying him, trying to figure out the angles. See the forest from the trees. Good luck to her because, honestly, he wasn't concrete on his own motivations now.

"You have flour..." He reached over and wiped the smudge on her chin with his thumb.

Their physical distance hadn't actually changed, but he felt closer. Like it was just the two of them in the world close. He started to sway in to her, let that pull between them win. Her gaze dropped to his lips, and that's when he knew she wanted to kiss him, too. One kiss couldn't hurt. It might be what he needed. What they both needed. Maybe it would be the worst kiss and he wouldn't have to think about her any more because he'd know they didn't have chemistry – that he was just getting caught up in nonsense again.

Or it would possibly be the best kiss of his life and confirm all the feelings that he was too scared to admit swirling in the depths of his mind. He had to find out.

His head dropped down farther, and he was just closing his eyes for the view of the fireworks.

"Smells great in here." Trent came stomping in from the mud room covered in remnants of the tree they'd undoubtedly chopped down.

Henry pulled back and cleared his throat. Lorelei turned back to the counter and continued adding cups of flour to her mix.

"Did I interrupt something?" Trent glanced between the two of them as his boys came running past, still covered in dirt and snow from the mountain and headed straight for their video game in the downstairs living room.

"Nope." Henry shook his head, trying to keep his voice light and not show the agitation he felt. "Get a good tree?" It better be the best tree they'd ever had and ever would have to ruin that kiss.

"Sure did." Trent probably picked out the tallest he could carry. "Are we decorating tonight?"

"No. Tomorrow night. Lorelei and I have plans tonight."

She glanced at him quickly and the ends of her lips turned up as she continued her work on the dough. "Let it sit out in the garage overnight and then we'll bring it inside after dinner and decorate."

He was going to meet her parents tonight. There was a ball of nerves in his gut that both couldn't wait for dinner and was shouting that he was making a huge mistake. Nothing like the holidays to make a person anxious.

Chapter Four

Lorelei opened the door to her parents' home without knocking. Henry had picked her up. She'd tried to just give him the address, but he'd insisted. She didn't know what to make of that – and she was trying not to read too much into it. She didn't want to make an assumption that would lead her imagination down the wrong path. This was already odd on a lot of different levels.

She knew Henry respected her mother; Francis Bristow was a star to him. So maybe he'd wrangled this invitation on his own. Lorelei, however, was wise to her mother's ways. There was no doubt she'd bulldozed the conversation where she'd wanted it to go. And as much as Lorelei wanted to accuse him of using her to meet Francis, when she'd turned in his kitchen to let him have it, he'd looked so, so not conniving. Instead he was seeing *her*, as if she were the only one that could touch his heart. A raw connection had sparked and she'd nearly let him kiss her.

Her goals and motivations had started to blur when she'd looked into his light blue eyes.

This was all a little too weird. Even going over to his house earlier to help his mother with cookies had felt like an overstep. Henry had stuck around the entire time, perched at the island and happy to taste when they'd needed it. He hadn't rolled up his sleeves and baked, but he'd stayed. That counted for something.

Lorelei led Henry to the right, where the wide expanse of a kitchen took up half the room. Next to the kitchen was a living room area centered on a giant entertainment wall that held a seventy-inch television. Off to the left was the dining area.

"Where's Dad?" Pentatonix's "Little Drummer Boy" played in the background.

"He had to go out of town. He'll be back before Christmas." Her mother, dressed in black slacks and a deep emerald turtleneck, didn't bat an eye at the news. As a well-respected business strategist for Fortune 500 companies, Phil Sullivan had been traveling for as long as Lorelei could remember. She had to give her dad credit though: not one time had he ever not been home when he said he'd be.

"Francis Bristow Sullivan, meet Henry Hale of Hale Law." Her formal introduction was on purpose. "My boss" wasn't a title that would apply for much longer.

Francis finished scraping the mash potatoes into a ceramic red ornate bowl then stuck her hand out. "Pleased to meet you."

"You as well." Henry didn't smile, but the apple of his cheeks was a little fuller and his eyes lit up. He was loving this but maintaining the control she was used to witnessing.

Lorelei held in a laugh. It was always amusing when people met her mother. To Lorelei, she was just Mom – a mom she'd rarely seen in the courtroom doing her thing but who had always been at the dinner table and at her school debate tournaments and track events. Wow. And here Lorelei was barely keeping clean clothes on the hangers while she launched her career, and thank goodness she didn't have a fish because that thing would be belly up.

"As we all know, your father is the cook in this house—" Francis hugged Lorelei and kissed the top of her head "—so I made my favorite dish."

"You didn't." She smiled at her mother. "I have been dreaming about your meatloaf lately." The way her mother made meatloaf, something that should be easy to replicate but wasn't – Lorelei had tried and given up after attempt number four literally oozed out of the pan – was everything good about her childhood.

"Sounds delicious," Henry chimed in.

Geez, for a minute, Lorelei had forgotten he was standing there. "You're in for a treat."

Francis sat at the head of the table, Lorelei to her left and Henry to her right. The table was already decked out in the festive holiday set her mother had used ever since she could remember.

"Have you watched any good movies lately?" Her mom looked between the two.

"I don't know the last time I went to a movie." Henry placed a red napkin in his lap.

"She means scary or horror flicks specifically. It's all she likes." Lorelei scooped up mashed potatoes on her fork. "I've just been watching the old steadfast ones on Netflix these days." In between reading briefings and prepping for trial.

"I would not have pegged you for a scary movie fan." Henry's gaze roamed over her face and her body started to warm.

"It's a tradition we started when I was a little too young to be watching those types of shows."

"What?" Francis shrugged. "She needed to be aware of the world. Do you watch them?"

"No," he laughed, "that's the one genre I don't watch much of. No interest in horror especially."

Francis started laughing and caught Lorelei's gaze. "Do you remember when you got kicked out of school for scaring your classmates?"

"What?" Henry chuckled. "I have to hear this story."

"Nah. That's the whole of it." They'd gotten so close to getting through this dinner without anything embarrassing from her childhood coming out.

"My little girl, you were in what, the seventh grade?" Francis's brows pulled together as she studied Lorelei's face. "Yeah, seventh, and she wanted to be scary."

"Just scary?" Henry's eyes danced as he grinned as her.

"I believe the words the principal used were *terrifying* and *disturbed*."

"It wasn't that bad. Wusses." She shook her head and took a drink of her wine.

"You had blood dripping off of your sweet little cheeks."

"I liked realism in my murderous makeup." It wasn't much of an excuse; looking back on the pictures, she wasn't sure how she'd made it all the way to school in the first place – someone really should've called the cops on her during her ten-block trek.

Henry was staring at her now, shaking his head slowly, as an emotion flitted across his eyes – admiration perhaps?

"What? I am who I am." She sipped her wine.

"I'm seeing that more and more." He stabbed at a chunk of meatloaf on his plate.

"I got really good at costume makeup. I only use my powers for good now."

"Have you seen her collection?" her mother asked.

"Mom." The makeup story was one thing. That was her past.

"She has scary masks. She collects them to this day."

"How does one collect scary masks?" Henry's courtroom voice was in full swing, only this time there was a playfulness behind it. He was certainly more laid back tonight than at his own family dinner. Tingles flipped in her belly. She shouldn't have noticed that fact, or liked it, or start thinking of Henry in any way other than as her boss and the man that could give her a promotion.

"One buys them at Halloween shops and scary shops from time to time." She tried to wipe her dumb happiness from her face, but she couldn't.

"There's a decently scary Halloween store in Buffalo. You'll have to check it out sometime. I still might have a Krampus mask from a prank I pulled on Trent years ago. It wasn't dripping-blood-from-your-face scary though."

His blue eyes shined back at her, and her breath caught before she remembered why they were having dinner with her mom. Henry wasn't her boyfriend. She was allowing him into her world so that he could see she was partner material.

"It's not often Lorelei brings a man she's dating over." Her mom broke the moment.

Lorelei choked on her sip of water. "We're not dating, Mom. I told you that very specifically." She couldn't even glance at Henry to see his reaction to her mother's intentional slip. Make no mistake, Francis knew they weren't dating, and she'd be discussing that with her mother later. If anyone should understand about being professional in the workplace, it was her mother, who'd always prided herself on her reputation.

"How do you like working with my daughter?" Francis changed the question without a hint of apology in her voice.

"She's an exceptional lawyer."

When he gazed at her, a heat started in Lorelei's belly. One she hadn't experienced with him before. Was she starting to like him? No. Nope. Not a good idea and not possible. Henry was her boss, soon to be equal, and nothing more. If she wanted to date someone, there were plenty of eligible bachelors she knew or could probably meet somewhere. When she had the time to get dolled up and go out. She could date anyone else in the world, just not Henry.

She broke their moment by looking down at her half-eaten pile of mashed potatoes.

"That she is." Francis rubbed her shoulder. "I'm so proud of my baby girl."

That was enough of that. "Did I see hot chocolate on the stove?"

"Yes." Her mother got the hint. "It's been in the Crockpot this whole time, so it'll be perfect. Why don't we move to the salon? Your father decorated the yard again. It's so festive. I love it."

Lorelei put her silverware on her plate and started to pick it up.

"Don't worry about it. I'll get it later." Her mother waved her palm a couple of times.

They each took a cup, filled it with the liquid that had been warming on the stove, and headed to the back of the house which was one of Lorelei's favorite places.

She stepped down onto the porch that her parents had windowed in about five years ago. The backyard was dazzling. Lights wrapped around all of the trees along the edges of the fencing, with lighted deer in one corner, a manger set up in the other, and white-it snowflakes strung across the entire length of the yard.

"Mom, this is amazing." They could still hear the holiday music inside; and Lorelei's chest filled with the wonder of Christmas, just like when she was a child. This was truly her favorite time of the year.

"Isn't it? We've been enjoying it all month." Francis sat in a comfortable, padded wicker chair to the right of a wooden end table and put her feet up, crossing at the ankles.

Lorelei sat next to her and Henry on her left. Snow fell lazily from the sky, giving the lights a winter haze. She could stay here all night.

"Where were we? Oh yes, when is my daughter going to make partner?" Francis gave Henry a polite smile, but her stare was serious.

Welp, this had gone from a beautiful moment to a mortifying situation in less time than it took for a parent to be shamed on Instagram for posting a picture of their baby.

Henry's cool posture turned rigid. The light between his eyes darkened for a second "We've made some considerations. I'll be looking at options and making a decision in the near future."

Something wasn't right. She blew on her cocoa while watching him then gingerly sipped. Was he not going to name a partner, or was he not going to name her? She hadn't even considered the latter possibility. There were three other lawyers in the office: Diana, Paul and Diego. None of them had a record as good as hers, and none of them billed as much as she did. Her chest felt heavy as her mind spiraled. Would he bring in an outsider? That was unacceptable. She'd have to leave. There was no way she could stay if she was looked over for partner for no good reason. And if he had one, she'd love to hear it.

She clamped her teeth together until they hurt and watched him for any sign that she was right or wrong.

"You're right about him." Her mother nudged her arm. "Always the warrior diplomat. The nickname fits."

"Mom." This was enough. She had to stop reading into Henry, and her mother really needed to stop whatever agenda she was working. What was her mother's angle tonight – to talk her daughter out of a job? Because that's what she was one comment away from doing. Henry valued professionalism just as much as Lorelei.

"You have a nickname for me?" Henry asked, his blue eyes sparkling in the holiday lights.

She let out a breath as her spiral halted. Had his gaze always calmed her down?

"Maybe." She captured her bottom lip with her front teeth. For once, the person squirming tonight wasn't her.

"Let's hear it."

"Hale the Conqueror." She could barely say the three words without smiling so widely her cheeks hurt. "It's meant as a compliment."

"I see." A smile crooked to one side of Henry's face, causing a dimple.

He was so darn cute. She'd never noticed the dimple in his smile before. She'd never noticed a lot about him before.

Time to call this night quits. She couldn't afford to get caught up in any kind of moment or see him in any other light other than as her boss.

"It's getting late." She nodded to Henry as she set her cup of hot chocolate down and stood. "We're going to head out."

"Thank you for a lovely evening, Mrs. Sullivan." Henry stood and put his palm on Lorelei's back as they filed out of the sitting area.

His touch was unexpected, and as much as she hated to admit it, welcomed. Her flesh tingled. This night had not been a good idea – she should've squashed it the minute she heard he'd spoken with her mother.

His hand on her could mean nothing. She hoped it meant nothing. She was 90 percent sure of that.

"Look at that." Her mother was right behind them. They stopped and turned toward her. "You two are under mistletoe."

"Since when do you put up mistletoe, Mother?" Lorelei looked around for the blasted sprig. This was just like her mom to scheme even though she'd explicitly told her Henry was her boss five times before they'd even arrived.

"I always put it up. You just never have a reason to use it." All said with a smile. Typical. "It's tradition."

Her belly fluttered. How embarrassing. She was thirty and fine with being single. She didn't need to look desperate to kiss her boss. He could surely come up with an excuse not to kiss her. But was that a good or a bad thing?

She gazed at him, trying to non-verbally communicate that he was the one who needed to bow out. She had no clue what to do next.

Instead of arguing, he shrugged. "Who are we to argue with tradition?"

Henry's hand cupped her cheek and gently tilted her lips up to his. She closed her eyes as he pressed his lips against hers ever so smoothly. His warmth engulfed her and then was gone all too quickly. She'd barely had time to take in their physical connection.

She opened her eyes, and he was staring back at her with an emotion she hadn't seen before from him. His gaze was gentle, it cradled her. Soft and warm.

His hand left her cheek, and she made an effort not to shake with a chill.

"Shall we?" His eyes were back to being on the cold side of friendly. Had all of this just been to be sociable? They'd certainly moved beyond co-workers with that kiss.

Ugh. Here was a problem she wasn't seeking. Henry was a great catch, and he'd be easy to fall in love with. On the other hand, and most importantly, she was his subordinate and she wanted to be seen as a professional, not some office hook-up. She wanted to make partner at the firm. Then maybe they could revisit the kissing. Or, by then they wouldn't be caught up in the lure of the holidays, so it would be a good thing if nothing more happened between them.

She nodded, hugged her mom goodbye after they made plans for Christmas Day, and was out the door and into the cold December night.

She followed him to the car. He was all toned meat at a solid six foot one. He was someone you could really put your arms around, and yet he seemed nimble like a fighter. And a fighter he was. In the courtroom. She wanted to see that fire in him now.

"Sorry about that," she said as she got into Henry's car. "My mother was in rare form tonight. She gets an idea in her head and it's hard to get it out."

"Don't worry about it."

"I don't want you to think that…" She paused to make sure she used the best phrasing. "I don't want there to be any confusion. That was all her doing."

He nodded and was silent. Whether it was a good silent or bad silent she wasn't sure. The one thing she was certain of was how much she wanted more of his lips. That kiss, that simple taste she'd gotten, was enough to make her question everything she'd thought about him before. But she wasn't going to throw away a career opportunity because of a man and his kiss. No. She was smarter than that.

Promotion. Get the promotion. That was her goal and she wasn't going to deviate. Not again. Not when she was so close.

Chapter Five

The sound of the doorbell reached Henry in the kitchen where he was helping his mom clean up the dinner dishes.

"You better get that." His mom took the rag from him and started drying the plates. He had a dishwasher, but she insisted doing the dishes by hand was faster.

He swung his front door open to reveal Lorelei. "Hey." His brows rose at the sight of the woman he hadn't been able to stop thinking about since he'd kissed her last night.

"She didn't tell you, did she?" Lorelei rubbed her hands together in the frosty evening.

"Nope." He moved to the side so she could come in out of the cold. There was no way he was turning her away. Another chance to kiss her had smiled upon him tonight.

"She found me on Facebook." Her forehead wrinkled. "Your mom said tonight was game night and you needed an even number of players." She searched his gaze. "I'm going to go. This is weird."

"Stay." He shrugged, hoping she didn't see the excitement in his eyes. "It really is game night."

"Okay." She started undoing the zipper on her coat. "What's the game?"

"Phase 10, Crazy Eights or poker. Something like that."

"I see." She nodded, pink spreading over her cheeks. "I can go. Really, this is just too…" Her words trailed off as she swiveled toward the door.

"No. Of course you should stay. Everyone knows even numbers are best." He should've found mistletoe and hung it up in his doorway today. Count that as a missed opportunity. He hadn't called her but he had thought about her all day. Her scent, the way she'd smiled at him last night on the couch while they'd laughed, the way his whole being felt lighter around her this week. Yeah, he wasn't letting her leave.

"What a friendly invitation." Her sarcasm was not lost on him. Nor was her likelihood of taking the opportunity to leave. He had no idea how she felt about that kiss.

He laughed. "I mean, please join me for game night with my family." He put his right hand over his heart. "Save me."

"I play to win." She eyed him before stepping past him in the hallway and continuing to the kitchen.

"I expect nothing less." He followed her intoxicating scent. "We all do."

"A family of lawyers," she chuckled. "I guess that's to be expected."

"Buckle up, buttercup." He winked. "You ain't seen nothin' yet." Ugh, he'd freaking winked. Was he from the Seventies all of a sudden?

"Are we playing in here?" She pointed to the table in the dining room.

"We are. Trent and Alicia are putting the kids to bed. I'll let my parents know we'll start soon." His mother had suspiciously disappeared from the kitchen. He wasn't about to let this get awkward – like it wasn't already, and they might never acknowledge that kiss – and he wasn't about to let her come over for a game night that didn't happen.

But when he returned to the dining room, Lorelei was gone. He stepped to the hallway. Relief caved his chest when he spotted her coat and purse slumped against the wall by his front door.

"Lorelei?" he called out, feeling a little silly.

No answer.

He headed back to the living room then farther down the hall then stopped abruptly at his open office door. He always kept the door shut, especially with guests around. He slipped his hands in his jeans pockets and stood quietly in the doorway. She was sitting at his desk and lazily moving side to side in his chair while she studied his wall of bookshelves and fiddling with his pen in between her fingers.

His home office was his sanctuary. When he was working an extremely intense case or on the weekends, he chose this spot. He smoothed out the front of his long-sleeved polo. His life was on full display in this room for Lorelei's judgment. Not even his bedroom was this intimate.

The last time he'd let someone this far into his world it had ended in disaster – his girlfriend of four years through college had cheated on him. Multiple times. After graduating, he'd thrown himself into work, made goals and gone a hundred miles an hour after them. Now he had his firm. People who worked for him. A solid reputation in a community he loved.

Intellectually, he knew the next step was to grow his firm – bring on partners to get to that next level that he was surely close to but unwilling to outright acknowledge.

He watched this beautiful woman at home in his chair and felt a crack start in his stone heart. He considered himself a good, genuine person. He didn't, however, wear his heart on his sleeve – he'd locked up that part of himself for a long time now. As he watched her nose scrunch at something she possibly didn't like on his shelf, he knew. He was in trouble. Or rather, his heart was. Because not only was Lorelei Sullivan an employee and therefore off of the potential list of women he could date, but it was not long before the sparkle in her eyes would dim. She was not going to take a career let-down well. He'd seen her take bad news; she was a ball of well-spoken fury. An inevitable moment he was not looking forward to.

"Judging me on my Star Wars figures?" He stepped into the space dimly lit by his green metal desk lamp.

"I'd be judging you if you didn't have them. No, it was the Hardy Boys books in the corner that perked my interest."

"I read them as a kid and look for them whenever I'm in a book or antique store." He and Trent had gobbled them up as elementary school children. He still had some of the copies from his childhood, although not all had made it through two boys and years of caring more about girls than books.

"Quirky." Lorelei cocked her head, studying him.

He felt like he was on stage in his own home. "Nostalgic."

He knew she was always checking for angles, seeking out what she wasn't seeing. He should probably be doing the same with her. He knew one of her goals – to be partner – but were there other aspirations he should be dialed into? Was she also playing him, the kiss somehow a ploy to manipulate him? What else would she gain by having a relationship with her boss – money? No, she made good money at the law firm. Standing? She was already very respected in the community, without people knowing who her mother was. His reputation wouldn't boost hers any. Leverage? But for what?

"I was a fan of Nancy Drew, myself." Playful brown eyes with flecks of green watched him. No malice to be found.

"Is that when your obsession with criminal activity started?" He shook his head and tsked.

"I could ask the same of you."

They were locked in a staring contest and he didn't know why. But he wasn't detouring or yielding. She was formative. But she was playing a game where she held no cards. And, yet, somehow he had an ominous feeling that they both were going to lose.

"This room isn't usually for guests." He stepped around the right side of his desk, blocking her view of his bookcase, and rested his backside on the side of his desk.

"I got that." She nodded to the empty space in front of his desk. "No second chair."

He'd not placed extra chairs because he'd not intended to be a host in the one place that was all his.

"Are you two playing or not?" His dad's yell was sure to have inspired a dirty look from Alicia, who'd spent the better part of the last hour wrangling her three children into a lull.

"That's our cue." Henry hefted himself from his perch and let Lorelei go out of the door first, shutting off his lamp after them.

"Any strategy I need to know going in?" she whispered as they walked side by side.

"Take no prisoners."

He had a strong suspicion they weren't only talking about a card game now.

–

"We're playing Pictionary?" Lorelei sat at the table and Henry took the chair to her right. The long, navy box had been placed in the center of the table along with legal notepads and pencils. She grabbed one of each. A ripple of excitement washed over her – she couldn't remember the last time she'd played.

"What about the incident of 2012?" Trent took the seat next to Henry on the oblong table.

"It's time we get over that." Viola sat next to Lorelei on the left. "And tonight we have an even number of people for three teams."

Lorelei glanced at Henry, a sly smile crooked to the side showing his dimple. An adorable dimple.

"No matter what they tell you, I never cheated." Henry sat back, resting his palm on his thigh.

She glanced down momentarily to the strong hand so close to her – how would it feel to have his fingers interlaced with hers? She drew in a breath at the thought of his palms grasping her cheeks last night. Really good. It would feel really good.

"Let's team up. Couples together." Dwight sat down next to Viola and Alicia claimed the seat between Trent and Dwight.

Lorelei felt a big stupid grin starting and stopped it as best she could. Henry just shook his head as he reached for his own paper and pencil. Apparently, they'd both given up arguing the point that they were not, nor ever had been, a couple. She didn't know what her future held. But she wasn't delusional about her present.

She helped set up the board in the middle of the table.

"Now, Lorelei," Trent started with a smile, "I know you work with his big guy, but if he tries to cheat, it's okay to tell us. Also, definitely don't whisper, because we won't go off of what other people are drawing to guess."

The game started when Dwight rolled first.

"You first." Henry set his pencil down and swiveled toward her.

"Are you sure?" She raised her brows.

"Trust me, we're better off with you drawing."

She took the hand off of the card: *Loveseat.*

Trent flipped the sand timer. "Go."

Alicia, Dwight and she all started to scribble. She drew an "O" in the corner for object then two dashes because, while it might technically be one word, she was going to draw it in two.

She drew a heart.

"Heart." Henry lowered his head and spoke quietly. "Red."

She shook her head and ran the pencil over the humps again.

"Love," he said, and his hot breath grazed her cheek sending a chill straight down her spine.

His gaze searched hers for a second then dropped down to her lips. Screw the game – she wanted to lean in and press her lips against his now.

"Love seat!" Trent yelled.

Neither she or Henry moved. They were in their own little bubble that she didn't want to pop.

The sound of dice rolling and Alicia gloating made them break and sit back in their seats.

"We'll get it this time." Henry took the card from Trent, glanced at it then passed it behind Lorelei to his mother.

"Go." Alicia flipped the timer.

Henry drew an "A" in the corner for action, then a circle with a ring around it.

She started calling out words, but close to him so hopefully only he could hear. "Circle, round."

He added stars.

"Space."

He nodded and waved his hand to keep going.

"Planet. Space."

He drew a rocket on the ring.

"Orbit!" she yelled and raised her hands.

"Yes." He mimicked her action, and she almost leaned in to hug him.

"See, we got this." His smile and lone dimple lingered.

Yeah, he may be talking about the game, but that wasn't where her mind as at right now. Because whatever this was between them, they certainly didn't have a handle on it.

-

Henry sat on the couch after game night and tried not to stare at Lorelei next to him. The light from the fire danced in her eyes. He hadn't been able to get their kiss out of his mind. Had she? If it had been a big deal to her then she was a great actress, because she seemed to have shrugged it off like she'd just placed a peck on an old friend out of tradition. He didn't want to be an old friend. He wanted to be a new flame. But that was never going to happen. At least not in the near future. Especially when she figured out she wasn't being named partner.

His skin prickled. Would she leave his firm when she didn't get what she wanted? If she left, they could date – if she didn't hate him, that was. But if she left then he wouldn't get to see her every day, go over cases and strategy with her, smell her perfume as he walked by her office.

This was a pickle. He'd not thought this through. Maybe he needed Lorelei more than he thought.

And tonight may be the last time she ever looked at him like he could do no wrong. Tomorrow was Christmas Eve, and the family would announce a new partner at dinner. He finished the wine in his glass and extended his arm over the top of the couch past her.

Still watching the fire, she leaned into the crook of his arm and put her feet on the couch, with her knees closer to her chest.

"What a long year," she said quietly.

"Sometimes I'd like to know what it is like not to work all the time. Then I remember I love what I do."

"A real catch twenty-two. Does your life ever bother you?" Lorelei asked.

"How so?"

"Working fifteen-hour days, barely acknowledging most holidays. Identifying with it. Dreaming about it."

"It didn't used to." Before this week, he'd not thought a part of his life was missing yet. He'd assumed there'd be dating, a family – all in due time. That time was feeling more and more like now.

"And it does now?"

"Something like that. Is being a workaholic bothering you?"

"No. And I think that's the problem. I love what I do. Really. That can be rare. I feel blessed in that capacity. I need to figure out a bit more balance, though, so I can keep up with my friends with our brunch dates. And there's other things I want to do in my life. Travel, for example. But right now feels good, like I'm where I'm supposed to be."

"Hale Law is lucky to have you. I'm lucky to have you. Mom wanted me to ask you to Christmas Eve dinner." Bold-faced lie. This is what he he'd been reduced to: asking his employee to dinner.

"Sure." Lorelei shrugged, only working herself more into his chest.

"You don't have plans?"

"We celebrate Christmas Day. Christmas Eve is a free-for-all."

He wanted to say something insightful, something profound. He had nothing. All he wanted to do was ask her if she'd leave him. Life was full of change, but he'd never cared. The only option was to look at all the angles, embrace it and work it to your good.

There were no good angles to her leaving. Because if she left Hale Law, it would be because she never wanted to see him again.

She'd become his opposing counsel.

Chapter Six

"This is perfect." Lorelei held a first edition Hardy Boys book in her hand.

She'd relaxed, read a book, caught up with emails to friends about the holidays and then started to miss being at Henry's for his random family holiday activities. She'd run out of laundry to wash, closets to organize and dishes to do, so going to the mall and getting her boss a Christmas gift other than the baked goods she'd made him presented a sound reason to leave the house.

"Those books are out there, but this is the only one I've had come across my desk in a while." Milfred looked over his wire-framed glasses and put his hands on the counter of his antique store in the mall. "The original volumes were all published in a cloth hardcover format with a color dust jacket. With the later ones, the pictures were all published on the cover itself."

"This is definitely like the other ones he owns." She was unreasonably proud of herself for finding Henry such a perfect Christmas gift. They'd never exchanged presents before; no one in the office had. This year felt different, like a gift was warranted. The books weren't necessarily hard to find, but she'd felt a brush of luck when she'd learned Milfred had one in stock.

"He's a special young man to you?"

She snapped her head up to look into the eyes of their long-time family friend. "He's my boss. I noticed his collection the other day and figured this would be a great gift and a way to garner some favor." It was half true.

Milfred knew her family, so he'd believe she was calculating shifting odds into her favor. And she'd even told herself that the entire way over. She'd called Milfred for an idea of where to get the books because it would help her career. Not her personal life and not her love life. She seriously needed to tattoo her primary goal on her hand or something, because every time she laid eyes on Henry, him being her boss was not the first thing coming to mind any longer.

He was different this week than the automaton she'd seen at the office for the last two years. Certainly he was more fun to be around. They'd not gone out many times with Silver and Fisher, but Henry had been fairly buttoned-up when they had. The most emotional she'd ever seen him was when they'd been at the hospital when Fisher's heart was failing. Henry'd tried to hold it together, but there'd been fear in his gaze and his knuckles were white at his side when he paced.

"Let me wrap that up for you." Milfred took the old book in the back, came out with it wrapped in cloth, and then wrapped it again in brown paper, even tying it with a string bow.

"Thanks, Milfred. You're the best."

"Tell your parents Merry Christmas."

"I will." She waved and headed out into the main mall area. She didn't need anything else. But she didn't exactly have a to-do list at home either.

Macy's was by the food court where she'd parked, so she wandered in there. Maybe she'd find a new blouse or two.

She lightly grasped the fabric of a white and black chevron pattern when she noticed a guy standing at a table that was filled with "add-on" stuff like jewelry, scarfs and gloves.

It was Henry. Her belly fluttered. What a happy surprise. She could turn around and leave the store right now and he'd never be the wiser. Or… she could go say hi and talk with him for a bit. She really wanted to see him again outside of work. There was no telling how he'd act when January third rolled around and they were all back at the office. How she'd act. They'd be on equal footing then. Was dating between partners at a law firm frowned upon professionally? She could continue to get to know him through the holidays, keeping it professional with no more kissing, and then if something happened when they were partners, so be it. They were consenting adults, after all.

She hid her new purchase in her bag.

"You've got to be kidding me." Lorelei sidled up to Henry, who was now holding a pastel painted scarf out in front of him and cocking his head to the side. "Put it back. That is not my color." She bumped his upper arm with her elbow.

He smiled back at her, and her chest tingled. "It's for my mom. What do you think?" He held it up under his chin and wiggled his brows.

"For your complexion, no. Hers, yes." She leaned over the display of accessories. "And these." She held up dangling light pink earrings to her ears.

"Beautiful."

Only he wasn't looking at the jewelry.

She held out the pair for him to take. Held her breath at the possibility of their fingers mingling. As he took them from her, his fingertips grazed hers, sending shivers through her arm and into her belly.

"You're a little late to the shopping game."

"Late? Shoot, this is early. Stores are open late on Christmas Eve because of guys like me."

"You need to get with the program. That's why online shopping and next-day delivery exists." She smiled at him. He made her happy.

"That's why you're in the mall right now? Because you have your shopping done?" He glanced down to her empty hands.

"Yeah, okay, you got me." She wouldn't be done until after the holidays. Silver, Maisy and she had started a tradition long ago of waiting until Christmas to hit the sales. Whoever got the best deal on a great gift didn't have to buy brunch that day.

"Are we talking all the shopping left to do or for a select few?" he asked as his gaze continued to peruse the table of gifts.

"I came up here for one gift today. You?"

"Not counting my mom now, thank you very much, that makes… everyone else currently in my home."

"I'm in." She shrugged. "What were you thinking for the others? Let's start with your brother."

"I was thinking about a nice set of pens for him."

"Okay. Practical. Anything else spring to mind?"

"Golf lessons. His putting could use some work."

She chuckled. "All good gifts. What about Alicia and the boys?"

"I was just going to pick out toys for the boys. Alicia said there's one show they all like and I could get them something pertaining to it – it's about a pirate or dragon slayer."

"There are a lot of shows out there with those characters. You should text her for specifics so you don't end up having to return something. What about Alicia?"

"I was hoping you'd help me when it came to her."

"I have no idea what she likes."

"Being that you're a woman, you already know more than I do. I'm guessing pens won't fly for her too."

"No. Not unless you want a dirty look and coal in your stocking next year."

"Oh, a woman who still believes in Santa."

"Darn straight. I'm not taking any chances when it comes to presents."

"Who are you here getting a present for?" he asked.

The roundabout nature of his questioning wasn't lost on her. He was trying to catch her off guard so she'd tell him. But she was on to his trickery.

"Right now, we have an Alicia problem."

"Now I'm intrigued. Complete avoidance."

"You're not getting it out of me, so move on, counselor." The present was, in fact, tucked in her purse, safe and sound. He wasn't getting it out of her. The find was too perfect to spoil. And now she didn't have to figure out how to entertain herself later. Her parents were at their annual friends' dinner party that she had no interest in attending.

"We'll see about that. The night is young."

"Back to Alicia. What does she do for fun?"

"Who knows."

"Let's head over to Bath and Body Works. They have nice candles." Not an endearing option, but she doubted he'd ever purchased something for his sister-in-law that meant anything.

They left Macy's and moved two stores down, closer to the food court. Her stomach growled. And she was fighting a bit of a headache, too, from way too many scents of flowers and white tea musk.

"That just leaves one. My father." Henry shuffled his bags around.

"What do you usually get dear old dad?"

"I'll probably circle back to that golf idea. Buy him some rounds at the local course."

She nodded. She shouldn't be surprised. Not everyone bought meaningful gifts for others. She stole a glance to her purse. Yet she'd purchased something fairly meaningful for him. Was it too much? Would it send the wrong signal? He might not be getting the book after all.

Her gaze drifted. "Well, look at that." She pointed to the cinema front riddled with old movie posters and festive garlands, adjacent to the food court. "They are showing Christmas classics on one screen all week. Let's see what's playing." She headed straight for the screen that listed the dates, times and movie titles. If he followed, terrific. If not, she had probably dodged a bullet and was going to a movie alone. Holiday movies were her favorite year-round.

He was still beside her.

"Dang, we just missed *It's a Wonderful Life*. Ohhh, *Family Man* is next." That was a great flick. She bit her lip at the irony – the movie was also pretty relevant to their lives, considering both of them were basically workaholics. "Oh my gosh, then *Die Hard*. Which is basically one of the best Christmas movies ever. Want to see a double feature?"

"Yes." There was no hesitation. She liked a man sure of himself. She'd never seen Henry anything but.

The whole afternoon felt like they'd slept in, had a great breakfast, decided to go shopping and now see a movie on a whim. What a great day – had that been what actually happened. But, instead, she was in this weird non-relationship that sort of felt like a relationship with her boss. Yeah, she was being real professional these days. She had to cut out this cycle they were in – could spending time with someone be called a cycle, or was it really just a series of events that led them to spend time with each other, get to know each other, and start to watch the clock when they weren't with the other person?

"Two tickets, please, for your next two holiday movies," Henry said to the teenaged girl behind the glass.

"Oh, no, you don't have to do that. If anything, it's my treat. It was my suggestion." Was it a date if he paid? Did he think it was a date? Did she want it to be a date? She surely wouldn't say no to holding his hand and kissing. Yep, this was exactly was she needed to squelch. "I'll get the food," she finished her train of thought as he opened the door and the wave of buttery goodness led her right to the counter.

"Do you want a pop?" he asked. He'd already thrown a pack of Junior Mints on the counter.

"Yes, root beer. And no butter on my popcorn."

"That'll be a double date pack with a Pepsi and root beer and," he swiveled his head, "anything else?"

He was so close that his juniper and oaky scent surrounded her and beckoned her closer. She didn't have to lean far to touch him, to put her lips against his.

"Milk Duds," she whispered as her gaze dropped to his lips before she turned away and focused on grabbing as many napkins as humanly possible so that the blush that was surely reddening her cheeks would go away and he'd just think she really liked the chewy chocolate candy.

The lanky boy behind the counter rounded up the food and put it in a black tray with a little section for each item they'd ordered.

She reached into her purse for her card and stretched out her hand right as the kid was taking Henry's.

Her brows wrinkled as she stared at him.

"My treat."

His treat. Yeah.

He picked up the tray and she opened the door to the first of three theatres in the mall.

She and Henry were among only a handful of couples in the giant room. The intimacy made it fun, like they could whisper as if it were only them there. They shared their candy, their arms touching the entire time.

She retrieved her mittens carefully from her purse so he didn't see the wrapped book. "I can't remember the last time I took time out to do something like this."

"What about with Silver and… who's the other gal? Macy?"

"Maisy," she corrected. "We go to brunch, but that's the only time I've seen them lately. I honestly cancel all the time on them now." The cold air was making it tough to take a breath, but she took one out of defeat anyhow. "I've been so focused on work, I've let a lot of things slide I shouldn't."

"I know the feeling."

"I'm not trying to complain," she quickly modified. She was not in the mood to give off a pathetic vibe and let that be his last taste of this night.

"It's hard when you get so focused on one thing," he finally chimed in and she was grateful to just stop talking.

It was late. The main mall had closed. More snow had fallen while they were inside. About three inches already was stacked perfectly on her car.

"I'm over there." She pointed to the end of the near-empty lot, which had been packed when she'd arrived. "It's freezing out here." She rubbed her hands together.

"I'm there." He pointed to the black Audi adjacent to hers and a row over.

They walked in silence, the light flakes falling away with each step. There was going to be a lot more white in town when she woke up in the morning, which was perfect because Christmas was only two days away.

"Do you have auto start?" he asked.

"Nope."

He pulled keys out of his pocket and pushed a button, causing lights to flash and his car to start. "Get in and start your engine. Hand me your scraper."

"It's okay, you don't have to do that."

He didn't say a word – his look said it all. He wasn't going to take no for an answer. She did as she was told and sat in her red Sentra, handing him her blue scraper. It had sleeted before settling into a perfect night snowfall, so she cranked up her defroster and watched him as best she could through her ice-drizzled windshield. He brushed off the snow layer and then scraped her windshield methodically. He didn't have to do this. He didn't have to care if she stood in the cold and made sure she had visibility. But he did. He was a man of action.

The rushing air soon turned warm – the lines on her back window started to appear. She sat facing forward even though Henry was on the passenger side clearing the windows. It was awkward to just sit here and let him clear her windows. She bent over to pick up some trash and stick it in her side-door pocket. Her car definitely needed vacuuming – this should be her next holiday project.

Being independent was something she'd never give up, but once in a while she longed for companionship. Someone who could run to the grocery store, throw in a load of laundry, talk about shows with her in real time. Having another person to lean on, who cared about the kind of day you were having or who could let you sleep in while they made breakfast wouldn't be so bad.

She watched Henry in her rear-view mirror now.

What am I doing? She slumped back into her leather seat that was hot now from the seat warmer. She was falling for her boss. The man she'd worked with for two years – that man. The man who was clearing snow off of her vehicle so she could stay warm. She was so screwed. She couldn't date her boss, or even her partner, and be taken seriously. She couldn't think of anyone who had made dating within the firm look like a good idea.

Nope. The relationships she'd known about hadn't ended well or inevitably were the topic of gossip for a while. The last thing she wanted was people up in her business, assuming they knew her life and talking behind her back. She valued privacy. Hello! She went years without mentioning who her mother was.

Henry tapped on her window with the tip of the scrapper. She opened her door and crawled out.

"Thank you." She tossed the scraper onto the passenger side floorboard.

"You're welcome." His nose and the tips of his ears were red. It was adorable.

They stood there as fluffy flakes fell around them. Neither said a word and neither looked away.

What was supposed to happen in this moment? Something was. It felt important. But she couldn't decide if she was ready to make the leap yet, so chances were good she wasn't. When they'd kissed before it was because of the mistletoe, and they'd been together this week basically due to happenstance. She couldn't afford to make a fatal error at this point. Not when she was so close.

"I'll see you tomorrow for dinner," she broke the silence.

"Yes." He nodded, an odd mix of emotions flitting through his gaze. "Drive home safely."

He turned and headed for his vehicle where the defroster had melted the snow and nearly cleared off his windows.

The cold nipped at the skin on her legs. She sat back down and closed her door as she watched Henry get in his own car.

She'd worked way too hard to have her career cheapened by a fling.

Unless Henry wasn't a fling.

Chapter Seven

Henry poured more wine into Lorelei's glass and then his. Christmas Eve was off to a swinging start. Except for the game of ping pong in his mind. He liked Lorelei, there was no denying that any more. Could they date and still work together? Was she going to want that when he didn't name her partner? Maybe he should take her on as partner after all. She would be the best choice. But then would she think it was because he wanted to date her. He had a sinking feeling there was no way this ended with him getting everything he wanted. If he ever decided what that was.

"Where'd you go yesterday?" Trent asked as he stuffed another cheese cube from the appetizer tray their mom had set out.

"Out for a while." Henry didn't want to go into his time with Lorelei. It was private.

"Anything special?" Trent waggled his brows and looked between Henry and Lorelei.

"Nope. Just some errands." He took a sip of his Malbec before either of them could spot his lie.

The day had been extremely normal – what he expected most couples did during holiday or the weekends: just be with each other. He'd succeeded in getting his shopping done – he'd ordered gift certificates to the golf course online, printed them and found some envelopes. He'd also succeeded in spending time with Lorelei like he probably shouldn't but was actively trying to figure out a way to make it happen again. After this evening, they had no plans or reasons to see each other outside of work. Fisher and Silver didn't return until New Year's Day, and that was just simply too far away. Maybe he could invite Lorelei to a festival or even her family's ranch. If she were a normal girl, he'd man up and ask her out. But the lines had become too gray between them, and he wasn't sure where he stood.

After he'd cleared the snow from her car last night, they'd had a moment. He'd felt a spark between them laced with uncertainty. The only thing he couldn't work out for sure was if that uncertainty was because she had feelings for him, too, or if she realized how inappropriate it would be to date her boss. The fact that they really shouldn't be together made him want to pursue her even more.

"What did you and the family do yesterday, Trent?" Lorelei stepped in after the silence went on a little too long.

"We hit up some parks, shopped downtown and then went around looking at all the Christmas lights in town. Some people really outdo themselves. The boys loved it."

"I bet it was beautiful with the snow." Her nose crinkled. "You know, I haven't even driven around this year. Usually I get out at least once to check them out."

Here was his opportunity. He could ask her if she wanted to go tonight. It would be the perfect excuse to get her alone again.

"I'll talk my dad into driving my mom and I around, blasting some music and drinking hot chocolate," she solved the problem before he could take advantage of the opportunity.

He was going to have to be more on his toes when it came to Lorelei.

"Thanks for having me over again, Mrs. Hale. Is there anything I can help with?" Lorelei asked.

"No, I think we're set. I just need to put some of it in serving dishes now. You and Henry can set the table."

"Will do." Henry picked up the Christmas dishes that were white with gold garland laced up and down the edges. "The silverware is there." He nodded to the counter where the glasses and napkins were lined up.

Lorelei was right behind him grabbing stuff.

"Do you switch who hosts Christmas each year? I don't remember you mentioning them being in town before."

"Yeah, we rotate. It's especially better since the boys were born. It's easier if Trent's family doesn't have to pack up the house to have Christmas. Every once in a while, though, they come down."

"That's nice."

"Do you always spend it at your parents' here, or do you prefer destination Christmases?"

"Right here in town. I love Christmas in Casper. I'm not averse to traveling for other holidays though."

"New Year's?"

"If it was somewhere good and I didn't have to fight the holiday crowds at the airport, it wouldn't be so bad."

OK, Buffalo was only a short drive up the interstate. He was going to have to work on his approach, but his plan definitely had merit.

–

Henry's dad stood at the end of the table and clicked his glass with his fork. "I'm glad to have my family here to spend Christmas. We may not always be in the same place, but we are forever in each other's hearts. And that's why I'm pleased to announce that we are naming a new partner to Hale Law."

Lorelei's stomach flipped. This was the moment. Everything she'd been doing – all the long hours, all the prep work and not seeing her friends much this year – it all was worth it for this moment. Her thudding heartbeat throbbed in her ears.

She glanced at Henry. Then froze. She'd expected to see him looking at her, smiling. Instead, his stare was fixed on his dad and a wrinkle had appeared between his brows. His lips were pressed together. Suddenly the thudding was replaced with a ringing.

"Alicia," Dwight continued. "Welcome to Hale Law. We are happy to have you."

Clapping commenced around the table, and just by muscle memory alone Lorelei's hands, too, were moving in front of her. Her eyes glazed over and all she saw were her failings. They gave the prize to a blood relative. They were a bunch of greedy, selfish, cliquish snobs. She was never going to make it in this firm. That was clear now. What wasn't clear was whether Henry had known all along or if this was just as surprising to him. Not that he should care about the firm in Buffalo, but if he had any intention of making her partner, now would've been the moment. Now. In front of all the partners.

All four of them.

She slowly turned her head to her left to look him dead on. There was a plastered sort of smile on his face. One of shock, really, like when you're not exactly happy at the news but should be. He sat in his chair like a stiff cardboard cut-out. She'd seen it before when he was trying a case where the odds weren't in his favor.

He didn't look at her. By now he had to know she was staring right at him yet he didn't move a muscle.

The clamoring of utensils on plates, people serving and requesting portion sizes commenced around them and still neither moved.

Yeah, he'd known all right. Maybe not about the Buffalo promotion but certainly the absence of hers. She glanced around the table at the festive green and red decorations and smiling faces. She didn't belong here. She never had. She'd forced herself into a dinner and let it snowball from there, all the while thinking she was doing herself a big favor. But what she had really been doing this entire time was making herself look like a fool and dragging her emotions into the fight. She was a complete dimwit who hadn't picked up on any signs that she wasn't partner material, or family, or, and this was the hardest of all, not someone Henry cared for beyond employee status.

"Excuse me," she whispered to no one in particular as she scooted the wooden chair back as quietly on the hardwood floors as she could manage and then placed her napkin on the seat. The last thing she wanted was to make a scene as she tried to leave as quickly as humanly possible.

She made it to the hall closet still dry-eyed and took her coat and purse, gathering it in her arms. There was no time to put it on. After drowning herself in whatever wine was in her kitchen, she was going to start looking for a new firm. She'd have her resignation on Henry's desk before Christmas was over. She was good at her job, dammit, and very employable. A downright asset. Any firm would be lucky to have her.

"Lorelei." Henry's voice from behind startled her as she shut the closet door.

There was no exit reason at the ready on her tongue. She just wanted out of here. She was done looking weak to the Hales. To Henry.

She took a deep breath and closed her eyes a couple of times, trying to dry any tears that thought now was a good time to appear. She turned around, setting her purse on the glass table against the wall. Someone leaving for a non-emotional reason would stop to put on their coat.

"It dawned on me that I should really be with my family for Christmas."

"Christmas is tomorrow." He spoke slowly, like he was testing the waters of her limits.

He'd already struck land.

"Then Christmas Eve," she ground out of a plastered smile.

"Listen, with my dad's speech and the whole partner thing—"

"Stop," she blurted. She couldn't. She couldn't listen to whatever lame excuse he was going to give. Any words short of "you're being named partner in Casper" were unacceptable. She slung her purse onto her shoulder.

"Go ahead." She met his stare straight on. Yes, she did want to hear this. From his mouth, in her own words, so she didn't have to spend hours tonight making up the excuse he was intending to use. This would save her wallowing time and hopefully get her to the moving-on stage a lot faster.

"This whole week." He put his hands in his pocket and shook his head as he looked at the floor for a second. "It started out innocently enough and then snowballed. I didn't stop your assumptions. I know I should've, but I didn't." He opened his mouth to say more, then stopped himself.

He looked earnest, he even sounded it. Like he believed what he was saying. Like he wanted her to trust his words, too. But there was no room for emotion in her journey any more. She shouldn't have let it, let him, in in the first place. If she hadn't gotten wrapped up in her feelings for him, she would've seen the writing on the wall.

"There is no partnership offer even remotely on the table, is there?" She summoned all the strength she had left and prayed for a little extra holiday luck that he may still have the right answer.

"No. Not right now. In the future, maybe. I don't know."

"Did I even have a shot with them? With you?"

He took in a breath. "No."

Her eyes widened and she stepped back.

"I told them I don't want a partner yet."

Her heart utterly sank so far into her chest she wasn't sure if she was able to even breathe. "You knew how badly I wanted to be named partner. And you used that." Lorelei didn't want to cry. It wasn't professional. It wasn't who she was. But nonetheless, a tear slipped down her cheek. A betrayal of her tough persona that she wanted so badly to have right now. Business wasn't supposed to be personal. Yet it had become that. And so much more.

"Lorelei, I'm sorry."

"Too little, too late." She stomped down the hall. "Merry Christmas."

"Please don't leave."

"Here's what you need to know." She whipped around to face him and cleared her throat. "You can consider this my formal notice. My desk will be cleaned out first thing in the morning." Her three open cases could be transferred to one of his other lackeys. She was done being the back on which he built his business and she profited none.

"It's Christmas tomorrow." The side of his jaw jumped as he put his hands low on his hips.

"I don't care." She clutched at her purse straps to stop the shaking she felt descending down her arms. "Second, anything that may or may not have started between us is over." The first part of her sentence started off so strong then weakened, but she got through it. She hadn't imagined the spark between them was so hot that it would scorch her when it imploded.

"Lorelei." His stern tone froze her. "I never promised you anything. I realize how this looks, and this week," he shook his head, "not everything was always cut and dried. As far as quitting with one day's notice, that is far from professional."

She made it all the way to her car in his driveway before the tears started flowing down her cheeks. She'd go in the morning to clean out her desk when no one else was around. That way it would be less embarrassing when she cried. And she wouldn't have to see him again. Wouldn't have to look into his eyes and see a glimpse of a life she'd dreamed about for a brief moment.

She'd meet him in the courtroom, no doubt. Then she'd be prepared. He wasn't going to break her twice.

Chapter Eight

The dawn of Christmas morning didn't catch him by surprise. He'd tossed and turned most of the night. It was stupid that he'd had high expectations of this day this year. With Lorelei around all week, and – he sighed. Well, she hadn't been wrong. Something had started between the two of them. Something that he was having a hard time letting go of. Granted, it was only twelve hours ago that she'd walked out. Usually he could wrap his head quickly around outcomes of cases and arguments either won or lost, but this all seemed surreal.

When had she gotten so under his skin?

Lorelei had been in his life for more than two years now, and all of a sudden he felt like he couldn't live without her in his arms full-time. There was a hole in his chest where she'd warmed him this week. Heck, maybe she'd had this effect on him the whole time and he never realized it.

Screw the pretense of professionalism. Not that she'd say that. The job was the only thing keeping them together, and that fact was on a lifeline considering she'd sort of quit last night. Sort of – there he was going fooling himself again. Her eyes had been full of rage. She'd definitely, for sure washed her hands of Hale Law.

Man, he'd messed up big.

He stood from the seat where he'd been perched all morning feeling sorry for himself. "I have to go." He had to get to the office before she did, stop her from clearing out her desk. He'd wait there all day, every day if he had to. He couldn't lose her. Professionally or personally.

"Where? It's Christmas," his mom said while she made a cup of coffee on the Keurig.

"I have to catch Lorelei."

"You never did say why she left dinner last night."

"Because I'm an idiot." He grabbed his keys from the counter, adrenaline causing him to clutch them a little too tight.

His mother's eyes turned soft and she nodded with understanding. "Think of a good speech."

No kidding. He reached the office in record time. He jogged into the building, swung through the glass door, and bolted for her office down the hall.

He braced both hands on the doorframe.

Gone.

She was gone. He was too late.

His head sank to his chest for a moment as his entire world shut down. She really had been serious. There was probably a letter sitting on his desk right now telling him off about his employment. He took a heavy step into her office – the red, orange, and yellow flower arrangement on the edge of her desk was gone, the turquoise office supplies that usually peppered her space were gone. The only thing of hers that still lingered was her scent and a wrapped, rectangular package.

He picked up the brown bundle tied with a bow. There wasn't a name on it anywhere, but it seemed like a sign she had left for him.

He pulled the string and undid the bow. He ripped into the brown flap and unwrapped the entire thing, flipping it over to see the front.

A chill ran down his spine. A Hardy Boy's book, *The Disappearing Floor.* What an appropriate name for what was happening to him right now. And the sweetest gift he'd ever received. She'd paid attention and gave him a present that actually meant something to him.

Ah, hell, she meant something to him. The world. She meant life to him.

He opened the book and red-marker writing caught his eye.

> *To Henry, thanks for the best Christmas ever.*
> *xo Lorelei.*

Guilt pinched at the sides of his eyes.

He clutched the book and stood. He had a place to be. Wherever she was. He had to try to win her back. He couldn't lose her for good. Not now. Not after finally realizing he loved her.

He ran back to his car and drove straight for her parents' house where she said she was spending Christmas Day. If she wasn't there, he'd go to her house and then start scouring the town until he laid eyes on her again and told her how he felt. It was the very least he owed her. And himself.

He'd never manned up with her this week and told her how he was feeling or asked what she thought of their exploring a relationship. Now it may be too late. Either way, he had to explain himself to her and hope and pray that she hadn't shut the door on them forever.

Lorelei poured another glass of water from her parents' Brita pitcher and sauntered back to the couch. She'd had way too much wine last night and today was saying no to the pitcher full of Mimosas her mom had made. Although if this hangover didn't go away soon, she was going to subscribe to the "hair of the dog" method next.

"Are you feeling well, sweetheart?" her mom asked as she sat near her on the couch.

She'd not told her parents about the blow up with Henry last night. She couldn't bring herself to look them in the eye and tell them she'd quit her job and had her heart broken. How stupid did that sound? Not to mention, if last night was any indication, no amount of wine was going to get Henry out of her head or heart.

"Yeah, Mom, just a lot going on. It's nice to have a relaxing day."

"We'll have lunch soon and open presents. Did you ask Henry if he wanted to join us today?"

"I sure didn't. He's got his own family stuff today. And, he's not my boyfriend. He's my boss." *Was my boss. Now he's the enemy.* She directed her next question to her father who was opening the paper. "Could we drive around and look at the lights later?"

"Absolutely, pumpkin. We haven't gotten out yet either to see what people have done this year." He smiled at her over the print. "The theme downtown is Cowboy Christmas this year, so the houses should be interesting."

They were watching *National Lampoon's Christmas Vacation*. Normally, she still found the old perfect Christmas movie funny. Today she did not.

The sadness she felt went down to her core. The trauma of it all was too much to process; there was going to be a lot of fallout from her actions. She had savings, but she didn't want to run through it. She'd made a list this morning of people she'd contact next week to set up meetings, but no one ever really looked to hire a new lawyer; it just sort of happened when the fit was right. For her, the fit was going to be right anywhere there wasn't a Henry Hale involved.

Even though she hated it, she could capitalize on her mother's good name and move out East; getting in with a well-known firm would give her a lot of experience. Then when she returned to Casper she'd come back better than ever. Henry was one person. She could move on. She would. And then nothing that happened this week would matter ever again.

She sighed. Who was she kidding? She didn't want to work anywhere else or with anyone else. She'd fallen asleep on her couch after all that wine, but then woke up with the sun and couldn't fall back asleep. Her mind wouldn't shut off. And she'd cried through a whole box of Kleenex in the car after packing up her office at the crack of dawn.

The doorbell rang and her father got up to answer. She heard mumbling of male voices and then the door shutting and felt a whoosh of cold air. She glanced over to the hall, expecting to see her dad coming back to the living room. Instead, she set eyes on Henry.

He was breathing hard and his normal coiffed brown hair was disheveled.

"What happened?" she asked, sitting forward, uncrossing her legs. "Is it Fisher or Silver?" What else would make him come over here?

"No, nothing happened. They are fine. Well, I assume, I haven't spoken to them in a couple of days." He rubbed the back of his neck. "But you are right, everything is wrong." Henry had a deer in the headlights look going on with the hair, wide eyes and terror flitting across his face.

Her dad sat down and her mother stood. "Henry, this is my husband, Phil. Phil, this is Henry, Lorelei's friend."

"We just met, Fran."

"It's nice you're joining us today," her mom continued, unfazed. "Can I get you a drink, Henry? We just started the movie."

"No, thank you, Mrs. Sullivan. I just need to speak with Lorelei."

"Henry, I think you should leave." Lorelei's words were clipped. She did not want to have any sort of conversation with him, let alone one in front of her parents. Ruining Christmas Eve wasn't enough for him, he had to come after the actual day now? He needed to leave her alone to wallow in her own self-pity.

"I can't. Not until we talk." He put his hands loosely on his hips.

"No." She stood and crossed her arms over her blue sweater. She'd worn her yoga pants because Christmas was a time to be comfortable in the Sullivan house. Now she wished she'd done her hair and makeup and put on a dress so that Henry could see what he was missing.

"Son." Her tall, fit father with a full head of white hair stood. "It's time you left."

Henry stepped to the side so that he could continue to hold her stare.

"I love you," he practically yelled.

Her dad stopped and turned back to Lorelei, his bushy white brows raised, then looked at Francis.

"We have a present to go find and wrap." Her mother grabbed her father's arm and dragged him toward the salon. They were probably still going to listen in. Great.

"What are you doing?" she asked. Was he drunk?

"I don't care if I embarrass myself in front of your parents, or you, or whoever. I need to talk to you."

"You've had a long time to talk to me. So far it hasn't been that impressive." She didn't budge. "You are aware it's Christmas, right? This couldn't have waited?"

He shook his head. "I was wrong to stonewall you out of becoming a partner. I'm sorry. I don't trust that easily, and the thought of relying on anyone is terrifying."

Nice words, but that's all they were – words. She shook her head. Three minutes ago she was mentally updating her resumé and rebuilding the brick wall around her heart.

"Please come back to Hale Law. To me. I was wrong."

"And if I don't love you back, is the partner offer off the table?" This was entirely too messy. Everything was connected now. The line between personal and professional had been decimated the first time they'd kissed. She couldn't work with him without loving him now that she'd opened that door. It would be too hard to see him every day, knowing they could've had something special, something real in this world.

Frustration started to knot her stomach. Why should she punish her career because of him?

She had to give him credit though, he didn't flinch at her comment about not loving him. There was hope in his eyes.

"The partner position at Hale Law is on the table permanently. You're an amazing lawyer, truly gifted. I'll get over my issues."

"How do you plan to do that?"

He stepped toward her. "One day at a time." He smiled and flashed his white teeth.

She almost melted but stopped herself. His charms no longer worked on her. She was impervious to Hale the Conqueror.

"I'll have to think about it." She squeezed her arms around her chest a little for comfort, mostly to stay resolute. "A lot has happened over this past week."

That was no lie. She couldn't process the new offer. She thought this door had been shut.

"Fair enough." Another step closer to her. "Let me submit the following for arguments. One, we work well together. We always have, especially when we needed to brainstorm a case problem. Two, we both have the same drive for success and a genuine love of the law. There is no one out there who is more dedicated. And that type of energy is infectious to be around. And, three, you're the only one I want to share the firm with, talk to about decisions and discuss the future with."

"Number three sounds awfully personal." All his numbers were delicious. He was the perfect partner for her.

He took another step. She could reach out and wrap her arms around him if she wanted. "It is because you are personal to me. I want to talk about my day with you and hear about yours. I want you in my space permanently. Everywhere. I want to go to movies with you, share inside jokes with you. I want to know your hopes and dreams so that I can make them come true. I want you as my partner, for everything in life. I love you. I don't want to have a firm if you're not in it, and I don't want to go another day without you knowing how sorry I am about last night and not being honest with you this week. I got caught up in getting to know you and didn't want it to stop. I knew you'd pull away, and I selfishly wanted all the time I could get with you."

"Quite a speech." She dropped her crossed arms and her hands fell by her side. "You hurt me. I let you in. I cared about you." She shook her head. He'd just bared his soul, but she couldn't even say the words out loud.

"I'm human." He reached down and laced his fingers with hers. "I can't say that I'll never mess up. Again. But I can promise that I won't make a stupid mistake like not telling you every day how in love with you I am."

Tears ran down her cheek. His smooth voice was too much. The way he looked at her with such openness. She'd never experienced this type of clarity before. She loved him. If she didn't tell him now, she could be making the same mistake he had this week, and it was unacceptable not to learn from others' mistakes.

She leaned forward and pressed her lips to his. For a second, peace flooded her soul and her chest felt lighter. Henry was the man for her. By his side is where she wanted to be.

She pulled back to look into his beautiful blue eyes. "I want our partnership agreement in writing."

"Done." He crooked a smile to the side and his one dimple appeared.

"I don't want any flack over being partner at Hale Law for any other reason other than I earned it." This point was unbelievably important to her.

"Done. It's the truth. People know you, they know your work ethic and respect it. No one will be surprised that you were named partner."

"I want the name changed to Sullivan and Hale Law."

"Don't push it."

A small chuckle escaped her lips. "And I don't want any of this half in, half out business. If we're doing this, we are both completely in with no deception and no out strategy."

He smiled and leaned down for another kiss. She happily obliged. She wanted to kiss him for the rest of her life. "I love you, too," she said into his kiss.

She'd never been so sure about anything in her life. And that was saying something.